Stratford-Upon-Avon Studies
Second Series

General Editor: Jeremy Hawthorn
Professor of Modern British Literature
University of Trondheim, Norway

Plotting Change: Contemporary Women's Fiction

Editor: Linda Anderson

Edward Arnold
A division of Hodder & Stoughton
LONDON   MELBOURNE   AUCKLAND

© 1990 Edward Arnold

First published in Great Britain 1990

Distributed in the USA by Routledge, Chapman and Hall, Inc.
29 West 35th Street, New York, NY 10001

British Library Cataloguing in Publication Data

Plotting change: contemporary women's fiction. –
   (Stratford-upon-Avon studies)
   1. Fiction in English. Women writers, 1945 – Critical studies
   I. Anderson, Linda   II. Series
   823.914099287

   ISBN 0–7131–6603–7

Library of Congress Cataloging-in-Publication Data

Plotting change: contemporary women's fiction/editor, Linda
   Anderson.
       p.   cm.—(Stratford-upon-Avon studies. Second series)
   Includes bibliographical references.
   ISBN 0–7131–6603–7
   1. English fiction—Women authors—History and criticism.
   2. American fiction—Women authors—History and criticism.
   3. American fiction—20th century—History and criticism.
   4. English fiction—20th century—History and criticism.
   5. Women and literature—History—20th century.
   6. Women in literature.
   I. Anderson, Linda R., 1950–   .   II. Series.
PR888.W6P67   1990
823′.914099287—dc20   90–204
                                                  CIP

Typeset in 10/11pt Garamond by Colset Private Limited, Singapore
Printed and bound in Great Britain for Edward Arnold, a division of
Hodder and Stoughton Limited, Mill Road, Dunton Green, Sevenoaks,
Kent TN13 2YA by Biddles Limited, Guildford and King's Lynn

Contents

Preface

Ten years ago, writing in a volume of the Stratford-Upon-Avon series entitled *Contemporary English Fiction*, Lorna Sage predicted the demise of a tradition of fiction writing which she believed women writers had helped to determine and which had in turn long sustained and nurtured their talents.[1] The tradition she referred to – a predominantly English tradition – had, she believed, thrived on the kind of sensitivity to detail and sense of connectedness to others which the woman, living 'in the home and her emotions'[2] could be said to have cultivated, though with little other choice, and then turned to her aesthetic advantage in fiction. The characteristic trope of this tradition was the woman in the drawing-room, positioning her writing within an interior also occupied by others, writing what she sáw. Sage believed that women's fiction in the 1970s, in step with other changes in women's lives, had arrived at a new but hazardous threshold: it could try to sustain a sense of continuity, keeping within its own well-tested limits by ignoring change, or it could move into the uncharted territory of a new subject – the woman defining her own life and fiction. Surveying the novel at that time Sage's essay expressed a sense of unease: for whilst reading signs of transition and sensing upheaval she also could not be sure in what form women's fiction would survive.

Ten years later the theme of change, anticipated in the 70s, has become a central focus for both critics and writers and the essays in this collection reflect and explore the diversity of directions taken by women's fiction in the decade between. Women's fiction, we can congratulate ourselves, now merits a whole volume of essays to itself and this critical visibility seems testimony to its current liveliness and status. The argument has moved on; women's fiction – now occupying its own space – has arrived.

Yet metaphors of journey, however appealing, may well be the wrong ones for us to use, since they threaten to erase the ambiguities of the shifts that have occurred and the openness of the destination. Change, we see

---

[1]'Female Fictions: The Women Novelists' in *Contemporary English Fiction* (London, Edward Arnold, 1979), pp. 66–87.
[2]Virginia Woolf, 'Women and Fiction', in *Women and Writing* ed. Michele Barrett,

now from our perspective in the 80s, is not an end result, the exchange of restriction for freedom, a feminine plot for a feminist one, but a process which, looked at in reverse and with new critical insight, reaches back into the very tradition defined by Sage. Women, Sage asserted in acknowledgement of their covert influence, are at 'the sensitive core of English fiction';[3] at the same time, however, women's writing has always existed illegitimately; the official story – the version that passes into history – is the one written by male writers. As Nancy Miller has argued, however successful or influential women writers may be 'literary *history* remains a male preserve, a history of writing by men'.[4] What this means for the woman novelist is that, inheriting a plot which is not her own, she must find ways of contesting her own silencing. Feminist re-readings over the last ten years, attentive to this different relationship of women to culture – inside it and yet denied subjective validation by it – have mapped a complex interplay in women's writing between imitation of the dominant fictions of the day and divergence from them.[5] By asking different questions – questions related to difference – what has emerged is a view of the woman writer less contentedly keeping to her separate sphere – and a particular kind of fiction – than powerfully straining against the boundaries that hem her in.

This view of the interrelationship of fiction and ideology and the woman writer's struggle through and against them provides a link with the present, as well as an important key to the concerns of many of the writers represented in this volume. The contemporary woman novelist may be able to unravel her situation with far greater clarity than of old: what she may be clearer about, however, is the entanglement of masculine fictions of desire and power in the constitution of what we take as universal truth. Her own truth-telling may depend on her acumen in seeing through stories as well as on her ability to make up new ones of her own.

The concept that weaves its way insistently through this collection of essays is 'intertextuality' and its relevance and importance to women's writing becomes increasingly apparent. Judie Newman recognizes that the specific definitions of the term, as applying to the way a text builds itself out of other texts, can have far wider ramifications, giving us a way of thinking about experience as already structured by the modalities of fiction. Women inherit stories, we could say, which are powerfully oppressive; part of that oppression lies in their unitary character, their repression of alternative stories, other possibilities, hidden or secret scripts. Juxtaposing stories with other stories or opening up the potentiality for multiple stories also frees the woman writer from the coercive fictions of her culture that pass as truth. If women's texts point to other

(Harcourt Brace Javanovich, New York and London, 1979), p. 46.
[3] p. 67.
[4] 'Emphasis Added: Plots and Plausibilities in Women's Fiction', in *Subject to Change: Reading Feminist Writing* (New York, Columbia UP, 1988), p. 27.
[5] See especially Sandra Gilbert and Susan Gubar, *The Madwoman in the Attic* (New Haven: Yale UP, 1979).

texts it is frequently with a sense of an imagined elsewhere, unacknowledged alternatives, other stories waiting silently to be told.

Doris Lessing, a writer whose lifetime's work has been involved with change both as a theme and a possibility, makes a wholly appropriate starting point for the collection. Ruth Whittaker lucidly surveys Lessing's fiction, starting with *The Children of Violence* series, and traces in her work a refusal of limits, of endings which make false promises of fulfilment, which impose limitations, shaped and sanctioned by society, to individual searching. By moving outside or beyond realism Lessing also liberates her characters from everyday reality into new possibilities for development; change can occur, she believes and she sets herself the task of exploring, from *The Golden Notebook* onwards, the means of making it happen. The alternative to change is bleak for Lessing; if we do not change we may not survive and her fiction has taken on a strongly prophetic character. Yet what Whittaker also notes running through Lessing's work, complicating and humanizing her distancing vision, is an important undercurrent of vulnerability.

Angela Carter is also a writer much concerned with change; where, however, Lessing seriously examines the mechanisms of change, the conditions of society and soul that make it possible or impossible, Carter plays with alternatives. Her novels, according to Elaine Jordan, are 'questioning journeys to no final home, which remember but are not detained by nostalgia'. Meaning for Carter is open-ended; it is both multiple and changeable. Carter creates new perceptions for her readers by displacing the accepted hierarchy of meanings, putting together stylistically and thematically what is usually kept apart. Jordan sees Carter as a writer frankly committed to radical analysis, knowingly moving us around in a world of intertextualites, sometimes deconstructing old fixed identities (and the stories which contain them), at other times experimenting with producing new subjects and new ways of overcoming the ideas and images that have up till now ruled (and narrowed) our choices. Her 'new fictions', according to Jordan, do not attempt to be more than that, are not solutions but different angles of seeing.

One of the most powerful stories within our culture is that of heterosexual romance; this form of romance is woman's destiny, so the story goes, and other forms of fulfilment, sexual or vocational, become invisible or marginal. As the critic Rachel Blau du Plessis has put it, it is a story that means 'entering into teleological love relations, ones with appropriate ends'.[6] In her wide-ranging essay on 'Contemporary Lesbian Feminist Fiction' Paulina Palmer argues that lesbian fiction is not simply about the representation of lesbians in fiction – women writers have been known to reproduce society's oppressive stereotyping – but about using the sign lesbian to deconstruct the concepts of naturalness and 'normality' which mask patriarchal definitions of experience. Palmer sees the power and distinctiveness of the genre – which can employ a variety of themes and

[6]*Writing Beyond the Ending* (Bloomington, Indiana UP, 1985), p. 15.

fictional approaches – as lying in the way it identifies 'the oppressive facets of heterosexual conventions and structures'. Whilst it shares themes and techniques with women's fiction generally, Palmer argues, this genre's specific insights and form of political questioning means that it should not simply be assimilated into it. Indeed the current climate of homophobia makes its separate existence all the more important.

All the writers so far talked about explore change by moving between a reality which is 'given', a social and mental topography which shifts and contracts as its fictional contours come into view, and an imagined elsewhere. As Penny Florence argues in her thoughtful essay on feminist science fiction, one of the problems facing the woman writer is precisely this 'present – future dynamic'; in order to move beyond present definitions and ways of thinking she also has to move through them. To talk about science fiction as a genre runs the risk of re-inscribing the restrictions of this kind of categorization; yet the appeal of feminist science fiction is precisely in the way it is not bound by convention but moves experimentally and experientially into 'other dimensions'. Florence argues that there is an important distinction between fantasy and feminist science fiction: science fiction is closer to mimesis; the exploration is less into 'what is real' than 'what the real is'. Consequently the narrative and thematic design of the stories is not escapist. Rather it frees us from the present so that we can begin to imagine it differently.

The short-story form is perhaps particularly suited, as Rosemary O'Sullivan suggests, to the exploration of potentiality through its emphasis on beginnings. Grace Paley's short stories manage with their precarious irony and humour to retain a belief that change, against the odds, always remains a possibility. In conversation with Rosemary O'Sullivan, Paley describes her own dislike of the fixing of meaning through theory or generalization; the fluidity of her own point of view depends partly on the importance of listening to her writing – what she sees as a necessary openness to the other's point of view – and her care for detail, the day-to-day hopes and worries of people's lives. Society's responsibility to children is at the heart of her political vision and it makes it a vision also rooted in the realities of women's lives. It is children, too, for Paley who make us believe in renewal, beginnings. 'They begin us', she says, 'again and again'.

'Do novels change lives', Alison Light asks, in her essay on Alice Walker's *The Color Purple* and if so 'what is the job of criticism in relation to those experiences?' Light shifts the emphasis away from the process of writing to the process of reading and examines the possible disjuncture between critical discourse and reading pleasure. The happy ending of *The Color Purple* can seem both 'deeply pleasurable and deeply suspect'. The pleasure of reading the book, Light found in her teaching, quickly turned into negative critique when the analysis of meaning learned through the study of 'English' was applied to it. How far, Light questions, does 'English' enforce 'Englishness' and either refuse to engage with difference or recognize it only in terms of lack and failure? A suspicion of the happy ending could be partly to do with misreading, therefore; even as we (white academics) reject liberal humanism and its claim to full subjecthood, we collude with it. The novel can mean differently to different groups. However Light also wants to validate the pleasure of the 'naive' reading, and the kind of uncritical identification which the novel invites: it speaks of and to important desires, she argues, which can also be politically mobilizing. Only a belief in ourselves as active agents in the world rather than fragmented subjects – the kind of belief which a text like *The Color Purple* gives us – allows us to 'get out there and do things'.

Judie Newman's essay on Alison's Lurie's novel, *Imaginary Friends* traces the knowing and complex ways the novel plays with intertextuality. The novel re-writes the story of the trance maiden – the heroine's name is Verena – which Newman sees as a 'topos with a fairly obvious normative patriarchal content' by making this Verena active in writing her own text (and destiny). The novel, according to Newman, generates irony by putting together two texts or systems of signs, that of the social scientists who are observing Verena and her sect and that of Verena herself, who skillfully receives messages, transcribed through automatic writing, which subvert their scientific and 'objective' observations. Who frames whom could be the question asked by the novel and Newman sees Lurie exploring serious questions about how cultural hegemony is established and how plausibility and normality are defined. Ultimately it may be no more or less than having the power to convince others that you are telling the truth.

My own essay is also concerned with whose version of the story passes into history and thus becomes history. Both feminism and post-structuralist theory have undermined history's status as truth. Yet women writers, whilst questioning the authority of history, have also evinced a powerful desire for women not to lose status, or rather the chance to gain it, as historical subjects. Women's re-writing of history must therefore confront both the danger of making history disappear before we have had a chance of writing ourselves into it and the ever-present danger of recuperation, of simply reconstituting reality as it is. Toni Morrison's novel, *Beloved*, I argue, attempts to imagine a new and different relationship between subjectivity and history, unsettling our notions of identity, language and history, whilst at the same time situating the characters within history and showing the ways it shapes and forms subjectivity. It is a novel which posits the re-imagining of history as an endless process for the unrecorded past, what has been repressed and forgotten, can also strangely come back to haunt us.

To go back to the beginning, this collection of essays moves beyond the 'English tradition' defined by Sage, intended, to be sure, only as a descriptive label, by including contemporary American fiction as well. Yet Alison Light's strictures about 'Englishness' can still sound a useful cautionary note for us. We need to go on acknowledging the exclusions and the limits of our reading, the narrow cultural base on which our theorizing and analysis rests, the differences among women which cannot be collapsed into Difference. These essays have much to say about the current achievements of women writers and the exciting new horizons of meaning they open up. Another collection in the future may throw its net wider and further and continue to revise our view of fiction by women.

Linda Anderson

Note

Life

Doris Lessing was born in Persia in 1918 of British parents, and brought up in Southern Rhodesia. She married and divorced twice, and has had three children. In 1949 she came to England, where she has lived ever since, although she is widely travelled. She was briefly a member of the Communist party, first in Southern Rhodesia, and then in England. In the late 50s she was one of the founder members of the Campaign for Nuclear Disarmament. In middle age she undertook psychotherapy with a Jungian therapist, and later became a student of Sufi. She likes cats.

Novels

The Grass is Singing (1950); *Children of Violence: Martha Quest* (1952); *A Proper Marriage* (1954); *A Ripple from the Storm* (1958); Landlocked (1965); *The Four-Gated City* (1969); *Retreat to Innocence* (1956); *The Golden Notebook* (1962); *Briefing for a Descent into Hell* (1971); *The Summer Before the Dark* (1973); *The Memoirs of a Survivor* (1974); *Canopus in Argos: Archives: Re: Colonized Planet 5, Shikasta* (1979); *The Marriages Between Zones Three, Four, and Five* (1980); *The Sirian Experiments* (1981); *The Making of the Representative for Planet 8* (1982); *Documents Relating to the Sentimental Agents in the Volyen Empire* (1983); *The Diaries of Jane Somers* (1984); *The Good Terrorist* (1985); *The Fifth Child* (1988).

Short Stories

This Was the Old Chief's Country (1951); *The Habit of Loving* (1957); *A Man and Two Women* (1963); *African Stories* (1964); *The Story of a Non-Marrying Man and Other Stories* (1972); *This Was the Old Chief's Country: Collected African Stories*, Vol. I (1973); *The Sun Between Their Feet: Collected African Stories*, Vol. II (1973); *To Room Nineteen: Collected Stories*, Vol. I (1978); *The Temptation of Jack Orkney: Collected Stories*, Vol. II (1978).

Plays

Each His Own Wilderness, in *New English Dramatists: Three Plays* ed. E. Martin Browne (1959); *Play with a Tiger* (1962) in *Plays by and About Women*, ed. Victoria Sullivan and James Hatch (1973).

Poems

Fourteen Poems (Northwood, Middlesex, 1959).

Non-fiction

Going Home (1957) Revised edition, 1968; *In Pursuit of the English: A Documentary* (1960); *Particularly Cats* (1967); *The Wind Blows Away Our Words* (1987); *Prisons We Choose to Live Inside* (1987).

Selected Interviews

Christopher Bigsby, interview with Doris Lessing in *The Radical Imagination and the Liberal Tradition* by Heide Ziegler and Christopher Bigsby (1982). C. J. Driver, 'Doris Lessing', in *The New Review*, 1, no. 8 (November 1974), 17–23. *A Small Personal Voice*, ed. Paul Schleuter (1975) contains interviews with Lessing by Florence Howe, Roy Newquist and Jonah Raskin.

Selected Criticism

Draine, Betsy, *Substance Under Pressure: Artistic Coherence and Evolving Form in the Novels of Doris Lessing* (Madison: University of Wisconsin Press, 1983)

Fishburn, Katherine, *The Unexpected Universe of Doris Lessing: A Study in Narrative Technique* (Westport: Greenwood Press, 1985)

Pratt, A. and Dembo, L.S. (eds.) *Doris Lessing: Critical Studies* (Madison: Univ. of Wisconsin Press, 1974)

Rubenstein, Roberta, *The Novelistic Vision of Doris Lessing: Breaking the Forms of Consciousness* (Urbana: University of Illinois Press, 1979)

Sage, Lorna, *Doris Lessing* (London: Methuen, 1983)

1

Doris Lessing and the Means of Change

Ruth Whittaker

Doris Lessing looks sibylline: remote, unfrivolous, sage. In the photograph of her on the jacket of *The Fifth Child* (1988) she is standing, hands on hips, looking both defensive and slightly resigned. 'Well, reader?' she seems to be saying, with some irony. Like many artists' faces, hers looks asymmetrical. The right side (i.e. left as you face her) looks grim, embattled, tired. The left side (i.e. right as you face her) looks wary, sensitive, vulnerable. I have seen her face light up with animation when talking with undergraduates, but in still photographs she invariably looks as if she is shouldering more responsibility than is good for her. Words like 'wise woman' and 'prophetess' recur in descriptions of Doris Lessing, and she appears to bear these labels with the detachment with which she has borne earlier categorizations such as 'Marxist' and 'Feminist'. 'And then I was *mysticism*, in quotes', she said once,[1] describing the response to her later work. Nevertheless, it must be quite a strain, being on the receiving end of all those weighty attributes; how can they allow for any vulnerability?

In this essay I want to attempt an overview of Lessing's work to date, to trace the route her search has taken her. Her fiction begins by exploring personal and social relationships which are gradually revealed as inadequate and limiting. It then shifts perspective and takes a much more detached view of the human race, which Lessing sees as doomed unless we

---

[1]Quoted by Ann Scott in 'Sufism, Mysticism and Politics' from *Notebooks, Memoirs, Archives* ed. Jenny Taylor (London, Routledge & Kegan Paul, 1982) p. 167.

Sprague, Claire, *Rereading Doris Lessing: Narrative Patterns of Doubling and Repetition* (Chapel Hill, NC: University of North Carolina Press, 1987)
Sprague, Claire and Tiger, Virginia (eds.) *Critical Essays on Doris Lessing* (Boston: G.K. Hall, 1986)
Taylor, Jenny. (ed.) *Notebooks/Memoirs/Archives: Reading and Rereading Doris Lessing* (London: Routledge & Kegan Paul, 1982)
Thorpe, Michael, *Doris Lessing's Africa* (London: Evans, 1978)
Whittaker, Ruth, *Doris Lessing* (London: Macmillan, 1988)

Journal
Doris Lessing Newsletter ed. Linnea Aycock at California State University, Fresno, California, 93740.

learn to evolve and change. Her later fiction explores the nature and mechanisms of change, and in this phase of her work there is a sense of urgency and frustration: either we learn to transcend our earth-bound limitations, or the race dies, either physically or psychically. Lessing takes on the role of a present-day Cassandra; perhaps that is why she looks so care-worn in her photographs. In looking at her work, I am interested in the discrepancy I see running through her writings: that between the serene, detached voice that has asked real questions and found some of the answers, and what I can only call the voice of an insecure little child crying out for affection. There seem to be two personae beneath the surface of her novels – the one who lives in the cool Canopean air, and the child-like figure, evidently mortal, anxious still about its identity, disappointed that its pain has had so little effect. Lessing's fiction is a quest for ontological solutions, but it is also a quest for identity. These subtextual voices sometimes alternate, sometimes clash, sometimes cancel each other out.

To begin with, I am haunted by Lessing's descriptions of her childhood house in Southern Rhodesia, which are echoed in descriptions of Martha Quest's house in Zambesia. In *Going Home* she gives a long and beautiful description of that house, which was made of indigenous materials. It had a skeleton of wooden poles, mud walls, earth floor and a thatch of wild grasses.

> A pole-and-dagga house is built to stand for two, three, four years at most; but the circumstances and character of our family kept ours standing for nearly two decades. It did very well, for it had been built with affection. But under the storms and the beating rains of the wet seasons, the grass of the roof flattened like old flesh into the hollows and bumps of the poles under it; and sometimes the mud-skin fell off in patches and had to be replaced; and sometimes parts of the roof received a new layer of grass. A house like this is a living thing, responsive to every mood of the weather; and during the time I was growing up it had already begun to sink back into the forms of the bush. I remember it as a rather old, shaggy animal standing still among the trees, lifting its head to look out over the vleis and valleys to the mountains. (*Going Home* Ch. 2)

Eventually her parents left the house, which later became over-run with ant-hills, then by fire, and finally subsided back into the bush, as if it had never been. But its organic image is very deep and powerful, and has remained 'home' in Doris Lessing's mind, even though she has lived mainly in London for the last forty years. In *Going Home* she wrote 'I worked out recently that I have lived in over sixty houses, flats and rented rooms during the last twenty years and not in one of them have I felt at home. . . . The fact is, I don't live anywhere; I never have since I left that first house on the kopje.' (Ch. 2) I find this almost unbearably painful to read. What has happened to the needs of that person who lived in that living house, who listened to the sweeping winds, who took the space of those landscapes and skyscapes for granted? What happens to someone whose early home no longer exists, and who, in addition, leaves the country of her childhood? I suppose I'm asking what it feels like to be deracinated, to live in exile. Maimed, I should think, almost literally 'cut off'. But also clear-sighted about a new environment, with a vision unblurred by habit and unquestioning familiarity, both deficient and advantaged, bereft and privileged.

Homelessness propels us outwards, and so sometimes does the failure of personal relationships. For us all, the primary relationship that is doomed to some kind of failure is that between parent and child. The theme of misunderstanding between mother and child lies like a dark, cold vacuum at the heart of Doris Lessing's work, and what is interesting is her recurrent re-working of the relationship throughout her fiction: May and Martha Quest, and Martha and Caroline in *Children of Violence*; Anna and Janet and Molly and Tommy in *The Golden Notebook*; Dorothy Mellings and Alice in *The Good Terrorist*; Harriet and Ben in *The Fifth Child*. From varying viewpoints both parents and children see each other as monsters: demanding, repressive, rapacious. Surrogate relationships fare better, such as Kate Brown and Maureen in *The Summer Before the Dark*, the Survivor and Emily in *The Memoirs of a Survivor*, Jane Somers and Maudie in *The Diaries of Jane Somers*. Doris Lessing allows characters without blood ties to be relieved of the emotional pressures of such closeness and, as often happens in real life, the safe distance between them enables them to achieve some true rapport.

Throughout Lessing's fiction the relationship between Martha Quest and her mother is the most powerful. Although Mrs Quest is horrendous, even when softened by the mitigating understanding of the narrator, her relationship with Martha is the most vital in *Children of Violence*, more compelling even than the sexual bonds between her characters. I imagine that the character of May Quest is largely taken from life as she is far too unreasonable, too infuriating not to be believable. A more imaginary character would have been made more muted and palatable and 'realistic'. Even after May's death in *The Four-Gated City*, the relationship re-emerges in *The Memoirs of a Survivor*, where Lessing looks not just at her own childhood, but at her mother's also, calling the novel in the blurb 'an attempt at autobiography'. Emily, May, and the Survivor become interfused, as Lessing again tries to understand, through her writing, the losses that motivate her work.

We are first introduced to the roots of this emptiness in *Martha Quest*, the first volume of *Children of Violence*. The novel begins with Martha in adolescent rebellion against her parents. But, as Nicole Ward Jouve has pointed out,[2] we are not given any account of Martha's childhood to prepare us for this abrasive relationship. (This is tackled twenty-two years later in *Memoirs*.) In *Martha Quest* Lessing begins to explore the theme of

[2]Nicole Ward Jouve, 'Of Mud and Other Matter – The Children of Violence' from *Notebooks, Memoirs, Archives*, p. 98.

repeated patterns, both their apparent inevitability, and the need to break them. Martha reads theories of child development which vary in their emphasis. One stresses the irrevocable influences of pre-natal experience; another the trauma of birth, and a third the irreversible effects of the first five years of life:

> . . . the feeling of fate, of doom, was the one message they all had in common. Martha, in violent opposition to her parents, was continually being informed that their influence on her was unalterable, and that it was much too late to change herself' (*Martha Quest*. Pt. 1 Ch. 1)

Nevertheless, perhaps motivated by this sense of doom, all the protagonists in Lessing's novels do seek to change themselves, in an attempt to cast off this sense of already being accounted for, done for. Martha's early attempts are predictable. She tries to thwart her parents' academic expectations of her by a variety of psychosomatic illnesses, and she rejoices in her emergent sexuality. Mrs Quest cannot cope with her daughter's growing up. She looks with alarm 'at the mature appearance of her daughter's breasts and hips. She glanced at her husband, then came quickly across the room, and laid her hands on either side of the girl's waist, as if trying to press her back into girlhood.' (*Martha Quest*, Pt. 1 Ch. 1) When Martha makes herself her first evening dress to go to a local dance she expects, but of course does not get, an acknowledgement of her adulthood, a ritual setting-free. After her escape to the town, her subsequent engagement is greeted with abusive letters from her mother. Her marriage is, however, a relief to Mrs Quest, and her pregnancy is greeted with malicious triumph as if it heralded the death of Martha's attempts at individuality: 'You won't have time for all your ideas when the baby is born, believe *me*!' (*A Proper Marriage*, Pt. 2 Ch. 2)

In *Landlocked* we begin to get a picture of May Quest from the narrator, rather than simply of her mother as perceived by Martha. We learn of May's difficulties with her own mother, and of her defiance of her father to become a nurse in the First World War. In *The Four-Gated City* this narratorial understanding is extended. As readers, we begin to see May Quest as frustrated and pathetic, yet also as courageous and not without her own reasons to be angry at the way life has turned out for her. But Lessing does not extend these insights to Martha, or, when Martha does get anywhere near to expressing a kind of understanding, Mrs Quest rejects any suggestion of a truce. In her mother's eyes Martha goes from bad to worse when she leaves her husband and child, has lovers, and remarries. But even leaving Africa for England does not free Martha of the feelings of emotional claustrophobia that her mother engenders in her. When Mrs Quest announces that she is coming to England to visit her daughter, Martha has a breakdown at the thought of it. The visit is awkward, with unsuccessful attempts by Martha to persuade her mother to accept her as she is. It ends with Mrs Quest pouring out years of bitterness and resentment to her daughters's psychotherapist. May leaves for Africa the next day, and Martha never sees her again. Their final exchange is a mutual look of 'ironic desperation'.

Children who are badly parented seldom make good parents themselves. Martha is initially delighted with her baby, though it is hours before she is allowed to hold her, and we are told a 'faint warning voice from the well of fatality did remark that a girl child was in the direct line of matriarchy she so feared.' (*A Proper Marriage*, Pt. 2 Ch. 3) The warning, like a self-fulfilling prophecy, is justified. The screaming baby is fed strictly according to the clock, and later on Caroline and Martha have terrible battles about eating. Martha breaks her daughter's will by leaving her alone at mealtimes, and the account of the strained, unloving atmosphere is painful to read. Lessing allows Martha very few glimpses of joy or fulfilment in motherhood. 'You bore me to extinction, and that's the truth of it, and no doubt I bore you. . . . you and I are just victims, my poor child, you can't help it, I can't help it, my mother couldn't help it, and her mother. . . .' (*A Proper Marriage*, Pt. 3 Ch. 2) By keeping herself emotionally independent of Caroline (which is what her treatment of her amounts to) Martha is able to leave her daughter when she leaves her husband. She is also able, temporarily, to convince herself that by leaving Caroline she is freeing her from the inevitable misery of being a daughter in relation to her mother. Martha comes to realize the naïvety of this; the damage has already been done even before she leaves, as well as by her leaving.

In Lessing's early novels the majority of women make substantial emotional investments in relationships with men. Parents and children may let you down, it is implied, but surely friendship, social and sexual, will supply answers, integration, wholeness? Through Martha it is possible to chart the series of expectations and disillusionments with regard to sex and marriage in Lessing's fiction. Her first experience of sexual intercourse is imbued by her with mystic, almost alchemic qualities: it will be the moment when 'the quintessence of all experience, all love, all beauty, should explode suddenly in a drenching, saturating moment of illumination.' (*Martha Quest*, Pt. 3 Ch. 3) When this does not happen with sex Martha, like a member of an apocalyptic sect, simply alters but does not lessen her expectations. With Douglas, her first husband, she told herself: 'Love was the key to every good; love lay like a mirage through the golden gates of sex.' (*A Proper Marriage*, Pt. 1 Ch. 1) After she leaves Douglas, and a subsequent lover, Martha feels incomplete. Lessing gives us a description not only of Martha, but of the kind of woman who depends on a relationship with a man to give her an identity: 'If the man goes away there is an empty space filled with shadows. She mourns for the temporarily extinct person she can be only with a man she loves; she mourns him who brought her 'self' to life. She lives with the empty space at her side, peopled with the images of her own potentialities until the next man walks into the space, absorbs the shadows into himself, creating her, allowing her to be her 'self' – but a new self, since it is his conception which forms her.' (*A Ripple from the Storm*, Pt. 1 Ch. 3) This has a Lawrentian tone to it, and in Lessing's canon it is applicable to other women even when Martha grows beyond it. Anna Wulf echoes it, and so do Kate Brown, Jane Somers and Alice Mellings. Even Al. Ith, in *The Marriages Between Zones Three, Four, and Five*, temporarily suffers this kind of dependence after her submergence with Ben Ata. Lessing is not by these examples deriding the unity and sense of completeness which may be brought about by a close partnership, but she is making us aware of the quiescence and stasis this may produce. The dynamic of her work pushes far beyond such a narrow fulfilment. Her novels do not end with her heroines cosily married, since she is suggesting that this may be a false completion. It is merely, at most, a stage on the journey; to see it as an end in itself is to atrophy the vital need to seek further.

Nevertheless, the characters in Lessing's novels who initially see marriage and maternity as an end to searching are abetted by a complicit society luring people to conform with it, and thus to validate its own precarious assumptions. It is hardly surprising that Martha's allegiance to the ideals represented by sex, love and marriage are so strong, despite the simultaneous reservations she has about them. 'One saw a flattering image of a madonna-like woman with a helpless infant in her arms; nothing could be more attractive. . . . what everyone conspired to prevent one seeing, was the middle-aged woman who had done nothing but produce two or three commonplace and tedious citizens in a world that was already too full of them.' (*A Proper Marriage* Pt. 4 Ch. 1)

Mrs Quest's heartfelt cry at the end of *Martha Quest*: 'It's *such* a relief when you get your daughter properly married!' is nothing to do with whether or not Douglas is a suitable husband for Martha; simply that she has achieved what her mother sees as a ritual completion. Thus, at the end of *A Proper Marriage*, when Martha tells her mother that she is leaving Douglas, May Quest turns on her, 'hands lifted in fists' and cried 'I always knew you'd come to this.' After shouting abuse at Martha 'she cried out in complete despair, from the heart ''And what will people say?'' For this was the kernel of the matter.' The narrator goes on: 'Martha went home with the feeling that she had accomplished another stage in that curious process which would set her free.' (*A Proper Marriage*, Pt. 4 Ch. 4)

Martha's quest for freedom is continued in *A Ripple from the Storm* in which she pursues politics as if communism would reveal to her what she has previously sought from love. Lessing relates Martha's political life with some irony, allowing her gradually to realize the purely theoretical nature of the communist party in Zambesia. She marries the group leader, Anton Hesse, partly to give him citizenship, but also, one feels, because she cannot yet be on her own without feeling somehow deficient: 'who, next, would walk into the empty space?. . . . Meanwhile, she told herself, she must become a good communist.' (*A Ripple from the Storm* Pt. 1 Ch. 3) This novel ends with a sense of sterility and exhaustion. The original communist group disbands, and Martha is locked in a deadening marriage. The sterility is not only thematic, but in the tone of the narration too. Up to this point Doris Lessing has been a realist writer, albeit a writer of realism shot through with intimations of another world than this. But by this time her material is becoming inappropriate for the techniques of realism. An omniscient viewpoint, conventional syntax, a linear, causal narrative, simple chronology, comprehensible characters, non-reflexive subject matter: all these are increasingly inadequate to delineate the complex potential of Martha, the questions she asks and the solutions she seeks. Martha cannot 'move on', partly because at this stage of her writing Lessing's narrative techniques do not allow her to convey the dynamics of psychic growth. The linear convention of chronological story-telling 'And then, and then' has to give way to other methods. Instead of moving onwards in the hope of arriving, Martha has to move inwards. In order to facilitate this, Lessing interrupts the *Children of Violence* sequence, and takes apart the novel form in *The Golden Notebook*. In this book she explores the ways in which form can imprison the potential of its content, and how it can be freed. *The Golden Notebook* is a transitional novel, more about processes than finished products. It is an arduous, painfully creative book, like labour and giving birth, and it marks a distinct change in Lessing as a novelist. I don't know what happened to her at the end of the 1950s. But later, talking of the genesis of *Marriages Between Zones Three, Four, and Five*, she said 'When I was in my late thirties and early forties my love life was in a state of chaos and disarray and generally no good to me or to anybody else and I was in fact, and I knew it, in a pretty bad way.'[3] And in an interview with C.J. Driver she said 'I have been involved steadily in mental illness, either by knowing psychiatrists very well indeed (which is a euphemism for saying I had a long affair with one), or by being involved with people who were nuts.'[4] It is possible that that affair broke up around this time; certainly something traumatic, or some new combination of circumstances led Doris Lessing to perceive aspects of the unconscious, both in the individual and in society, which do not operate in a neat, linear fashion. What is born from *The Golden Notebook* are the techniques which will enable Lessing to portray Martha's new growth, which is inaccessible through the conventions of realism. Martha's development needs methods of writing which can accommodate multiple viewpoints, non-linear narrative, a time scale not bound to chronology, characters who need not be understandable, fragmented sentence structure and, above all, irrational subject matter. By employing these methods, Lessing not only shows the psychical development of her characters, she enables it. There is a strong sense that Lessing's liberation from realism is also Martha's freedom from the constraints of everyday reality.

[3]Doris Lessing interview with Christopher Bigsby in *The Radical Imagination and the Liberal Tradition: Interviews with English and American Novelists* by Heide Ziegler and Christopher Bigsby (London, Junction Books, 1982), pp. 203–4.
[4]C.J. Driver, 'Doris Lessing', an interview in *The New Review*, I, no. 8 (November 1974), pp. 17–23.

Lessing began to study Sufism in the early 1960s, and this may account for the relative suddenness of Martha's insights in *Landlocked*. She seems to have had projected onto her aspects of Lessing's own personal growth so that she appears to have changed dramatically and without adequate explanation between *A Proper Marriage* and *Landlocked*. Martha's affair with Thomas Stern clearly influences her, but it is not sufficient to account for her sudden telepathic and visionary experiences. Undoubtedly after *The Golden Notebook* Lessing's work changes focus. From showing her protagonists searching for completion in personal relationships, she shifts their attention to the possibilities and methods of transcendence. This is the dominant theme from the publication of *The Golden Notebook* in 1962 for the next twenty-two years, when she comes down to earth, as it were, and re-works a surrogate mother–child relationship in *The Diary of a Good Neighbour*. *Landlocked* marks the beginning of her emphasis on the need for people to change, and thus initially on the necessity of understanding what enables us to change. This novel is followed by *The Four-Gated City*, *Briefing*, *The Summer Before the Dark* and *Memoirs*, all of which focus on ways of distancing ourselves from this material world, and making some kind of spiritual discovery. *Canopus in Argos: Archives* is a study of the mechanism of change, and it is hardly an exaggeration to say that this theme obsesses her later work, both fiction and non-fiction. She is fascinated by the apparently irrational and unpredictable shifts in public opinion, and she explores these in various ways. In the Afterword to *The Making of the Representative for Planet 8* she talks about the Antarctic Expedition of 1910–12, led by Captain Scott. She raises the question of why Scott was a national hero in the early part of this century, and was then turned into an incompetent villain by the prevailing opinion sixty years later. She also cites the McCarthy era in America, and the rise and fall of the Gang of Four in China, as examples of the transience of accepted ideas. Examples are only too easy to find, but Lessing is interested in *why* opinion changes. She says 'A word can be a powerful drug for one generation, and as bland as milk for the next.' (Afterword). What frustrates her is our complacency in not trying to discover why these changes occur. 'I think there must be definite lifespans for ideas of sets or related ideas. They are born (or reborn), come to maturity, decay, die, are replaced. If we do not at least ask ourselves if this is in fact a process, if we do not make the attempt to treat the mechanisms of ideas as something we may study, with impartiality, what hope have we of controlling them?' (Afterword, *The Making of the Representative for Planet 8*).

There are several reasons given in Doris Lessing's work for the necessity of controlling the mechanisms of change. First, to prevent the repetition of negative patterns which seem to recur every generation. Climates of opinion may change, but patterns of behaviour persist. I have already mentioned this in a familial context in the *Children of Violence* sequence: May Quest, Martha and Caroline are all victims of bad parenting, a seemingly inescapable legacy. Lessing frequently shows how children refuse to learn from their parents' experiences and mistakes, and feel bound to go through the same patterns, to go over the same ground instead of moving on. The young invariably react against their parents' values, so that Martha leads a very unconventional life in response to her mother's tenacious hold on respectability. Julia Barr, in *Retreat to Innocence*, is jealous of her liberal, freethinking parents, and what she sees as their terrible strength. She ends up by marrying a dull, cardboard civil servant, in order to avoid their way of life. In *The Golden Notebook* Anna and Molly lead eccentric, irregular lives, with the result that Anna's daughter Janet wants to go to a traditional girls' boarding school, and to wear a uniform. Tommy, Molly's son, tries to commit suicide to avoid becoming the sort of person represented to him by his mother and Anna. In *The Good Terrorist* Dorothy Mellings and her daughter Alice despair of each other, and Alice symbolizes all the brainwashed followers of sects and movements who are unable to think independently. Throughout her fiction we see Lessing's irritation with the generation succeeding hers, and its refusal at least to consider what might be learnt from the struggles and failures of its elders. In Lessing's short story 'The Temptation of Jack Orkney' she voices this frustration: 'What he could not endure was that his son, all of them, would have to make the identical journey he and his contemporaries had made. . . . That humanity was unable to learn from experience was written there for everyone to see, since the new generation of the intelligent and consciously active youth behaved identically with every generation before them.'

A second reason to examine what causes change is to prevent catastrophe. In *The Wind Blows Away our Words* Lessing talks about our universal capacity for forgetting disasters: 'We cannot endure the memory of the worst that has happened – planets or meteors colliding with us, sudden shifts of climate, the sea level suddenly rising and drowning whole cities, civilizations. . . .' (Pt. 1) Catastrophes linger on in legends, but not in history, as though we cannot simultaneously live and be aware of former annihilations. Underlying Lessing's work is an apocalyptic tone which in *The Four-Gated City* is related specifically to a nuclear holocaust. But if we were able to understand what leads us to acts of self-destruction, Lessing suggests, we might be able to understand how to avoid them. And this leads to the third reason for understanding the mechanics of change, which is in order to learn how to change ourselves. From *The Golden Notebook* onwards, Lessing's protagonists are increasingly interested in ways of transcending the material world. Their individual egos lose importance as they begin to realize that we are all part of a universal consciousness which subsumes the limitations of personal identity.

Lessing's emphasis on personal change is related to her interest in the Sufi religion. In the 1960s she became a pupil of Idries Shah. One of the tenets of Sufi, in common with other esoteric religions, is the necessity of accelerating our own evolution. 'Sufis believe that, expressed in one way, humanity is evolving towards a certain destiny. We are all taking part in that evolution. Organs come into being as a result of a need. . . . What ordinary people regard as sporadic and occasional bursts of telepathic or prophetic power are seen by the Sufi as nothing less than the first stirrings of these same organs . . . So essential is this more rarefied evolution that our future depends on it'.[5] It is becoming understood that a large proportion of the human brain lies dormant, unawakened, unused. The feats of Shamans and Yogis are not achieved because they are a different species from the rest of us, but because they have, by specific techniques, worked on the potential that lies within us all. It is possible, for example, to teach people to become spiritual healers, by making them aware of their latent powers and how to utilize them. Lessing suggests that, if we are to prevent ourselves from annihilating most of the population of this planet, or to cope with survival after such a catastrophe, we need to cultivate these latent qualities. Seen from this perspective, her later fiction can be read as a guide to methods of transcendence.

For, having pointed out the urgent need for change, Lessing does not stop there, but goes on to give us practical methods of achieving it. The first necessity, she suggests, is to cultivate the ability to look at ourselves with detachment: '. . . making that deliberate step into objectivity and away from wild emotionalism, deliberately choosing to see ourselves as, perhaps, a visitor from another planet might see us.' (*Prisons We Choose to Live Inside*) She feels that writers, being natural observers rather than participants, are particularly well placed to view situations and people objectively, and she cites the authors of Utopian fictions, such as More and Butler, as examples of clear-sighted commentators. In her own novels, one of the first signs of a change in a character's perception is an ability to see fellow beings differently. In *The Four-Gated City* Martha describes her sea-voyage to England, where she sees all the passengers 'drugged and hypnotized' with food and alcohol and sex, to which, after four days, she also succumbs. After living in London, and working with Lynda who has extra-sensory powers, the human race begins to seem disgusting to Martha. A Swiftian apprehension of her fellow beings recurs in Lessing's novels from this point onwards: '. . . their eyes were half-useless: many wore bits of corrective glass over these spoiled or ill-grown organs; their ears were defective: many wore machines to help them hear even as much as the sounds made by their fellows: and their mouths were full of metal and foreign substances to assist teeth that were rotting . . . their guts were full of drugs because they could not defecate normally; and their nervous systems were numbed. . . . They lived in an air which was like a thick soup of petrol and fumes and stink of sweat and bad air from lungs full of the smoke they used as a narcotic, and filthy air from their bowels.' (*The Four-Gated City*, Pt. 4, ch. 2) Kate Brown also experiences this detached view in *The Summer Before the Dark*. She goes to the theatre and views the audience as 'animals covered with cloth and bits of fur, ornamented with stones, their faces and claws painted with colour. Everyone had just finished eating animal of some kind.' (Ch. 4) This impassiveness is carried

---

[5]Idries Shah, *The Sufis* (New York, Doubleday, 1964), p. 61.

further as Lessing's novels begin to centre on protagonists with increasing spiritual awareness, and who are shown to have a corresponding lack of investment in personal relationships. In *Briefing for a Descent into Hell* an agent for change is reincarnated into a man called Charles Watkins. Charles is remembered by his contemporaries for his indifference to other people. A school friend gives up a holiday for his benefit, and a woman sacrifices her career, but he is neither grateful nor reproachful; he is simply uninterested. By choosing a cosmic setting for *Canopus in Argos: Archives* Lessing allows her narrators literally to view the human race from the perspective of another planet. In *Shikasta* George Sherban (like Watkins, a disguised agent) is unemotional and cool. He distresses his lover, Suzannah, who wants more commitment than he is able to offer. In these novels the narratorial bias is steadily towards the impersonal. We have already seen in *Children of Violence* the disastrous consequences of seeking fulfilment from personal relationships. The varying narrators of *Canopus in Argos: Archives* endorse the fallacy of the personal as they record the emotional muddles of other races with serenity and dispassion. But occasionally a character is allowed a more emotional reaction, and we see the human race regarded no longer with disgust but with pity, as blind, ignorant and pathetic: 'Poor people of the past, poor, poor people, so many of them, for long thousands of years, not knowing anything, fumbling and stumbling and longing for something different but not knowing what had happened to them or what they longed for.' (*Shikasta*, last page).

Lessing's work reiterates the necessity of detachment from the influence of group processes. Jung points out that the process of individuation entails separation from a group, and that the changes wrought by crowd psychology are less long-lasting than those achieved by the individual. Lessing is interested in the power of group opinion, and in *Prisons we Choose to Live Inside* she devotes a chapter to this subject, called 'Group Minds'. She cites techniques of brainwashing, and the Milgram experiment, as examples of the difficulty of maintaining independent views under pressure. One of her favourite targets throughout her novels is our susceptibility to rhetoric, and she has spoken about the peculiarly disabling effect of certain words, such as 'fascist', which preclude further thought or reasoning. In *The Sentimental Agents in the Volyen Empire* there is a School of Rhetoric set up to train propagandists to incite others to action through rhetoric, whilst themselves remaining calm: 'a school for the use of power over others, for the crude manipulation of the lowest instincts.' To this end, examinations are held with students declaiming powerful speeches, wired up to record electronically their emotional reactions to key words such as 'friends', 'comrades', 'sacrifice'. A buzzer sounds when the reaction exceeds the prescribed limit, and then a student is failed. In the same novel there is a hospital for Rhetorical Diseases, where a group of young people are chanting

We shall overcome

We shall overcome
We shall overcome one day.

The narrator goes on to say: 'The tune of this dirge originated V-millenniums ago on Volyen during its time as a Volyenadnan colony, to express the hopelessness of slaves.' For Lessing it is clearly a song of impotent, sentimental indulgence, and its emotive qualities are what she most dislikes. In a review of a book by Idries Shah, she points out: 'We live in a society where emotionalism is prized; to say that something has moved us, is the equivalent of saying it is good, worthy, admirable. But the Sufis say that many of the 'higher' feelings we prize are merely crude emotionalism; and 'It is characteristic of the primitive to regard things which are felt strongly to be of importance.' And, again, 'the importance of something is in inverse proportion to its attractiveness.'[6]

The influence of the primitive is significant in Lessing's analysis of emotive words. In *Prisons We Choose to Live Inside* she examines the primeval power of the word 'blood', formerly associated with the protective qualities of ritual sacrifice. Leaders constantly implore their followers to 'fight to the last drop of blood', and, as Lessing points out 'It is not too much to say that when the word blood is pronounced, this is a sign that reason is about to depart.' (*Prisons*, Pt. 1) Marion Milner emphasizes this point in *An Experiment in Leisure* (1937): 'Under dictatorships vital images seemed used more deliberately for political purposes, primitive images of blood-brotherhood, of blood sacrifice for one's country, of an absolute father-god-dictator at the head of the nation.' Lessing is acutely aware of the atavism that lies under a cover of 'civilized' behaviour. In *The Fifth Child* a smug couple, David and Harriet, are living out an idyll of their own whilst relentlessly exploiting David's father and Harriet's mother. They congratulate themselves for having opted out of the mood of their time, 'the greedy and selfish sixties', but they are suddenly and sharply reminded of the savagery within them. Harriet gives birth to a wild little monster they call Ben. Ben embodies all the primitive brutality his parents are denying in themselves. He is their 'shadow' side revealed, and he is frightful. In this allegory Lessing seems to be saying how thin a veneer covers the powerful and barbaric forces within us, and that we ignore the primitive aspects of ourselves at our peril. Manipulators have always been skilful at utilizing the forces of the collective unconscious for their own ends. It is not a question of feeding people with ideas from outside, but of invoking and channelling the forces that are already there.

Lessing's sharpest attack on rhetoric comes in *The Good Terrorist*, where again she focuses on the political rhetoric she first undermined in *A Ripple from the Storm*. She implies that nothing has changed. *The Good Terrorist* is full of wonderful parody. The squatters (members of the Communist Centre Union) call each other 'Comrade' when they remember,

[6]Doris Lessing, 'Sufic Searches', *The Literary Review*, no. 49 (July 1982), pp. 10–11.

and their leader makes a speech consisting solely of catch-phrases strung together: 'We all know the criminal, the terrible condition of Britain. We all know the fascist imperialist government must be forcibly overthrown! There is no other way forward! The forces that will liberate us all are already being forged. We are in the vanguard of these forces, and the responsibility for a glorious future is with us, in our hands.' This novel is extremely funny, and most brilliantly observes the collective myopia of the sect mentality. But between the lines you can see Lessing's pain and disappointment that such a novel still needed to be written, and could still be so relevant to the 1980s.

Indifference to group opinion, an ability not to follow the herd, is one of Lessing's prescriptions for facilitating change. In *The Sirian Experiments* she explores the behaviour of a cool, dry, bureaucrat, Amien II. Amien II is gradually and subtly influenced by the planet Canopus, and, haltingly, she formulates to herself the theory that she is being used for a purpose, the changing of Sirian ideas. Through Amien II, her narrator, Lessing suggests that fundamental changes of ideas are brought into a group through a deviant individual who, if not thrown out of the group, will influence it. But even when we see this happen, we do not learn the potential usefulness of this phenomenon. Thus, in the Afterword to *The Making of the Representative for Planet 8* Lessing uses Southern Africa as an example of a situation where warnings by a few people were considered subversive and ignored. By the time these minority views were more widely accepted it was too late to prevent a war taking place in Southern Rhodesia, now Zimbabwe. She implies the likelihood of the same thing happening in South Africa, and regrets 'the waste of it all, the stupidity, the preventability neglected.' The question remains, however, who or what influences the individual in the first place to deviate from the prevailing climate of opinion or ideology? This is particularly interesting in view of Doris Lessing's own ability to absorb and transmit new ideas before they are generally received. From the accumulating evidence of her novels and other writings, it would seem that she believes that it is possible for individuals to 'tune in' to a higher consciousness, (possibly linked in her case with the practice of Sufism) which may alert an individual to what is about to happen. She seems to be saying that perhaps we really are influenced for change by forces of which we are ignorant.

Ways of being receptive to these forces are frequently described in her work. Dreams are perhaps the most common and acceptable way of introducing information about unconscious or irrational elements into a realist text. In Lessing's work they are extensively used to illumine both characters and the reader. In her first novel *The Grass is Singing* the dreams of Mary Turner illuminate the ambivalent feelings she has for her black servant, Moses. In *Children of Violence* Martha learns to use her dreams as a means of access to her unconscious motivations and desires, as does Anna in *The Golden Notebook*. Similarly, in *The Summer Before the Dark* Kate Brown is given a serial dream which runs parallel to her waking life. Lessing uses the dream symbolism very skilfully, making it act as counterpoint to the realist action. It is both a motivating force for Kate, and a commentary from her unconscious on her conscious behaviour. The vital relevance of dreams is emphasized by Charles Watkins in *Briefing*, and he tries to explain their importance to his psychiatrist: 'Is that it? Your dreams or your life. But it is not *or*, that is the point. It is *and*. Everything is. Your dreams *and* your life.' Lessing does not allow Watkins to live out this conviction. His vision is blotted out, and he is returned to a half-life.

Madness is shown to be another method of getting in touch with forces or powers beyond everyday comprehension. In Lessing's novels what is ordinarily seen as madness is revealed as a state of heightened perception or receptivity. Lynda Coldridge, in *The Four-Gated City*, is telepathic, and hears voices. Charles Watkins undergoes a psychical journey similar to that described by R.D. Laing in *The Politics of Experience*. Both characters are treated by psychiatrists in ways which attempt to deny or destroy their special powers. Some of Lessing's characters, such as Martha Quest, Anna Wulf and Kate Brown, voluntarily undertake a period of 'letting-go', of confronting the worst in themselves, and allowing a kind of temporary madness to engulf them. This brings them in touch with the repressed, 'shadow' side of their personalities, and allows them to work through it. Madness in Lessing's canon is always a situation of great potential, which can either be destroyed through conventional treatment, or used creatively if allowed to run its course.

In *Briefing for a Descent into Hell* and later in *Canopus in Argos: Archives* Lessing propounds the theory that change on earth is initiated by agents from other planets or civilizations. These people are often reincarnated for this purpose, and they have to try to retain their sense of mission despite many difficulties. In *Archives* the wise and benign Canopeans attempt to infiltrate less advanced planets to influence them for good. However fantastic these ideas may seem, I think it is important to remember that Lessing is not primarily an imaginative writer, and that these ideas are commonplace to ufologists and to those who study arcane religions, where this theory recurs. To quote just one example about the legend of Atlantis: 'The knowledge of the Atlanteans came from *another galaxy* and was brought by those who became the first rulers of Atlantis. Some of those Extraterrestrials returned to their home; others remained on earth to carry out a mission . . . The Atlanteans will reappear openly when Atlantis rises. They are now scattered all over the continents.'[7] The task of Charles Watkins in *Briefing* is to be 'an assisting of the Earth's people through the coming Planetary Emergency, in which all life may be lost.' Charles dimly remembers another existence, a memory of course shared by seers and poets throughout the ages. Lessing is simply re-stating what Wordsworth, for example, clearly sets out in 'Intimations of Immortality':

Our birth is but a sleep and a forgetting:

---

[7]Robert Charroux, *Lost Worlds: Scientific Secrets of the Ancients* (Glasgow, Fontana, 1974), p. 90.

The Soul that rises with us, our life's Star,
Hath had elsewhere its setting,
And cometh from afar:
Not in entire forgetfulness,
And not in utter nakedness,
But trailing clouds of glory do we come
From God, who is our home.

In Lessing's fiction the agents for change are sometimes in danger of forgetting their mission. They are tempted to succumb to what she often describes as the doped or drugged state of earthly existence. Charles Watkins is defeated by psychiatrists who return him to his wife, 'cured'. The Canopean agents in *Canopus in Argos: Archives* are generally more successful.

Although Doris Lessing advocates change both in individuals and in collective attitudes, she does not deny the difficulties of achieving it. In her beautiful and lyrical novel, *The Making of the Representative for Planet 8* she shows a race resisting change despite being put under terrible pressure, indeed threatened with annihilation. But it begins to realize that it is only such a powerful threat that will stimulate the necessary evolution: 'We were learning, we old ones, that in times when a species, a race, is under threat, drives and necessities built into the very substance of our flesh speak out in ways that we need never have known about if extremities had not come to squeeze these truths out of us.' One of the truths the people of Planet 8 come to know is the relative unimportance of the individual, or even of the species. What has actually materialized – their planet and its race – is shown to be only one aspect of how things are: '. . . possibilities that had not been given actuality in the level of experience we had known, had experienced . . . hovered just behind the veil, potentials, what might have been or could have been. . . . Myriads there were, the unachieved possibilities; but each real and functioning on its own level – *where* and *when* and *how?* – each world every bit as valid and valuable as what we had known as real.' This visionary passage has significant implications in relation to change. If unrealized, latent actuality is really valid and functioning at its own level, we do not need to see change in terms of loss, or experience it as a violent wrenching away from a certain course or mode of life. Rather, it's a question of expanding our perception to see potentialities that are already there, 'just behind the veil'. For the inhabitants of Planet 8 the hope of rescue from disaster (and with it the retention of their own identities and roles) has to be abandoned. It is only when they accept that they may not be able to fulfil the potential they're aware of, that they are able to become part of potentialities hitherto unknown to them. After much tribulation they are themselves changed, and they transcend the limitations of Planet 8.

After the mystic qualities of *Archives*, Lessing surprised her readers by the realistic, earth-bound tone of the Jane Somers novels, *The Diary of a Good*

Neighbour and *If the Old Could* . . . What is perhaps more surprising is that in the three novels which follow *Archives* she re-works old themes: mother and daughter relationships (albeit surrogate ones), a love affair between a man and a woman, and the activities of a small political sect. The hold of these themes on Lessing is tenacious, and she seems unable to shake them off. The publication of the Jane Somers novels under a pseudonym suggests an anxiety about her name, fame and identity. Despite her rationale for the experiment, what comes through is the nagging doubt of the insecure child: 'Am I any good without my famous name?' The answer, in terms of sales and recognition, was 'no', and this must have been painful. Interestingly, these novels must have been written at the same time as the *Archives*, and they deal with the messy aspects of human existence that are so cleanly excised from the clear Canopean air: ageing, degeneration, death. It is almost as if the maintenance of the detached perspective, the serene overview, was too much of a strain to maintain without some kind of safety valve in the form of realism. Lessing's best book is *The Memoirs of a Survivor* precisely because in it she admits the defenceless little child she excluded from the *Children of Violence* series, together with the enlightened, serene but battle-scarred survivor. Both were given understanding, both given their due. They were of course one and the same person, and they exemplified the paradox of humankind: we are both vulnerable and strong, we struggle and we survive, we are mortal and immortal.

Having achieved this synthesis in *The Memoirs of a Survivor* and, differently, in *The Making of the Representative for Planet 8*, Lessing needs to have the confidence to work with it again. She is apparently writing her autobiography, and maybe this will be the vehicle she needs to accommodate both the wise woman and the needy child. Meanwhile, Doris Lessing continues to remind us of the urgent need to change and, simultaneously, of the unremitting atavism of human nature. It is a thankless task, but then so was Cassandra's.

Note

Angela Carter was born in Britain in 1940, educated in medieval literature at Bristol University, and has worked in Britain, Japan, the US, and Australia. She has earned her living by writing, producing eight novels since 1965, as well as journalism, radio plays, three collections of short fictions, and an exercise in cultural history. She is actively interested in the moving image, and two films have been made from her work, *The Company of Wolves* and *The Magic Toyshop*. Her fiction can be called a kind of literary criticism (she has called it that), but it is also true that she has a large following among readers of Science Fiction. Her work is often categorized as fantastic or Gothic, but considered as a whole – consciously alert and unconsciously rich – it constitutes one of the most intelligent, committed and imaginative reports and critiques of the mid to late twentieth century, its myths, folklore, theories, fashions and cultural inheritance. It seeks to reflect changes, and to precipitate them: in women, and men, and on behalf of women, and therefore of us all.

Works
Shadow Dance (originally *Honeybuzzard*), (Pan Books 1965)
The Magic Toyshop (Heinemann 1967, Virago 1981)
Several Perceptions (Heinemann 1968, Pan Books 1970)
Heroes and Villains (Heinemann 1969, Penguin Books 1981)
Love (Hart–Davis 1971, Chatto & Windus 1987, revised)
The Infernal Desire Machines of Dr Hoffman (Hart–Davis 1972, Penguin Books 1982)
The Passion of New Eve (Gollancz 1977, Virago 1982)
Nights at the Circus (Chatto & Windus 1984, Pan 1985)
The Sadeian Woman: an exercise in cultural history (Virago 1979)
Nothing Sacred (Virago 1982)
Come Unto These Yellow Sands, 4 radio Plays (Bloodaxe Books 1985)
Fireworks (Quartet 1974, Chatto & Windus/Virago 1987, revised)
The Bloody Chamber (Gollancz 1979, Penguin Books 1981)
Black Venus (Chatto & Windus 1985, Pan Books 1986)

Select bibliography
Lorna Sage, 'A Savage Sideshow,' *New Review* IV, 39/40 (July 1977)
E.C. Rose, 'Through the Looking Glass: When Women Tell Fairy Tales,' in E. Abel, Hirsch, Langland, eds., *The Voyage In: Fictions of Female Development* (US, University Press 1983)
P. Duncker, 'Re-imagining the Fairy Tale: Angela Carter's Bloody Chambers,' *Literature and History* X, 1 (Spring 1984)
John Haffenden, 'Magical Mannerist,' *Novelists in Interview* (Methuen 1985)
Interview with Kerryn Goldsworthy, *meanjin* XLIV, 1, (Adelaide, March 1985)
Anne Smith, 'Myths and the Erotic,' *Women's Review* 1 (November 1985)
Suzanne Kappeler, *The Pornography of Representation* (Polity Press 1986), pp. 133–7
Robert Clark, 'Angela Carter's Desire Machine,' *Women's Studies* XIV, 2, 1987
Brian McHale, *Post-modernist Fiction* (Methuen 1987)

2

Enthralment: Angela Carter's Speculative Fictions

Elaine Jordan

'A city built of hubris, imagination and desire . . .' As we are, ourselves; or, as we ought to be.

Nights at the Circus, p. 97

I

History tells us that every oppressed class gained true liberation from its masters through its own efforts. It is necessary that woman learn that lesson, that she realize that her freedom will reach as far as her power to achieve her freedom reaches. It is, therefore, far more important for her to begin with her inner regeneration, to cut loose from the weight of prejudices, traditions, customs. The demand for equal rights in every vocation of life is just and fair; but, after all, the most vital right is the right to love and be loved.

Emma Goldman's words, from *The Tragedy of Woman's Emancipation* appear as part of the postscript to Angela Carter's *The Sadeian Woman*. We may accept the call to liberation through our own activity, but loving, or getting oneself loved, may be the very thing that stands in the way of acting against tradition and custom, and the prejudices of those we love. Toni Morrison's first novel, *The Bluest Eye*, exemplifies feminism's suspicion of romantic love, when Pauline Breedlove's fascination with what she sees on the silver screen makes her forget 'lust and simple caring for.'[1] The same novel gives wonderful expression to a woman's desires and to a maternal care which is intimately and life-savingly experienced in spite of burdened irritation and scolding: 'somebody with hands who does not want me to die.'[2] But lust and caring and the immense seduction of

I have been the beneficiary of an intemperate and generous correspondence with Angela Carter, which has informed some aspects of what I have written. I would also like gratefully to acknowledge discussion with many students, in particular Ros Kayes, who suggested that *Heroes and Villains* could be read as a rewriting of *Frankenstein*.

[1] Toni Morrison, *The Bluest Eye* (London, Panther Books, 1981), p. 113
[2] Morrison, *The Bluest Eye*, p. 16.

being cared for, like romantic love, may still stand in the way of free action. It is also true that Emma Goldman, like anyone with a programme for action, lays women under an obligation even as she aims to liberate them: Woman 'must learn'.

Love is the positive term against which oppressive sexual relations are defined, in *The Sadeian Woman*. Angela Carter at one point writes as if it exists naturally before social codes come into operation:

> The moment they succumb to this anonymity, they cease to be themselves, with their separate lives and desires: they cease to be the lovers who have met to assuage desire in a reciprocal pact of tenderness, and they engage at once in a spurious charade of maleness and femaleness (p. 8).

But when reading *The Sadeian Woman*, it is easy to forget this base in the possibility of heterosexual love being tender and reciprocal, because of the violence with which Carter here revalues the conventional ranking of wife and prostitute, mocks long-suffering, and desecrates the mother. Carter's 'Exercise in Cultural History' uses Sade's writing to expose twentieth-century feminine roles of victim and dominatrix, and to espouse his cause of sex for pleasure not procreation as far as she can take it before turning on her precursor: the libertine is never free because his excitement depends not on his human object but on the existence of an authority to defy. He can never accept or enjoy free love:

> In his diabolic solitude, only the possibility of love could awake the libertine to perfect, immaculate terror. It is in this holy terror of love that we find, in both men and women themselves, the source of all opposition to the emancipation of women (p. 150).

At the end of *The Sadeian Woman* as at the beginning freedom is identified with love, so that this work in fact challenges my fear that love makes for caution. But its last sentence, the one I've just quoted, is not really easy to read. There is a flickering possibility, not that 'We are all terrified of love, and this is why women and men alike resist real emancipation', but that 'love is a holy terror' – something mischievous and perverse and intense, quasi-sacred, still exciting to the libertine – and *this* is the source of continued enthralment. Where unequivocal assertion is needed there is a stylish equivocation producing at least a moment of bafflement. The Utopian peroration for free love is made outside the text and in the words of another woman: 'Postscript: Red Emma replies to the Madman of Charenton.' The main text itself is as terrified or embarrassed as the rest of us, thinking of love. And this is quite proper: it needs to be spoken for, but it is not unproblematic given the debris you have to wade through to get there.

The kind of caring recognized in 'Someone with hands who does not want me to die' seems to answer to 'need' rather than the perverse and chilling 'desire' (what I want, what I hate) that has haunted analysis since Lacan. It is this base in knowing herself cared for that keeps Toni

Morrison's narrator Claudia sane, its absence for Pecola that means she goes mad in a world of fantasies. Something like it is fundamental to active identity, to well-being in the world. Value for such a foundation is hard to combine with projects that unsettle learned assumptions and familiar affections. Hard but not impossible.

II

Explaining Angela Carter's ways of writing, I'm often tempted to make analogies with male writers – with Swift for her unstable irony, with Voltaire for her rational impiety, with Blake for persistent radical questioning. *The Passion of New Eve*, for example, is peppered with bits of Blake and draws on the same hermetic sources as he did, alternative religion as a site of resistance to power. A comparison can be made between Carter's historical situation as a writer, and the account given of Blake's by David Erdman in *Prophet Against Empire*:[3] a window opened briefly in the 1790s by the French Revolution, on radical possibilities, rolled back by international hostilities and Tory repression. Though I make such comparisons, I really have no problem in saying that Angela Carter writes as a woman:

> The Women's Movement has been of immense importance to me personally and I would regard myself as a feminist writer, because I'm feminist in everything else. . . . growing into feminism was part of the process of maturing. . . .

> There is a tendency to underplay, even to completely devalue, the experience of the 1960s, especially for women, but towards the end of that decade there was a brief period of public philosophical awareness that occurs only very occasionally in human history; when, truly, it felt like Year One. . . . I can date to that time and to some of those debates and to that sense of heightened awareness to the society around me in the summer of 1968, my own questioning of the nature of my reality as a *woman*. How that social fiction of my 'femininity' was created, by means outside my control, and palmed off on me as the real thing. ('Notes from the Front Line', p. 69)[4]

The mood of Angela Carter's fifth novel, *Love* which was written in 1969, predates her time in Japan which confirmed her in questioning what it could be, to be a woman or a man. In her Afterword, on *Love*'s republication in 1987, she calls it 'an almost sinister feat of male impersonation,' and continues the lives of its personae from her different perspective nearly two decades on. This is one example of her instructive lack of anxiety in acknowledging change, in the world and in her own awareness

---

[3]D.V. Erdman, *Prophet Against Empire* (Princeton, 1969).
[4]Angela Carter, 'Notes from the Front Line,' *On Gender and Writing*, ed. Michelene Wandor (London, Pandora Press, 1983), pp. 69–77.

and ways of writing. The account of her personal history within a larger history which I have quoted is jeered at by Janet Watts in the *London Review of Books*, 8 December 1988, as the sort of gullible Sixtiespeak at which the young of the 80s giggle. My kids don't – in fact, the jeering generation is as much produced in journalist discourse as anything else. The young are uncertain, they attach themselves to available identities, like anyone else. Janet Watts is reviewing Sara Maitland's collection of women's reminiscences of the 60s, *Very Heaven*, which she criticizes for their self-absorbed, muddle-minded frivolity, ignoring any larger sense of politics and history. Although oral and feminist history have invited us to think beyond what newspapers and official histories record, Angela Carter is a bad person to pillory on such grounds. She acknowledges the journal as 'the most traditional of all women's literary forms', but 'has a strong resistance to telling people about myself.'[5] In interviews, she rarely fails to relate moments in her career to the political possibilities, both at the moment of the interview and of the writing discussed. The flagrant element of quotation in 'Notes from the Front Line', which Janet Watts seems to miss, makes a valuable connection between Carter's discourse of herself in the 60s, and the liberatory aspects of the discourse of the French Revolution, which in England was that of Blake and Mary Wollstonecraft (an antagonism of potential comrades which has not yet been seriously explored). We, by which I mean women and the post-modernist 90s, need writers self-conscious and world-conscious enough to harness our enjoyment of sardonic quotation to active hope and energy, rather than a journalist who only belatedly recognizes her censoriousness in relegating hope and energy to the sphere of remembrance, and then has nothing more to offer than saying, without any recantation, that she's sorry.[6]

Each of Angela Carter's longer fictions represents a process of change. They are questioning journeys to no final home, which remember but are not detained by nostalgia – 'Eve on the run again,' as *The Passion of New Eve* puts it (p. 169). Women on the road, escaping the last enthralment. How very difficult it is to say that, without sounding as if you mean Marilyn Monroe in *Bus Stop* or *Some Like It Hot*. Angela Carter writes as a reader of texts and signs, and animates readers to a similar active response, resisting passive consumption that wastes away time and life. She accepts open-endedness, the possibility of different readings of her work, and she is not without contradictions. In 1980 she wrote of the attraction, for groups excluded from 'the power-political high spots,' of rewriting myths to 'accommodate ourselves in the past,' myth being 'more malleable than history.' But this assumes a certain freedom from myth, for historical discourse; and she is not over-optimistic about the revision of myths as a political tactic: 'It is, after all, very rarely possible for new ideas to find adequate expression in old forms.'[7] In 1983 she is more conscious of

[5]Interview with Kerryn Goldsworthy, *meanjin* 44, 1, (March 1985)
[6]Janet Watts, 'Viva Biba,' *London Review of Books*, 10, 22 (8 December 1988), pp. 15–16.
[7]Angela Carter, 'The Language of Sisterhood,' *The Fate of the Language*, ed. L. Michaels and C. Ricks (University of California Press, 1980), p. 228.

writing on the 'front line' of change, than of finding accommodation in a
fixed history:

> (Reading is just as creative an activity as writing and most intellectual
> development depends upon new readings of old texts. I am all for
> putting new wine in old bottles, especially if the pressure of the new
> wine makes the old bottles explode). . . .

> I personally feel much more in common with certain Third World
> writers, both female and male, who are transforming actual fictional
> forms to both reflect and to precipitate changes in the way people feel
> about themselves.
> ('Notes from the Front Line,' pp. 69, 77)

Excitement about 'demythologizing' was historically specific, a thing of
the 70s. It operated like a myth itself, having the power to activate; it's not
dead yet, I hope.[8] Angela Carter has tried at times to draw a distinction
between folklore, produced by the people to make their lives more
exciting, and myths, designed to make people unfree. I don't think that
will really hold, except as a way of showing (as in my previous quotation)
whose side she's on. Some myths have more power than others, overtly or
covertly; the more veiled they are, the more dangerously perhaps they lie
coiled in and round the psyche and behaviour. Whether a myth is
liberatory or oppressive depends on the existing power relations, the
company it keeps, the context of its use.

III

My experience of reading Angela Carter's work is of being entertained,
enthralled, jolted – and drawn back to second and third readings in which
I realize how much of a structure her fictions have in experimenting with
particular sets of pre-texts. Robert Clark has taken her to task for not
wanting to be over-conscious of what she's doing.[9] I think rather that she
wants to cover her tracks. 'Wolf-Alice', the final story in *The Bloody
Chamber*, could be taken as a training manual in Levi-Straussian anthro-
pology and the Lacanian mirror stage: in 'wild reasoning', the derivation
of a sense of time from women's periods and of selfhood from objectified
images, and the sacrifice of animal existence to human relations of subject
and object. Saying that far from exhausts the story, in which a wild girl,
not socialized into disgust, humanizes a male monster, the werewolf or
psychotic that wolves would reject for preying on his own kind – yet
another go at 'Beauty and the Beast'. Carter has a strong habit of radical
rationalism, and a tendency to produce slogans and maxims, converted to
satiric and subversive purposes. So Marianne in *Heroes and Villains*

---

[8]Roland Barthes, 'Myth Today,' in *Mythologies* (London, Jonathan Cape, 1983), pp. 135,
137, 157.
[9]Robert Clark, 'Angela Carter's Desire Machine,' *Women's Studies* XIV, 2, (1987),
pp. 151–2.

derides herself when she starts to think in gnomic sentences like those the myth-maker Donally chalks up. Can you take down the master's house with his tools? Well, you'd use any tools available, but your own way. Carter's work makes imaginative desire play over intellectual constructs, and intellect work with myths.

'The genesis of the story was something discarded in the final version,' Angela Carter said in an interview with Anne Smith, talking about her researches for 'Black Venus'.[10] A degree of oblivion, of deletion, is crucial to writing: the sign we make rises on the ashes of what we want to forget or destroy, both consciously and unconsciously. This is part of Angela Carter's writing process to an extreme degree, and this produces one of the strongest effects of her work (when it's not inhibited) – the reader's retroactive response. Something like *zeugma* – the yoking together within the same syntax of incompatible elements – is Angela Carter's most characteristic device. Walser in *Nights at the Circus* notes 'A skipping-rope of egg-shaped pearls, which she banked' (p. 11). Starting from mid-sentence, Fevvers's pearls are precious, to be handled like the eggs they look like; but being so outsize they're valued at no more than a child in a playground would give for them: the sentence swings like a skipping rope from one extreme to another, play and calculation, the fragile and the gross, coming to a stop with Fevvers's actual respect for cash value, though by this point, with a fairground dizziness, she may seem to be putting eggs and skipping ropes into the safe-deposit. Carter puts together what should properly be kept apart: a sumptuous carpet and dog turds, in *The Passion of New Eve*, (p. 90), to take an example that makes my housewifely gorge rise.

I have written elsewhere of the way in which Angela Carter's short fictions offer three for the price of one: on how 'The Bloody Chamber' rewrites the Bluebeard story as a critical homage to Colette, for example.[11] 'Peter and Wolf' in *Black Venus* revises Prokofiev's parable (whose primary purpose is to teach children the instruments of the orchestra), but also the story of the Fall in Genesis; once you've seen it, it's written all over it. I didn't see it until ten minutes before I had to take a Community Education class on the story – the realization redeemed me from my panic at how my class of housewives would take Peter's prolonged fascination with the accidentally, unconsciously displayed genitals of his girl cousin, nurtured as a wolf. It would have been all right for me to say 'Some feminist theorists think that women should take over the representation of women's bodies': they had quite enough respect for me as the expert representative of the academy, and probably plenty of reservations about which they kept their own counsel. The fact remained that the story turned on a boy looking and looking, and if any of them felt offended I

10'Myths and the Erotic,' interview with Anne Smith, *Women's Review* I, (November 1985), p. 28.
11Elaine Jordan, 'The dangers of Angela Carter,' to be edited by Isobel Armstrong & Maud Ellmann, proceedings of the conference at Southampton (July 1988), [2].

did not want to appeal to my institutional status and tell them there was nothing natural about their response, they were just ideologically conditioned. My own involuntary second look, my retroactive response to the story's concealed origin, gave me more confidence. The effect of the Fall in Christian discourse was shame at sexual difference, producing cultural differences of women and men. The boy's horror at seeing the girl's difference (which he experiences as guilt, compounded by the death of his grandmother from the wolf-girl's bite, since he was responsible for finding her) motivates him to learn to read, to learn Latin, and to decide to become a priest. 'On this rock do I build my Church.'[12] At the cost of her life, his grandmother had tried to teach him that the alien child of the wild was after all kin, however much of an unholy mess that made in the house. This is the opposite of what the grandfather teaches in Prokofiev's *Peter and the Wolf*, where the boy learns that the undomesticated beast must be kept outside the gate, or captured. The only female in that story is the duck who gets eaten.

Carter's use of wolves and other beasts in her stories reminds us that we are animals, and, in the tradition of the fable, says that animals may have more sense than us, when we think ourselves most sophisticated. This complicates the first two versions of 'Beauty and the Beast' in *The Bloody Chamber*, 'The Courtship of Mr Lyon' and 'The Tiger's Bride' – raising the question of whether we are to read the beasts as men, or as instructively better than men. I think Mr Lyon is a man, in the last instance, but the Tiger is better than that. In 'Peter and the Wolf' shock and guilt make the difference between female and male yawn wider than the difference between human and animal, initially; and it's important that readers should share something of this shock, or wonder. The boy refuses his grandmother's transgressive wisdom, and chooses the male initiation rite of learning Latin, the *sermo patria*, leaving the village and his mother tongue behind. But he is vouchsafed another look. Leaving for the seminary, he sees his cousin again, across water, suckling some cubs. He wades the water to embrace her, overcome with emotion – but she's off at once, back to the wild. Possibly this parodies the baptism of Christ: the hairiness of the wolf-girl associates her with images of Mary Magdalen, modelled on John the Baptist. In that case, the boy is not acknowledged by the father, but himself acknowledges the mother. The scene replaces the intended initiation; he continues his journey, but now his destination is the open world not the seminary – away from home and kin, but also away from paternal discipline. His knowledge now can incorporate kinship with the woman and closeness to animal existence; he has no need for alienating structures to maintain barriers against the facts of life.

My students might be affronted with good cause at the textual display of a girl's private parts. But in so far as their sense of what was proper depended on Christian culture, I could say that the Bible depended quite

---

[12]See W.J. Ong, *The Presence of the Word*, quoted in *No Man's Land I: The War of the Words*, S. Gubar & S. Gilbert (Yale University Press, 1988), pp. 252–3.

as much on the reminder of sexual difference, the woman's body as a forbidden book; though it took some sort of shock to make that clear – an initial stunning, a delayed realization. To be sophisticatedly unmoved by Peter's observations, cauterized by culture, was to be obtuse. Peter's second chance in Carter's story revises the first glance and restores the ordinary fact of our animal origin and dependence on maternal nurture, which can then be left behind. His status in the story is double: it is a parable of anyone's maturation in view of the facts of life, and also a mockery of biblical misogyny. Some readers are more shocked by the transgression of the boundary between animal and human, than by the boy's horror at seeing where he comes from, as I found when I studied the story again with a group within the university. Well, it's fantasy; if you want to be literal, conceivably the girl is fostering the cubs. I don't mean to suggest that everything can be neatly justified and closed off. Fictions like this deliberately leave you arguing, and continuing the story to your own satisfaction.

IV

I have mentioned Robert Clark's criticism of Angela Carter in *Women's Studies*. I did not mean to: it is motivated by a disposition to find fault, patronizes when it approves, suppresses material from an interview with Lorna Sage (on which it draws heavily) when such material would counter his criticisms, reads carelessly and therefore misinterprets, and is factually inaccurate – not a petty matter when interpretation must depend on accurate reading, however selective, and when such a harsh judgement is derived from the interpretation. Clark's criticism in fact reads like a sinister piece of female impersonation:

> Her primary allegiance is to a postmodern aesthetics that emphasizes the non-referential emptiness of definitions. Such a commitment precludes an affirmative feminism founded in referential commitment to women's historical and organic being. . . . her fascination with violent eroticism and her failure to find any alternative basis on which to construct a feminine identity prevent her work from being other than an elaborate trace of women's self-alienation. (p. 158)

On such grounds, which ignore her own statement of where her primary 'allegiance' lies, Clark would cast out the most brilliant and exciting of women writers who is also frankly and intelligently committed to radical politics and analysis, 'attempting to grapple with the real relations between human beings,' whose writing is devoted to 'investigating the social fictions that regulate our lives' ('Notes from the Front Line,' p. 70). What Angela Carter does in her writing and stimulates in her reader is feminist affirmation. She works from specific experiments rather than from a single assured base towards a single Utopian goal. She knows that, given differences of class, culture, race, opportunity, 'there is a fictive quality about the notion of a "women only" experience' ('The Language of Sisterhood,' p. 231). She is well aware of how such fictions can serve political purposes, by producing identification and solidarity. It is also true that notions of the feminine, of what is proper to and for women, have enslaved us.

The 'historical and organic being' of women is true enough, as true and real as anything ever is, but it is not fixed as a necessary identity that must be referred to. We are speaking or writing subjects, in discourses that precede us and go on; we participate in them and can produce new ones (I derive the term 'speaking subject' from the work of Julia Kristeva, and from psychoanalysis more generally). Some of these discourses produce 'selves' – indeed the end of *Nights at the Circus* indicates that the production of new selves, as well as the deconstruction of old fixed identities, is very much part of Angela Carter's discourse. Terms like 'self-alienation' and 'self-discovery' assume that we are essentially fixed as pre-given selves, that we can find, even when we don't know them. The alternative term to 'self', the 'speaking subject', is not alienating but realistically gives us some choice (in the light of how we're conditioned and affected) of where we want to speak, read and live from, right now. If identifying yourself as an 'I' in language seems to forget the body, is 'the self' any better in that respect?

I meant to cast Clark out from consideration. But antagonism animates, whereas appreciative commentary is inert, and represses the motives that make it seem necessary. I don't in fact think Carter is unquestionable, nor that she would want to be; I am driven to positive advocacy by misreadings that drive me wild, and by what lies behind them, secretly working. I want to put Clark to work for me, as the bit of grit that may make a hopeful pearl. The attractions of Carter's style, he writes, 'put the reason to sleep, thereby inhibiting satire's necessary distancing of the reader from both the text and the satirized illusions' (p. 159). How is 'the reason' to be rescued from his dismissal of 'the critical activity' which, he claims, Carter appeals to as 'a good in itself', linked to no political action? (p. 153) This is absurd – who is politically committed, if she is not? She did not speak, in the passage he quotes, of 'criticism' but of the need to produce 'a critique of our lives' through 'a critique of our symbols'. Clark introduces a familiar and extraneous critique of 'liberal late-bourgeois criticism', rather than reckon with Carter's rational argument at this point. The confusion he finds in Carter is a confusion in his own categories; he juggles with the terms alienation/distance and reason/criticism because he is committed to finding against Carter, partly because he feels seduced by her 'style' (which he therefore depreciates as cheaply commercial) and partly on behalf of 'women's historical and organic being – for which he speaks.

V

Angela Carter's fictions are a series of essays: attempts, trials, processes. Though in general Clark runs through them chronologically, he doesn't begin in order but sensationally/censoriously, as *The Sun* or *The Star* might, with 'The Company of Wolves' and the grandmother's appalled and threatened vision of the wolfman's genitals: 'Ah! huge.' Which I think is funny. In the next story 'Wolf-Alice' (there's never only one story) the werewolf is found 'scuttling along by the churchyard wall with half a juicy torso slung across his back' (*The Bloody Chamber*, p. 162). Now, in so far as 'juicy' momentarily invites us to experience necrophagy as tempting (like 'cadavre provencale' in the next paragraph), does that mean most of us are actually tempted? The momentous horror of the werewolf's bollocks or whatever, in 'The Company of Wolves,' belongs to the fear of sex which granny would teach Little Red Riding Hood. I have begun this article as tendentiously as Clark, with a good and heroic granny, in order to establish that Carter has nothing against grannies *per se*. Her revision of the fairytale has one obvious project, to question and reverse the age-old wisdom that wolves rather than prohibitive mentors are to be feared, and that sexual initiation is a kind of extinction. The film of *The Company of Wolves* makes the mother wiser than the grandmother in this respect. Clark takes for granted the representation of an unafraid girl enjoying sex, and wants to interpret the force of that as 'the standard patriarchal opposition between the feral domineering male and the gentle submissive female': 'The girl burst out laughing: she knew she was nobody's meat.' (*The Bloody Chamber*, p. 158). That effect, it seems to me, was worth producing. The death of the granny is not an assault on real old women; it is the death of what the granny represents in this particular story, the imposition of fear on the girl. Why make a woman represent that imposition? Well, it's in the initial story; and also, it does happen. The point is to rewrite one story and the regulation of women it represents. Perhaps after all you do really need to have lived as a woman – to have feared and suspected and walked in the middle of the road – to enjoy the possibility of this revision enough. Of course it does not say all that can be said on the subject; the fact that *The Bloody Chamber* offers various versions of the Beauty and the Beast metamorphosis declares that none of them can be the whole story. Carter contrasts the linguistic world of 'The Company of Wolves' with that of 'The Erl-King' – the former is a world of ambiguities where meanings can be changed, whereas the latter is 'transparent', with no way out of the cycle of oppression and violence (*The Bloody Chamber*, p. 113).

Having established 'innumerable rapes or near-rapes in Carter's writing' as his topic, Clark goes back to *The Magic Toyshop*. That Carter can be a fierce and reckless writer, 'terrorizing the imagination,' is one of the reasons that I like her, but her second novel is one of her more benign. Clark's account of it utterly fails to acknowledge its most important argument for me. Melanie's inital narcissism – the ready-made poses she adopts before her mirror, in her pubertal fantasies – is ready-made to collude with the scenarios her Uncle Philip, the cultural puppet-master, wants to play out, especially the rape of Leda by the Swan. He hopes that the enactment of this classical and Yeatsian scenario will also entice his son Finn to rape his cousin Melanie, and bring her down a peg or two, since he thinks her defunct parents were a cut or two above him. Melanie and Finn do end up sleeping together, in exhaustion and for the mutual solace they may offer each other (pp. 173–7). Sexual relation can be simply that, without the gothic excitement of rape. Finn is exhausted because he has destroyed his father's construction, his pride and joy, the puppet swan, the rapist. His rebellion on his own personal account has the side-effect of rescuing Melanie, though she's had her own experiences to go through. She learns for herself that sexual relations need not be a violent affair of aggression and submission, but a negotiation of mutual needs. Clark writes:

> The world of the everyday domestic interior is revealed as a stiffling [*sic*] network of repressed emotions, the antidote to which is the escape into a world of all that is illicit, incestuous, pagan, animal, sensuous; in literary terms, a world of the gothic and of the romance. (p. 150)

But, it is Philip's house which demonstrates not only how stifling, how ridden with fear, anger, transgressive desire and deception, families can be, but how the discourses of gothic, romance and classical/modernist myths are constructed as interior escapes from such everyday domesticity – discourses powered by familial feelings. Carter's stories do not replace realistic experience with literary fantasy, but offer other scenes, other imaginations of what could be made real. Nevertheless writing and reading are also real actions and experiences. In the end Melanie and Finn escape to confront a future which is open, unwritten, potentially quite different. It is the opposite of 'The Loves of Lady Purple', from *Fireworks* (1974, 1987), where the puppet woman destroys the puppet master only to re-enact his scenario because she knows and can construct no other. *The Magic Toyshop* has to do with overcoming the Oedipal and cultural incentives which make 'the threat of rape . . . constantly enticing' (Clark, p. 150). Clark is unable or unwilling to read Carter's earliest attempt to release heterosexual relations from the family romance and the threat of rape. I admit that Carter does not do this by preserving silence about rape and its enshrinement in culture high and low. Clark goes on to reduce *Heroes and Villains* to one scene of threatened gang rape, which the heroine, Marianne, prepares to resist by pretending she doesn't exist. As Joanna Russ has indicated in *The Female Man*, the protest 'Non sum' (Martin Luther's) can signify two things: 'I don't exist' and I'm not that, what you make of me.'[13] The distinction is vital, for feminism. Clark equates Marianne's response with those of Melanie in *The Magic Toyshop* and Eve in *The Passion of New Eve*: 'the usual response of the characters to such situations . . .'. I want to say two things about Clark's position. The first is that there are situations in which neither physical nor moral resistance will save the victim from humiliation or annihilation; where you will not even be accorded the tragic statement of your cause or your

[13]Joanna Russ, *The Female Man* (New York, Bantam Books, 1975: London, Women's Press, 1985), p. 59.

individuality, which literature encourages us to think is the case. Dreams and fictions are ways of protecting the psyche against destructive anxiety, against the fear of annihilation. Cunegonde in Voltaire's *Candide* casually and flourishingly reappears after rape and disembowelment: 'mais on ne meurt pas toujours de ces deux accidents.'[14] Of course if this were for real she would be dead; and it would be appalling for anyone else to say of or to Cunegonde, 'Well, you don't always die of such things.' She says it of herself. The relevant virtue is that of surviving and putting the past behind you if you can; of carrying on unhumiliated under the greatest possible threat to your surviving integrity as an agent not an object. Narratives which mention this possibility are necessary. To have someone in your personal history who does not want you to die also helps.

My second response to Clark's judgement on ways women may respond to rape is by way of continuing our mutual antagonistic journey through Angela Carter's stories. Melanie, Marianne and Eve are very different figures in different projects: it's no good treating them as if they were some universal Woman. *Heroes and Villains* (1969) is a more ambitious and complex enterprise than *The Magic Toyshop*. It explores a social group emerging from the needs of sheer survival and at risk of domination by mythopoeia. Donally, a renegade Professor, manufactures rituals to consolidate the rule of his pupil Jewel over his gypsy tribe. Intervening in this process with her own history and problems, Marianne incarnates Carter's will as a storyteller to 'do it back', to represent a man as the object of a woman's desire:

> See how he nak'd and fierce doth stand,
> Cuffing the Thunder with one hand;
>   While with the other he does lock,
> And grapple, with the stubborn Rock;
>   From which he with each Wave rebounds,
> Torn into Flames, and ragg'd with Wounds.
>   And all he saies, a Lover drest
> In his own Blood does relish best.
>   (Andrew Marvell, 'The Unfortunate Lover' – epigraph to *Heroes and Villains*)

Heroes and Villains is not most importantly 'an allegory of the post-holocaust future and of the late-sixties hippy opposition to conventional life' ('Angela Carter's Desire Machine,' pp. 150–1). You might just as soon call it a re-reading of Rousseau. Carter hasn't much time for 'eepies', for playing at personal freedom in an oppressive social system. She is concerned for possible transformations of conventional life, and, in this novel, with how academics (to speak only of them) treat and fantasize about cultural 'others', in this case gypsies. Marianne is a daughter of the Professors and estranged from her own desire, so that 'He' is embodied as

---

[14]*Candide* (Geneva, Librairie Droz, n.d.), Ch. 7 (1759).

a Stranger, a Barbarian – like the enthralling lovers of Elinor Glyn's romantic novels, or the Sheikh of early Hollywood fantasies. The actual rape of Marianne by Jewel is a version of such fantasies. Nevertheless, Jewel is terribly afraid of her, and she fails to save him from self-destruction after her presence has forced consciousness of cultural division and choice upon him.

We are not supposed to identify with Marianne, not altogether. Spiteful and solitary as a young child, her significant characteristic is her inalienable anger. She is never overwhelmed, though that is the only account Clark is prepared to give of her; never utterly at anyone's mercy, because she is adventurous and desirous of experience. She is unafraid: when at risk, she gets very cross. Once again, such a representation seems to me something that was worth trying on, and it's something Clark doesn't notice. She's in touch with her anger; but not with her desire. Melanie threw away the relics of her enthralment to dangerous desires (*The Magic Toyshop*, p. 189), but Finn became a companion, not a relic. Marianne's Unfortunate Lover remains, for her, an object; he can't live, in relation to her. In the end, she is all set to take over his role and that of his mentor Donally. She will become the barbaric Tiger Woman Donally has designed but failed to produce, articulated with the more deliberate, conscious role of the Renaissance ruler. Like Machiavelli's Prince, she intends to save herself by ruling through fear, subjugating the Barbarians. Some acknowledgment of this conclusion might reasonably have been asked of Clark; but the only thing he wants to recognize is a girl threatened by rape. A woman's desire for a man (I don't mean 'any man') is not taken up again in the longer fictions, in any positive sense, until *Nights at the Circus*.

VI

The Infernal Desire Machines of Dr Hoffman (a title which is an outrageous imposition and which I will therefore refer to hereafter as *Hoffman*) is the first of a planned trilogy of speculative fictions; the second volume is *The Passion of New Eve*. I have learned not to ask what is the third volume: choose your own, or acknowledge that Angela Carter evades conclusion (with Robert Louis Stevenson and his donkey, and Fevvers, 'to travel hopefully is better than to arrive,' *Nights at the Circus*, p. 279). The dedication of *Hoffman* waves goodbye, I think, to the barbaric, anarchic or revolutionary band of brothers whose opinions have hitherto haunted Angela Carter's fictions, in *Love*, for example, in 'Elegy for a Freelance' in *Fireworks*, and in *Heroes and Villains*. They had served their purpose as objects of desire or as transgressive identifications, stepping-stones to writing radically as a woman. The role of active revolutionary conscience falls to Lizzie, in *Nights at the Circus*, while her figurehead Fevvers is both an economic opportunist, and more given to spasms of Utopian sentiment (pp. 279–82). *Heroes and Villains* was already exploring the relation between myth, desire, and social control. Having driven out the father figure Donally, Jewel will not go to the Professors to be scientifically and sociologically analyzed (a process which would destroy what he *is*, both as culturally other and as the object of Marianne's desire – though to put it like that is to erase Carter's gorgeous Creature, whether naked or bedizened). He self-destructs, like Mary Shelley's Monster; though his tribe goes on.

Hoffman (1972) represents a power struggle between the positivist laws of science upheld by the Minister of Determination, and their subversion by the poet-physicist Dr Hoffman. The truth is, as the paradox poet-physicist suggests, that this story is so evocative and so acute in its response to contemporary Western culture that summarizing its significance is likely to make a fool of me, falling into the easy oppositions it subverts. I accept that. The Minister can represent both conservative common sense, and Marxist claims to be scientific, emerging historically out of positivism. Hoffman is both the surreal, liberatory opposition to both, and capitalist control of desire through the media. The city controlled by the Minister is originally 'thickly, obtusely masculine. . . . [It] can only be admired or bargained with and . . . settled serge-clad buttocks at vulgar ease as if in a leather armchair' (p. 15). Hoffman, the father of fantasy, feminizes the city, makes it beautiful; but in fact he and the Minister are brothers really. Their war makes the world we live in.

The Minister will allow no gap between signifier and signified, outlawing 'that shadowy land between the thinkable and the thing thought of' (p. 206). Dr Hoffman's technologically transmitted images proliferate along this borderline all the more powerfully for being officially prohibited. It's worth noting that E.T.A. Hoffmann's tale 'The Sandman' was the provocation for Dr Freud's meditation on 'The Uncanny', on that which is disturbing because all too close to home; and the suspicion of whatever is too lifelike, which Coppelia's wonderful doll generated in 'The Sandman', is reproduced here (p. 18).[15] Hoffman's control of the imaginary through forces equivalent to the mass media offers the increase of choices that Jewel had desired, as a release from merely surviving. In the real world of appearances, subjectivity and desire may resist bureaucracy, logical reason and the claims to cultural authority of science. But this is precisely the area by which we can be controlled. The narrator of *Hoffman* is Desiderio, which means that the speaking subject is the object of desire, as the text tells us, and the one who desires. He is our guide, passive and vulnerable like one of Walter Scott's heroes. An agent of the Minister of Determination, his dream and also his alter-ego is Albertina, Hoffman's daughter. Though she changes shape and gender, the imaginary is female in this representation, while the agent of reason, however disaffected, is male (a gendering which is drastically, surgically, altered in *The Passion of New Eve*, the successor to *Hoffman*). Desiderio is bored by the meaningless plurality of the city haunted by Hoffman's ghosts, the endless options which mean no real choice at all. Like most of

---

[15]'The Sandman,' *Tales of Hoffman*, (London, Penguin Books, 1982), pp. 121–2.

us, according to Carter, he has some idea of what's substantively real and what's not, enough to be dissatisfied with surrogates.

Clark patronizes and dismisses this enterprise: 'one of the most interesting attempts to escape literary naturalism and show through allegory the determining factors of late capitalism . . . but a parody that has no discernible point of departure or of arrival' (p. 154). When has Angela Carter ever been in thrall to naturalism? She has always been trying to include appearances, dreams, imaginative experience, within her definition of materialism – the phantasmagoria in and among which we lead our real lives, which Marxism has had such difficulty coping with. It seems to me a remarkable, a major exterprise; not to be sniffed at. Fictional and fantastic, it nevertheless speaks to my condition, raising questions about experience in the world in ways which attempts to transcribe experience do not, necessarily. The various interviews with Lorna Sage, Anne Smith and John Haffenden, and her personal statements in Michelene Wandor's *On Gender and Writing*, are revealing about Angela Carter's history and ways of working, which inevitably say something about mid to late twentieth-century experience; but are chaotic, ultimately, in comparison to the fictions. These interviews usually reveal at some point an irritation, an impatience to be working out some more specific project.[16] In *Hoffman* she explores desire, as what could be most liberating, and how it delivers us over to various enthralments. Hoffman with his machinery of gross images is finally tracked down in a citadel of high-bourgeois good taste (no surrealist he) in whose basements desire is clinically processed. Desiderio reluctantly commits himself to rationality, though his dreams are haunted by the woman who is variously Sade's valet Lafleur, a Generalissimo, and a Baudelairean scarlet woman, a bouquet of burning bone.

Clark's criticism, for all his spots of lip-service to anti-naturalism, is based on a demand for rational representation of socio-economic and historical real relations: a position akin to the one from which Carter wrote in 'The Language of Sisterhood' when she saw history as fixed and unaccommodating. Feminist historians (Natalie Zemon Davis, Catherine Hall, Leonore Davidoff, Ludmilla Jordanova, for example) have shown how our histories of popular protest, ideology and socio-economic relations change when women are at long last written into the account. It does also seem to me that the complicity of entrenched social and economic power with the arts, the entertainment industry and the trap of 'sexual liberation' is a valid point of conclusion, though to make such a point coolly is less animating than the final discovery of Hoffman. Clark's appeal to the authentic experience of real women is an attempt to articulate a static and exclusive Marxism with the most restrictive forms of feminism, whose positive definitions of what women are or should be trap us in traditional

[16]Lorna Sage, 'A Savage Sideshow,' *New Review* IV, 39/40, (July 1977); John Haffenden, 'Magical Mannerist,' *The Literary Review* (November 1984), pp. 34–8, reprinted at greater length in John Haffenden, *Novelists in Interview* (London, Methuen, 1985), pp. 77–96; Anne Smith, 'Myths and the Erotic,' *Women's Review* I (November 1985), pp. 28–9.

definitions. Angela Carter writes from the thick of Marxism's self-critique in the light of both twentieth-century experience, and psychoanalysis: there is hardly a theoretical debate of the past twenty years that she does not subject to imaginative exploration. Her narrative does not belong to authentic history, she reminds men like Clark, as the Russian Revolution approaches in *Nights at the Circus* (p. 97): but she is offering experiments in overcoming ideas, images, representations that have determined our options for thinking and feeling. Indeed the Revolution did not succeed in revolutionizing desire, or the condition of women in relation to sexuality, reproduction and childcare, as the work of Alexandra Kollontai shows: her 'Make Way for the Winged Eros!' haunts about *Nights at the Circus*.

The ghosts with which the media, and education, populate our lives may be purely present as 'experience' or 'knowledge' for many, part of the chaotic and arbitrary stock of conditions of life. In *Hoffman* Angela Carter traces the history of Reason and Desire in literary and philosophic representation, from the Enlightenment through to psychoanalysis and its postromantic consciousness of the unconscious – Enlightenment seen from its dark side, its blind spot. *Hoffman's* serial episodes explore our conventions and classificatory myths. To classify, to include and exclude, is human, all too human – for example, as Maxine Hong Kingston's *The Woman Warrior* suggests, to the traditional Chinese those who are not Chinese may be ghosts, horrible but not all that real. It is only of the Centaurs, in Section 7 of *Hoffman*, that it can truly be said 'nothing human was alien to them because they were alien to everything human' (p. 175). *Hoffman* explores pornography, the Gothic, fairy tales, horror films, boys' imperial adventure stories, anthropological idylls according to Rousseau or Levi–Strauss, and the fantasies of philosophy, the world as Will and Idea. The grotesque Count represents Sade and Nietzsche, dressed up as Dracula, but he is also like Marianne in *Heroes and Villains*, in so far as he embodies the solitary will inspired by an idea of itself, seeking perverse gratification no matter what. This option of individual assertion and transgression is acknowledged as one mode of resisting Hoffman's control of desire – it can be aligned also with Norman Mailer's 'Bring out the psychopath in yourself' – but it is rejected here, as the band of brothers had been, as sado-masochistic, in thrall to what it defies, and as antipathetic to any social ideal. The narrative position – that is, 'Angela Carter' – remains committed to socialism and to feminism. What conclusion to such a desire can there be, in present conditions, but continuing struggle, intelligent resistance along with kindred spirits?

Angela Carter also persistently refuses Utopian social idylls, the antithesis of individual will, as points of closure. The River People and the Centaurs in *Hoffman*, what Donally would make of Jewel's gypsy tribe in *Heroes and Villains*, the Finno-Ugrian culture in *Nights at the Circus*, are samples of the primitivist dreams of Rousseau and Levi-Strauss: coherent societies where belief, ritual and social practice offer no space for individual doubt and speculation. It's all inscribed as carefully and indivisibly on the consciousness as a tattoo on the skin. These are societies without *angst* (except for what they provoke in their aliens), without a gap between sociality and the psychic – a home for the children of God, the lost traveller's dream under the hill, as Blake and Yeats said. Fantasies dominated by the law of the same, whether that is patriarchal or, inversely, as in Mother's desert underworld, matriarchal. A persistent typology of characters in Angela Carter's writing links societies dominated by some absolute ideal of scientific reason, with societies dominated by magic ritual and theosophy (divine wisdom). Her makers and maintainers of myth are aligned with her scientists – Donally and Uncle Philip, and Mother in *The Passion of New Eve*, and Mme Durand in *The Sadeian Woman*, are akin in their will to experiment with people and their consciousness, to transform and dominate. It is in the light of such closed systems that Angela Carter's insistence on the dialectical openness of her fictions has to be understood: whatever her rational or unconscious programmes, readers have to jump off from where they're at (though my own position is often quite close to hers, because of the similarities in our personal histories, so that I want to insist on my version of her meanings). Even antagonism to what Carter is saying may be productive, covertly. It has to be said, however, that though women are powerful at the expense of men in Mother's desert laboratory, in all the primitive idylls women are oppressed.

VII

Angela Carter's scenarios are sceptical but not pessimistic. They are ways of looking with lively intelligence and imagination at ideas of the individual and the social in terms of the interests of those who have been colonized and marginalized, driven to the edge of what is held to be reasonable and commonsensical, and turned into ideals or horrors there. The demythologizing business is not only a rational process but a making of new fictions which do not pretend to be more than that: to be of use in asking some questions of the contemporary moment in the light of historical possibilities before taking to the road again, thinking, writing, again. Neither in an unstable, polymorphously perverse, world of differences (which would deny any specific identity for women), nor in any fixed social system, is there any absolutely safe place for women.

Robert Clark acknowledges Carter's representation, in *The Passion of New Eve*, of how femininity is and has been variously constructed. But he is also confused by it, and what he doesn't want to know reveals itself in his misreadings. He has already objected to what he misread as a mixing of the naturalistic and the Gothic in *The Magic Toyshop*; now he objects that Zero the male monster has a historical correlative, in Charles Manson, while Mother in her desert hideout Beulah, he says, has none, but is 'an image of feminine society that exists only in male chauvinist nightmares' (Clark, p. 157). This seems to me impossibly naive and literal-minded. The episodes centred on Mother and on Zero are fantastic propositions and experiments, equally real and unreal: that is, for both one can recognize a reference to texts, including media reports, which offer programmes for life (radical feminist prospectuses for segregation and the inversion of power relations; and the assertion of masculine transgression by the beat generation and its heirs). What Clark does not notice is the joke inherent in Zero's name: as in *The Sadeian Woman* (p. 4) he is the sign for nothing, by which women are represented in graffiti. 'Zero' satirizes the power of the phallus, which Carter suggests is an arbitrary sign, as in Greek comedy and as in the wooden leg he straps on (he cannot abide to be seen naked). His power depends utterly on the persistence of his harem's will to believe in him: 'But his myth depended on their conviction: a godhead, however shabby, needs believers to maintain his credibility. Their obedience ruled him' (*The Passion of New Eve*, p. 99).

Eve is a narrative device, as passive as Desiderio because like him she is a way for the reader to pass through possible options, as it were experimentally. Because of this non-realistic function she does not resist Zero, but his harem could, if they would only choose, if they wanted to. Angela Carter does not simply query masculine representations: she mounts a critique of women's 'feminine' behaviour, and of some feminist programmes. 'Mother' in *The Passion of New Eve* is inversely phallic, female to the nth degree. Clark assumes that Her rape, castration and conditioning of Evelyn the 'male chauvinist' is meant by Carter to produce a New Eve, a 'feminist alternative,' 'whose self-fertilized child will "rejuvenate the world" ' ('Angela Carter's Desire Machine,' p. 156). This is not quite the case. Eve escapes from Mother's programme before she is fertilized by her own/Evelyn's sperm; she escapes becoming a Virgin Mother, produced hermaphroditically out of her or himself, to experience a fantastically condensed version of a woman's life in Zero's harem, which is only maintained in existence by the women's belief in his ideas which condition their desires. The point of this section is to be aggravating: why don't they do him in, or at least run away? Its repulsiveness revises the rape fantasies of *Heroes and Villains* – hence the ultimate put-off, the dog turds on the carpet. Eve is impregnated by Tristessa, the screen goddess who is a man, the incarnation of his own fantasy of womanhood. Their love-making in the desert, taking turn and turn about in terms of the pleasures of activity and passivity, intensification and dissolution (I know Robert Clark thinks all this is neither here nor there!) enacts the royal marriage envisioned by alchemists, by Jung, by Sade. It is a fantasy of heterosexuality at its most reciprocal and bisexual, which leads to the conception of a child, as only heterosexuality can do without technological intervention like Mother's. This is not the most important thing to Eve at this point. She is in the grip of romantic love, the delirious and lucid *Liebestod*, since Tristessa is instantly killed by the Boy Soldiers (a fantasy out of William Burroughs's 'Wild Boys'). Eve is only prevented from dying beautifully on Tristessa's desert grave by an accidental collision with and escape from Mother's troops, who speed her on and out of all these myths and into a representation of 'historical time'.

What is going on here matches Julia Kristeva's imaginative account

of 'Women's Time,' which acknowledges that different feminist programmes (the claim to equal rights, radical feminist calls for inversions of
power and what may be considered to be power, and the deconstructive
dismissal of the *opposition* of feminine and masculine as 'metaphysical')
do exist contemporaneously in a way which calls linear accounts of the
historically significant into question.[17] (The daring and unparallelled feat
of undoing the opposition Woman/Man may be performed by consider-
ing in theory and practice the differences within rather than between
women and men, through psychoanalytic theory, and awareness of lesbian
and homoerotic desire and bisexuality, and the generally unfixed character
of gender identity, with which we are all familiar). Carter like Kristeva
counters Mother's archaic slogan that 'Woman is Space, Man is Time'
(that is, 'Man does; Woman is' – or, men are politically and economically
significant, while women reproduce and alleviate) by writing a story of
how women, and 'the Question of Woman' or more properly of gender
difference, have now irreversibly entered any adequate account of history.
Mother's scientific technology worked on a mythical base: she should be
compared to Mme Durand, the Enlightened Scientist as Phallic Mother, in
The Sadeian Woman, pp. 111–15. Eve runs from both science and myth.
Into 'incomprehensible political chaos,' Clark says (p. 158). Why should
it be so incomprehensible? Since this is an exploratory fiction, a sort of
allegory of options, which evokes recognitions of past, present and future
possibilities? The most oppressed woman, black Leilah, who has been
shown at the beginning producing alienated models for her existence in
the mirror, is revealed as having been always an active agent and now
enters the 'historical time' of the novel as a guerilla leader in a new
American Civil War. That represents one possibility, which doesn't fit at
all with Clark's final claim that Carter merely reproduces an unhappy
consciousness, alienated from awareness of its own oppression and real
interests. As a writer with a revolutionary socialist will she cannot *describe*
what has not happened, only give some space to hopes. The future lies
open at the end of *The Passion of New Eve*, as at the end of most of
Carter's fictions. 'Mother' withers away, like Lenin's state in *The State and
Revolution*, a necessary phase but one that has to be superseded. Mother
ends up as the cheery but decrepit old woman on the beach (p. 177): this is
the end of myths of the Mother. Eve will be a mother to someone not yet
representable, whom she may love but who will go on to live beyond her
imagination and will: though prehistory, Evelyn's own and that of
humanity, can be replayed like a reel of old film (ontogeny recapitulating
phylogeny, as they used to say), that film can be remade. The end of *The
Passion of New Eve* looks to an unknown future, one which inevitably
includes the possibility of new films, more myth-making. 'Woman' enters
history, rewrites it with herself in it, and tells more stories, as she's always
done.

---

[17]'Women's Time,' *Signs* VII, 1 (Autumn 1981), pp. 5–35

VIII

'The best weapon against myth is perhaps to mythify it in its turn, and to produce an artificial myth.'[18] *Nights at the Circus* writes out, erases, a number of myths, including ones by which Angela Carter was once enthralled, as a reader and writer – Sadeian liberation by sexual transgression, or the idea associated with Albertina in *Hoffman*, of Yin and Yang, and sexual conflict as 'what-makes-the-world-go-round.' It also has more directly positive elements, 'founding prospective history' (Barthes, 'Myth Today', p. 137). The mythologist, Barthes wrote, has to cut himself (*sic*) off from those who are entertained by the myths he deciphers, 'condemned to live in a theoretical sociality. . . . His connection with the world is of the order of sarcasm' ('Myth Today', p. 157). Carter's sarcasm against enthralling fantasies may be alienating, except for those who delight in finding a kindred spirit: it could be comprised in Bakhtin's judgement on post-Romantic carnival, as private, bitterly isolating.[19] I've hesitated so far to introduce such theories, in dread of carnival's liberating potential getting frozen by academic use (and of course carnival is always in the market-place – yesterday I saw a price tag in a clothes shop, 'Authentic Carnival', it promised). But clearly *Nights at the Circus* is a carnival of writing, containing 'the protocols and styles of high culture in and from a position of debasement.' Fevvers, by 'putting on' one variety of femininity with a vengeance, does suggest 'the power of taking it off' (Mary Russo, 'Female Grotesques', pp. 218, 224).

I want to celebrate what *Nights at the Circus* has in common with 'women's fiction', where it is not sarcastic but Utopian. The brutal Strong Man acquires a sensibility. Jack Walser, originally a sardonic contemplator like Desiderio, is knocked on the head, taken apart, and puts himself together, in the wake of the New Woman, as a man who can love and is worth loving. Carter offers a love story with a romantic ending, in bed not marriage:

> [Jack] was as much himself again as he ever would be, and yet that 'self' would never be the same again for now he knew the meaning of fear as it defines itself in its most violent form, that is, fear of the death of the beloved, of the loss of the beloved, of the loss of love. It was the beginning of an anxiety that would never end, except with the deaths of either or both; and anxiety is the beginning of conscience, which is the parent of the soul but is not compatible with innocence. (p. 293)

My son Matthew insists that I insert here something of a love letter from Karl to Jenny Marx, after thirteen years of marriage:

> Great passions which, because of the proximity of their object, take on the form of small habits, grow and reassume their natural dimensions

[18]Barthes, 'Myth Today', p. 135.
[19]Mary Russo, 'Female Grotesques: Carnival and Theory', *Feminist Studies/Critical Studies*, ed. Teresa de Lauretis (University of Indiana Press, 1986; London, Macmillan, 1988), p. 218.

by the magic effect of distance. Thus it is with my love. You only need to be removed from me – if only by dreams – and I know at once that time does to my love for you what sun and rain do to a plant: it makes it grow. My love for you, as soon as you are far away, appears as what it is, a giant wherein all the energy of my mind and all the character of my heart is concentrated. I feel a man once more because I feel a great passion. The complexities in which study and modern education involve us, the scepticism we must necessarily bring to bear on all subjective and objective impressions, are perfectly designed to make all of us small and weak and petulant and undecided. But love, not the love of Feuerbach's Man nor Moleschott's metabolism, nor again love of the Proletariat, but love of the beloved and more particularly of you, makes a man a man again . . .

Karl Marx, 21 June 1856 (*Marx in his own Words*, ed. Ernst Fischer, tr. Anna Bostock (London, Penguin Books 1970), pp. 25–6

Fevvers is Alexandra Kollontai's Winged Eros, or Sade's Juliette lifted up to a human level, as Apollinaire imagined her, with wings (*The Sadeian Woman*, p. 79); no longer 'rationality personified'. Sustained by her adoptive mother and companion, Lizzie, as well as by the marketability of the feminine and the freakish, she can afford a heart of gold, like Mae West in Hollywood. Her happy ending with Walser is far from being the only one. In a fit of jealousy she had tried to set Walser up with the victimized girl, Mignon; having another go at playing Good Fairy, she helps Mignon develop a career as a singer from which Mignon takes off through a love affair with the pianist and lion tamer, the hitherto mute and unresponsive Princess of Abyssinia. This Lesbian idyll, which restores her voice to the black woman, as Toussaint the black man has already regained his, is achieved before the heterosexual happy ending. This is not to say that black women always have to be linked to lesbianism in feminist critiques and representations, or that black women and men don't have great voices, which can be heard in their variety even through oppression, without stars like Fevvers amplifying them, but Angela Carter would have been wrong in her most optimistic revolutionary novel, if she had not said something of the sort.

In *Nights at the Circus* for the first time in the longer fictions, Carter's narrative voice is multiplied, the chronology rumpled (beyond her very common device of saying what happened and then elaborating that bare and often shocking information), not only to interpolate individual stories but also to give different versions of the same events, from different perspectives. 'True love', till death, the real romantic thing, can triumph because the nineteenth century and its confining institutions, as well as the pieties of nostalgic peasant resistance, have been blown away, fantastically. In Carter's most amazing and blasphemous tour de force, the discourses of clowning and of Christianity are yoked, by way of the primary school classic 'Lord of the Dance' and the idea of Christ as a whore, who gives himself to all, at a certain price (this scandalous conception can be traced to Sadeian scholarship and to negative theology, the anti-Catholicism, which haunts about French 'theory').[20] Angela Carter's active atheism insists that there is no 'buffer' between ourselves, whoever we may be, and our relation to all others, right here and now. The otherworldly pessimism of Buffo, king of the Clowns, is whirled out of the text's vision of possibilities, in a carnival denial of the wisdom that we have suffering always with us, beyond our human power to change. Nevertheless, something of the twentieth century as we know it survives, as Jack's concussed wild reasoning surmises: 'I see a man carrying a . . . pig. . . . The upper part of this man's apparel mimics the starry heavens. The lower part, by a system of parallel bars, represents, perhaps . . . felled trees . . . He brings light, and he brings food, but he also seems to bring . . . destruction . . .' (*Nights at the Circus*, p. 261). Colonel Kearney, the proprietor of the Circus, is still in business, his motto, 'Never give a sucker an even break.'

It may be that in trying to show that Angela Carter produces rather more than mindless entertainment I have cited an excess of intertexts. Perhaps one day I will be doomed to produce an annotated Carter. I want to end by quoting an unpublished paper by Clare Brant, of St Hugh's College, Oxford:

> A myth only works, culturally speaking, if it is an exclusive interpretation; it convinces by positing one story for each phenomenon. Narrative plurality would create tolerance, which contradicts myth's function as propaganda for an ideology. So biblical mythologizing, for instance, starts with singularity: 'In the beginning was the Word.'

Along with that, Maxine Hong Kingston:

> 'The difference between mad people and sane people,' Brave Orchid explained to the children, 'is that sane people have variety when they talk-story. Mad people have only one story that they talk over and over.'
> *The Woman Warrior*, (Pan Books, 1977), p. 143

Brave Orchid isn't unquestionable: she contravenes her own principle so that the one story she tells for her sister is disastrous. But that doesn't put the principle out of action.

---

[20]Jane Gallop, *Intersections* (University of Nebraska Press, 1981), p. 92. The relevant parts of *Nights at the Circus* are II, 4, and III, 7, which Christopher Norris has compared to Derrida's 'The Double Session', in *Derrida* (London, Fontana Books, 1987) pp. 46, 51–2.

Note
Studies of Lesbian Feminist Theory
Important works include: Charlotte Bunch, 'Not for Lesbians Only', in Bunch and Gloria
Steinem, eds., *Building Feminist Theory: Essays from Quest* (New York, Longman, 1981),
pp. 67–73. Sue Cartledge and Joanna Ryan, eds., *Sex and Love: New thoughts on old
contradictions* (Women's Press, 1983). Hester Eisenstein, *Contemporary Feminist Thought*
(Unwin, 1984), pp. 48–57. Joan Nestle, *A Restricted Country* (New York, Firebrand, 1987).
Radicalesbians, 'The Woman Identified Woman', in Anne Koedt, Ellen Levine, Anita
Rapone, eds., *Radical Feminism* (New York, Quadrangle, 1973), pp. 240–5. Adrienne Rich,
Compulsory Heterosexuality and Lesbian Existence (*Signs: Journal of Women in Culture and
Society*, V, 4, 1980; Onlywomen Press, 1981). Elizabeth Wilson, *Hidden Agendas: Theory,
Politics and Experience in the Women's Movement* (Tavistock, 1986).

Lesbian Feminist Criticism
Patricia Duncker, 'Writing Lesbian', in *Papers of the Conference 'Homosexuality, Which
Homosexuality?'* (Amsterdam, Free University/ Schorer Foundation, 1987), II, 32–46.
Catherine R. Stimpson, 'Zero Degree Deviancy: The Lesbian Novel in English', in Elizabeth
Abel, ed., *Writing and Sexual Difference* (Brighton, Harvester, 1982), pp. 243–59.
Elizabeth Wilson, 'I'll Climb the Stairway to Heaven: Lesbianism in the Seventies', in Sue
Cartledge and Joanna Ryan, eds., *Sex and Love: New thoughts on old contradictions*
(Women's Press, 1983), pp. 180–95. Bonnie Zimmerman, 'What has never been: An
overview of lesbian feminist criticism', in Gayle Greene and Coppélia Kahn, eds., *Making a
Difference: Feminist Literary Criticism* (Methuen, 1985), pp. 177–210. I discuss many
lesbian novels (e.g. Nicky Edwards's *Mud*, Aileen La Tourette's *Nuns and Mothers*, Kate
Millett's *Sita*, Anna Wilson's *Cactus*) in my book *Contemporary Women's Fiction: Narrative
Practice and Feminist Theory* (Hemel Hempstead, Harvester-Wheatsheaf, 1989).

Contemporary Lesbian Feminist Fiction
1 *Fiction on the theme of Coming Out*. Rita Mae Brown, *Ruby Fruit Jungle* (Vermont,
Daughters Inc., 1973). Maureen Craig, *All That False Instruction* (Sydney, Angus and
Robertson, 1975). Marge Piercy, *Small Changes* (USA, 1972; New York, Fawcett Crest,
1974). Nancy Toder, *Choices* (Watertown, Mass., Persephone Press, 1980).
2 *Fiction about Motherhood, and Relations between Mothers and Daughters*: Dodici
Azpadu, *Saturday Night in the Prime of Life* (USA, 1983; Onlywomen Press, 1987).
Maureen Brady, 'Early Autumn Exchange', in *The Question She Put To Herself: Stories*
(California, Crossing Press, 1987). Jan Clausen, *Mother, Sister, Daughter, Lover: Stories*
(Trumansberg, Crossing Press, 1980; Women's Press, 1981); *Sinking Stealing* (Women's
Press, 1985). Michèle Roberts, *A Piece of the Night* (Women's Press, 1978). Jeanette
Winterson, *Oranges are not the Only Fruit* (Pandora, 1985).
3 *Comic and Satiric Fiction*: Lisa Alther, *Other Women* (USA, 1984; Harmondsworth,
Penguin, 1985). Ellen Galford, *The Fires of Bride* (Women's Press, 1986). Kate Hall, 'The
Two Spinster Ladies', in Jan Bradshaw and Mary Hemming, eds., *Girls Next Door* (Women's
Press, 1985). Anne Leaton, *Good Friends, Just* (Chatto & Windus, 1983). Anna Livia,
Accommodation Offered (Women's Press, 1985); *Relatively Norma* (Onlywomen Press,
1982). Joanna Russ, *The Female Man* (USA, 1975; Women's Press, 1985); *On Strike Against
God* (USA, 1980; Women's Press, 1987).
4 *Thrillers and Detective Fiction*: Rebecca O'Rourke, *Jumping the Cracks* (Virago, 1987).
Barbara Wilson, *Sisters of the Road* (USA, 1986; Women's Press, 1987) and other novels.
Mary Wings, *She Came Too Late* (Women's Press, 1986). Other contributors to the genre
include Sarah Dreher and Val McDermid.
5 *Fiction by Black Women and Women of Colour*: Becky Birtha, *Lovers' Choice* (Women's
Press, 1988). Barbara Burford, *The Threshing Floor* (Sheba, 1986). Suniti Namjoshi,
Feminist Fables (Sheba, 1981); *The Conversations of Cow* (Women's Press, 1985). Gloria
Naylor, 'The Two', in *The Women of Brewster Place* (USA, 1980; Methuen, 1987). Ntozake
Shange, *Sassafrass, Cypress and Indigo* (USA, 1982; Methuen, 1987). Alice Walker, *The
Color Purple* (USA, 1982, Women's Press, 1983). A useful critical study is Barbara Christian,
Black Feminist Criticism: Perspectives on Black Women Writers (New York, Pergamon,
1985).

3

Contemporary Lesbian Feminist Fiction: Texts for Everywoman
For *Cambridge Lesbian Line*
Paulina Palmer

1 Introduction: Themes, Categories and Questions

In subtitling this essay on contemporary lesbian feminist fiction *Texts for Everywoman*, I take my cue from the American theorist Charlotte Bunch. Bunch, seeking to emphasize the relevance of lesbian feminist critiques of heterosexuality and patriarchy to all women irrespective of their sexual orientation, calls the paper she wrote on the topic *Not for Lesbians Only*.[1] Like Bunch, I wish to stress the fact that the novels and short stories which I discuss in this essay are of interest not only to readers who identify as lesbian or bisexual but to *all women*. The comprehensive nature of their appeal stems from the variety of the themes they treat which are pertinent to feminism in general. These include critiques of patriarchal power and male violence, analyses of mother–daughter relations and women's community, and debates about sex and relations between women.

Lesbian fiction produced in the late 70s and the 80s forms, in many respects, a marked contrast to the fiction written in the early 1970s at the start of the Lesbian Feminist Movement. Authors such as Rita Mae Brown and Marge Piercy, writing in the early period, generally utilized the form of the *bildungsroman* and concentrated, somewhat narrowly, on the theme of Coming Out. Today, as we shall see, developments in lesbian feminist theory and in the field of women's fiction make a far wider range of themes and genres available. Modifications have also occurred in the

---

[1]*Building Feminist Theory: Essays from Quest*, ed. Bunch and Gloria Steinem (New York, Longman, 1981), pp. 67–73.

---

6 *Other works of fiction mentioned in this essay*: Andrea Dworkin, *Ice and Fire* (Secker & Warburg, 1986). Nicky Edwards, *Mud* (Women's Press, 1986). Jennifer Gubb, *The Open Road: Stories* (Onlywomen Press, 1983). Aileen La Tourette, *Nuns and Mothers* (Virago, 1984). Sara Maitland, *Virgin Territory* (Michael Joseph, 1984). Caeia March, *Three Ply Yarn* (Women's Press, 1986). Marge Piercy, *The High Cost of Living* (New York, Harper & Row, 1978). Lesley Thomson, *Seven Miles from Sydney* (Pandora, 1987). Anna Wilson, *Cactus* (Onlywomen Press, 1980); *Altogether Elsewhere* Onlywomen Press, 1985). Barbara Wilson, *Ambitious Women* (New York, 1982; Women's Press, 1983). Elizabeth Wilson, *Prisons of Glass* (Methuen, 1986).

area of style. While the realist mode continues to be popular, a move towards anti-realism is discernible in a number of texts. Changes, moreover, are taking place in the general public's expectations of the lesbian writer. The stereotypical image of her as white, affluent, middle-class and living in the city, prevalent in the first half of the century, is starting to be challenged.[2] Black women and women of colour, such as Becky Birtha, Barbara Burford and Suniti Namjoshi, and women with working-class and country roots, such as Caeia March and Jennifer Gubb, are making an increasingly important contribution to the treatment of lesbian themes. A distinctive feature of lesbian fiction today, one which makes it attractive to a wide female readership, is its portrayal of women whose existence the dominant culture marginalizes or ignores. Black women, women with working-class and country backgrounds, the middle-aged and the elderly, play a central role in many novels and short stories.

It is not possible for me in the space available to discuss examples of all the different topics, genres and styles which writers employ. However, I hope in the following pages to give the reader an insight into the diversity and vitality of contemporary lesbian fiction, as well as pinpointing some of the problems and contradictions which it reveals. Many of the novels which I discuss will probably be unfamiliar to readers. This illustrates the way lesbian writing is marginalized by both academia and the popular press.

A major problem facing the critic is the term *lesbian feminist fiction* and the problems which it raises. Bonnie Zimmerman's statement that 'Lesbian criticism continues to be plagued with the problem of definition'[3] applies equally to the realm of fiction. What criteria should the critic adopt in defining a novel or short story as lesbian?

An obstacle to answering this question is the debates and controversies which at present surround the sign *lesbian*. Is the sign primarily erotic in emphasis, or is it political? Is lesbianism to be defined solely in terms of sexual practice and orientation, or are experiences of woman-bonding and feminist camaraderie also to be included, as Adrienne Rich advocates in her controversial essay *Compulsory Heterosexuality and Lesbian Existence*?[4] And what about the lesbian herself? Is she the deviant, erotically subversive figure associated with 'the underworld, the underground, the unconscious, . . . the excitement of danger',[5] whom Elizabeth Wilson admits haunts her own imagination? Or is she, on the contrary, the heroic,

---

[2]For reference to the topic, see Bertha Harris, 'The More Profound Nationality of their Lesbianism: Lesbian Society in Paris in the 1920s', in Phyllis Birkby and Jill Johnston, eds., *A Lesbian Feminist Anthology: Amazon Expedition* USA, Times Change Press, 1973), pp. 77–88.

[3]'What has never been: an overview of lesbian feminist criticism', in Gayle Greene and Coppélia Kahn, eds., *Making a Difference: Feminist Literary Criticism* (London, Methuen, 1985), p. 183.

[4]*Signs: Journal of Women in Culture and Society*, V, 4 (1980), 631–60. Reprinted Onlywomen Press, London, 1981.

[5]'Forbidden Love', in *Hidden Agendas: Theory, Politics and Experience in the Women's Movement* (London, Tavistock, 1986), p. 181.

politically right-on feminist whose vision and energy are the inspiration
of the Women's Movement, and who leads her sisters to challenge male
oppression and build women's community – as Beth does in Marge
Piercy's *Small Changes* (1972), and Moira in Margaret Atwood's *The
Handmaid's Tale* (1985)? Or is she an intriguing combination of both
these stereotypes?

Another obstacle to the definition of *lesbian feminist fiction* is the
ambiguity of the term itself. What precisely is a lesbian feminist novel? Is
it one written *by* lesbians, *for* lesbians or *about* lesbians?[6] All these criteria
prove unsatisfactory when put to the test. The first fails to take into
account the shifting nature of desire and sexual identification. As Patricia
Duncker observes:

> Our sexuality is something we invent, or re-invent, day after day,
> according to our circumstances and the political and sexual pressures
> upon us. In short, Lesbians are made, not born.[7]

It thus makes no allowance for authors such as Sara Maitland (*Virgin
Territory*, 1984) who write from a bisexual position, and others such as
Michèle Roberts and Piercy whose position shifts from lesbian to
heterosexual from one novel to another.[8] The second criterion is equally
untenable. Whereas some writers no doubt do address a primarily lesbian
readership, others (especially ones who treat the theme of Coming Out)
write for a mixed audience. They offer the reader, again to quote Duncker,
'an explanation of how the writer's sexuality was formed, articulated and
expressed'.[9] The third criterion is also to be rejected as unsatisfactory. It
ignores the fact that lesbian feminist perspectives are identifiable as much
by a political critique of heterosexuality and male power, as by an analysis
of love between women. This helps to explain why Jennifer Gubb's collection of short stories *The Open Road* (1983), though devoid of characters
who identify as lesbian and making no reference to erotic relations
between women, may arguably be called a lesbian text, whereas Fay
Weldon's *The Heart of the Country* (1987), despite the fact that it is
recounted by a narrator who admits to falling in love with another woman,
may not. The two novels make fascinating material for comparison, since
the writers' aims and interests are remarkably similar. Gubb and Weldon
both concentrate on deconstructing conventionally romantic images of
country life, forcing the reader to confront the harsh, cruel facts of rural
poverty and male dominance. Both, moreover, relentlessly, accumulate
illustrations of male acts of brutality perpetrated against women and

---

[6]See Patricia Duncker, 'Writing Lesbian', in *Papers of the Conference 'Homosexuality,
Which Homosexuality?'* (Amsterdam, Free University/Schorer Foundation, 1987), II,
32–46; and Zimmerman, 'What has never been'.
[7]'Writing Lesbian', p. 42.
[8]Piercy's *The High Cost of Living* (1978) and Roberts's *A Piece of the Night* (1978) are
lesbian in stance. Piercy's *Fly Away Home* (1984) and Roberts's *The Visitation* (1983) are
heterosexual.
[9]'Writing Lesbian', p. 37.

animals. Notable differences are discernible, however, in the writers' tones of address and authorial stances. Gubb's talent lies in deconstructing images of *the monstrous* and *the other*. She gives the impression of writing from the margins, presenting us with a view from 'the periphery of patriarchy'[10] and creating 'a dialectic between freedom and imprisonment'.[11] These attributes are described by the critics Susan J.Wolfe and Zimmerman as distinctive features of lesbian writing. Weldon adopts a totally different position. Her savage denunciation of patriarchal power, though radical feminist in the general sense of the term, reflects a perspective which is firmly heterosexual. She treats heterosexual relations as the only viable option for women.

My evaluation of Gubb's collection of stories as 'a lesbian feminist text' is also influenced, I admit, by an external factor. The collection is published by the Onlywomen Press, a small London-based press which specializes in the publication of lesbian feminist writing. This raises the interesting question of the part which publishers and packaging play in determining the reader's response to a work of fiction.

The category *lesbian feminist fiction*, though raising a number of problems, is none the less indispensable in both literary and political terms. As Catherine R. Stimpson cogently reminds us, 'Lesbian writers have worked under the double burden of a patriarchal culture and a strain in the female tradition that accepted and valued heterosexuality'.[12] Novels and short stories which, since they treat themes which are relevant to women, are loosely described as 'feminist', are not necessarily free from heterosexual bias and the prejudiced or inaccurate representation of lesbianism to which it gives rise. Zimmerman, in her discussion of the topic, cites as examples Doris Lessing's *The Golden Notebook* (1962) and Lisa Alther's *Kinflicks* (1976).[13] The two novels, in different ways, present sexual relations between women as inauthentic and pathetic. Works of fiction published more recently which reveal similar signs of prejudice are Lessing's *The Good Terrorist* (1985) and Emma Tennant's *The Bad Sister* (1978). The two novels, associating love between women with hysteria, self-destruction and incidents of violence, disparage and discredit lesbianism. They are oppressive in effect, contributing to the backlash against the Lesbian Feminist Movement which is currently taking place in the UK. The category *lesbian feminist fiction* is necessary to challenge these examples of bigotry with a fairer representation of the topic. While not necessarily presenting all lesbian relations in a positive light, writers should aim to deconstruct prejudiced myths and stereotypes, not endorse and perpetuate them.

Lesbian feminist fiction also has social and political significance in a

---

[10]Susan J. Wolfe, 'Stylistic experimentation in Millett, Johnston and Wittig' (1978), paper presented at MLA, quoted by Zimmerman, 'What has never been', p. 198.
[11]Zimmerman, 'What has never been', p. 202.
[12]'Zero Degree Deviancy: The Lesbian Novel in English' in Elizabeth Abel, ed., *Writing and Sexual Difference* (Brighton, Harvester, 1982), p. 243.
[13]'Is "Chloe Liked Olivia" a Lesbian Plot?', *Women Studies Forum*, VI, 2 (1983), 172.

wider, more general sense. Alison Hennegan in her Introduction to the Women's Press collection of short stories *Girls Next Door* (1985) comments on the vital educational and social function which it performs:

> People learn from fiction. They look to it for information, reassurance, affirmation about the ways in which other (fictional) people feel, believe, act and – most important of all, it sometimes seems – love.[14]

As Hennegan implies, novels and stories treating lesbian themes, published by the feminist presses and reviewed in the pages of the magazine *Spare Rib*, provide an invaluable source of information, solace and support for women who are in the process of discovering their lesbian or bisexual orientation or who seek to learn about the topic. The positive representations of lesbian relations which they contain challenge the incidents of prejudice and bigotry which, in the oppressive political climate of the 80s, are becoming increasingly commonplace. They counter, at least to a degree, the heterosexual bias of the media, press and educational system. This bias has been appropriately described as '*the* perceptual screen provided by our [patriarchal] cultural conditioning'.[15]

Lesbian help-lines and support groups, recognizing the educational value of works of fiction, sometimes use them as a resource. The provincial help-line to which I myself belong owns a small library of novels and stories which we lend out to callers. Women living in isolated, rural areas are especially glad to borrow them. With the notorious Clause 28 of the Local Government Act now become law, the role which fiction performs in providing women with information, reassurance and support is likely to increase. The Clause, as readers are no doubt aware, effectively sanctions discrimination against lesbians and gay men. It threatens the funding of help-lines and community centres and discourages the discussion of homosexuality in schools. It also discriminates explicitly against lesbian mothers and their children by describing their family units as 'pretended'.[16]

[14]Jan Bradshaw and Mary Hemming, eds., *Girls Next Door: Lesbian Feminist Stories* (London, Women's Press, 1985), p. 3. See also Derek Cohen and Richard Dyer, 'The Politics of Gay Culture', in Gay Left Collective, ed., *Homosexuality, Power, and Politics* (London, Allison & Busby, 1980), pp. 172–86.

[15]Julia Penelope Stanley, 'The Articulation of Bias: Hoof in Mouth Disease' (1979), paper presented at National Council of Teachers of English Convention, quoted by Zimmerman, 'What has never been', p. 179.

[16]Section 28 (previously Clause 28) of the Local Government Act was sponsored by a group of Tory backbenchers and, despite considerable opposition, came into force in the UK on 24 May, 1988. It prohibits local authorities from (a) promoting homosexuality or publishing material that promotes homosexuality, (b) promoting the teaching in maintained schools of homosexuality as a pretended family relationship or (c) giving financial assistance to any person for either of these purposes. Sarah Roelofs points out that 'Section 28 is not an explicitly prescriptive law, but an intimidatory one. Until there has been a judicial judgement to establish exactly what constitutes "the promotion of homosexuality" Section 28 cannot be implemented. This has not stopped some local authorities from trying to implement it, effectively fabricating the law in the process. Other authorities have responded positively, using the occasion to issue public statements reaffirming their lesbian and gay

The political implications of lesbian feminist fiction, outlined above, are something of a mixed blessing, possessing both advantages and disadvantages. On the credit side, they give the writing of a lesbian text, whether a piece of fiction or theory, a sense of urgency and importance. On the debit side, however, by prompting the demand that writers create positive role-models for readers to emulate, they result on occasion in representations of lesbian relations which, as Elizabeth Wilson complains, are insipidly idealized and bland.[17] The issue of 'role-models' in works of fiction is a complex one, involving questions of narrative strategy as well as aesthetics. I do not agree with the wholesale condemnation of the practice expressed by academic critics such as Toril Moi.[18] Moi's perspectives strike me as narrow and élitist. In my opinion, we benefit immensely from the portrayal of the strong, independent women who appear in the fiction of writers such as Jan Clausen, Barbara Wilson and Jean Winterson. All three writers succeed in creating characters who, far from being extravagantly idealized, possess a convincing mixture of contradictions, weaknesses and strengths. In contrast, other writers such as Nancy Toder (*Choices*, 1980) use clumsy tactics and strategies. However, the proportion of works of lesbian fiction which lack verisimilitude and complexity is, in actual fact, quite small in comparison with texts which are skilfully crafted and emotionally complex. We shall now move on to discuss a selection of these.

2   The Problematization of Heterosexuality, and Critiques of Male Power: Michèle Roberts, Anna Wilson, Gloria Naylor

In her essay *Not for Lesbians Only* Bunch describes 'a critique of the institution and ideology of heterosexuality as a cornerstone of male supremacy', combined with 'a commitment to women as a political group',[19] as constituting the twin poles of lesbian feminist politics. Literary critics emphasize the significance of these ideas to the role of the lesbian writer. Zimmerman suggests that the lesbian's woman-identified perspective, leading her to challenge patriarchal control and male defini-tions of experience, 'assigns her a specific vantage-point from which to criticize and analyse the politics, language and culture of patriarchy'.[20] Sandy Boucher sees the lesbian writer as engaged in deconstructing

---

equality policies.' (*Spare Rib*, 192, June 1988, p. 42) For discussion of Section 28 and its implications, see the following articles: *Times Educational Supplement*, 1102 (18 Dec., 1987), p. 13; *Spare Rib*, 188 (March, 1988), p. 16; *The Guardian*, 15 March, 1988, p. 18, and 1 June, 1988, p. 19. For information about lesbian lines in the UK phone London Lesbian Line, 01 – 251 – 6911, Monday and Friday 2 – 10 p.m.; Tuesday, Wednesday, Thursday 7 – 10 p.m.

17'I'll Climb the Stairway to Heaven: Lesbianism in the Seventies', in Sue Cartledge and Joanna Ryan, eds., *Sex and Love: New thoughts on old contradictions* (London, Women's Press, 1983), p. 192.

18*Sexual/Textual Politics: Feminist Literary Theory* (London, Methuen, 1985), pp. 47–8.

19*Not for Lesbians Only*, p. 68.

20'What has never been', p. 178.

concepts of 'the natural' and 'the normal', exposing them as oppressive constructs created by a phallocratic culture. The critique the lesbian creates, as Boucher neatly phrases it, 'puts us a step outside of so-called normal life and lets us see how gruesomely abnormal it is . . .'[21] Here I shall discuss certain novels which explore the oppressive aspects of heterosexual conventions and patriarchal power, relating them to the theoretical perspectives which form their base.

A key topic in lesbian feminist theory is *the problematization of heterosexual relations as an option for women*. This is indebted, in part, to psychoanalytic commentaries on the development of the female subject. As Joanna Ryan points out, 'A strength of most psychoanalytic accounts is that they do not see a girl's pathway to heterosexuality as either straightforward or inevitable'. On the contrary, by emphasizing the fact that to become heterosexual a girl has to transfer her love from a female object (the mother) to a male one, it gives 'a view of women as pushed and pulled out of their original homosexual intimacy into an ambivalent and very incomplete heterosexuality, where men may be the exclusive and primary erotic objects but are for the most part emotionally secondary to women'.[22] These ideas, along with a critique of the structures of the patriarchal family and their oppressive and divisive effect on female relations, form the ideological basis of certain works of fiction. Michèle Roberts's *A Piece of the Night* (1978) is an interesting example.

The focus of Roberts's novel is the relationship between the central character Julie and her mother Claire. In portraying it, Roberts refers to psychoanalytic concepts of the pre-oedipal bond between mother and daughter, foregrounding the fact that the initial object of Julie's love is female. Julie, reconstructing in her imagination the experience of sucking her mother's breast, recognizes that 'This is my first love affair, . . . She is my world, and I am hers'.[23] Roberts gives a detailed analysis of the pressures and divisions which conventions of male primacy and heterosexual dominance impose on relations between both mother and daughter, and women in general. Julie perceives that, in the home, her father and brother stake prior claim to her mother's attention. And, whereas the bond between mother and son receives cultural and religious endorsement in the image of the Virgin Mary nursing the infant Jesus, there is no equivalent endorsement of the bond between mother and daughter. Julie also discovers that, if she is to fulfil patriarchal expectations of femininity, then she has to renounce a female object of love in exchange for a male. If she fails or refuses, she risks incurring the wrath and disappointment of her family and society as a whole. When, on visiting her mother as an adult, she reveals that she has left her husband and is living with a group of lesbian feminists, her mother is appalled by the news. She wonders where

---

[21]'Lesbian Artists', *Heresies*, 3 (1977), 43.
[22]'Psychoanalysis and Women Loving Women', in Cartledge and Ryan, eds., *Sex and Love*, pp. 203, 206.
[23]*A Piece of the Night* (London, Women's Press, 1978), p. 137.

she went wrong with Julie's upbringing, interpreting her choice of life-style as an implicit criticism of her own family-centred way of life – which in a way, of course, it is. Roberts describes the communal household where Julie lives as providing both a refuge from, and a challenge to, the patriarchal family unit which, she illustrates, survives on the exploitation of women's labour and nurturing skills. Roberts's represention of the life of the commune is, however, by no means idealized. She emphasizes the tensions and problems, as well as the emotional and practical support, which the women encounter.

Other writers besides Roberts also treat the theme of relations between mother and daughter, examining the oppressive aspects of the patriarchal family. *Saturday Night in the Prime of Life* (1983) by the American writer Dodici Azpadu concentrates attention on a family of Sicilian immigrants to the USA. Azpadu explores the rift which occurs between Concetta and her daughter Neddie when the latter leaves home to live in a lesbian partnership.

Roberts and Azpadu have in common the rejection of conventional concepts of 'realism' and 'character'. In other respects, however, their styles of writing are entirely different. Their novels represent, in fact, two contrary stylistic modes available to writers of lesbian fiction today. Roberts's novel, like Aileen La Tourette's *Nuns and Mothers* (1984), is rooted in a psychoanalytic approach to feminism. Its texture is dense and sensuous, introducing devices of intertextuality. The interplay between past and present and the interweaving of different female subjectivities which Roberts creates, appropriately reflect the symbiotic nature of relations between women which is one of her key themes. Azpadu's novel, in contrast, like the works of Gubb and Anna Wilson, has its ideological base in radical and revolutionary feminism. The writing is deliberately austere and stark. Characters are portrayed, first and foremost, as products of their social environment. Emphasis is placed on their entrapment in social codes beyond their control or on the heavy price which they pay to struggle free. Although Roberts's style of writing is the more immediately attractive, Azpadu's is, in my view, the more genuinely radical. Like Gubb and Anna Wilson, she successfully challenges and contravenes notions of women's writing as gracefully decorative and lush. Azpadu, Gubb and Wilson excel at understatement, foregrounding in a tersely grim manner the social and political imperatives of life.

Another facet of patriarchal power and heterosexual relations which writers of lesbian fiction explore is *male acts of violence perpetrated in the context of contemporary urban life*. To avoid a negative focus on woman as victim, they frequently accompany this with a reference to female strategies of self-defence. This particular *topos* has become very popular in recent years, with the result that it is acquiring the status of a genre – a very successful one, in fact. Piercy's *The High Cost of Living* (1978), Andrea Dworkin's *Ice and Fire* (1986), Anna Wilson's *Altogether Elsewhere* (1985) and episodes from Gloria Naylor's *The Women of Brewster Place* (1980) all represent versions of it. Thrillers such as Barbara Wilson's *Sisters of the Road* (1986) and Mary Wings's *She Came Too Late*

(1986), portraying the lesbian feminist sleuth investigating crimes of violence, also contribute to it. These writers, in their representation of male violence, reproduce the ideas of radical feminist theorists. Dworkin is, of course, herself a theorist. Like Susan Brownmiller and Sheila Jeffreys, they present rape and sexual harassment as a means for men to impose control on women and perpetuate a state of supremacy. Men, they suggest, are not innately violent but are conditioned into violent behaviour by the macho nature of contemporary culture.

Anna Wilson's *Altogether Elsewhere* (1985) is an impressive, if bleak, example of this style of fiction. Locating the action of the novel in the London Inner City, Wilson vividly evokes both the terror and the drabness of city life. She describes, in an impressionistic, rigorously honed-down style, 'decaying buildings, the city degenerating. Crushed waitresses leaning on smeared tables, people walking the streets without purpose'.[24] The novel focuses on a group of women, some hetero and others lesbian, who, disturbed by the increase in violent crime, transform themselves into a group of vigilantes. They patrol the streets at night, protecting women from molestation and assault. Dehumanized by poverty and the monotony of their jobs, they strike the reader as, to a degree, anonymous. They communicate with one another in tersely monosyllabic speech, and are distinguishable chiefly by the distortions which manual labour has wrought on their physique or by signs of youth or age. Male violence is, on the whole, hinted at rather than described overtly. The threat which male sexuality poses is powerfully symbolized by the figure of the giant snowman the boys build in the yard of the high-rise flats. The women, on approaching it, see 'vast genitals hang over them'. (p. 36)

The episode 'The Two' in *The Women of Brewster Place* (1980) by the black American writer Gloria Naylor also merits a reference here. The 'two' in question are Lorraine and Theresa. Involved in a lesbian partnership, they move into an apartment in the Place, a drab street in a derelict area of the USA. Brewster gives a disturbing account of the effects of the lesbian stigma, describing the incidents of prejudice and persecution which the women encounter. While their female neighbours use verbal methods of abuse, the men in the area, regarding their sexual preference as a threat to their virility, engage in a horrific enactment of physical violence.

3 Debates about Lesbian Continuum, Sex, Lesbian Relationships, and Bisexuality: Caeia March, Barbara Burford, Mary Wings

The Lesbian Feminist Movement has developed very rapidly in the past twenty years, producing theoretical perspectives of a notably radical and

---

[24]*Altogether Elsewhere* (London, Onlywomen Press, 1985), p. 112. References are to this edition and are in the text. Piercy's essay 'The city as battleground: the novelist as combatant', in Michael C. Jaye and Ann Chalmers Watts, eds., *American Urban Experience: Essays on the City and Literature* (Manchester University Press, 1981) is relevant to novels about urban violence.

challenging kind. The controversies which these have provoked among feminists, though disruptive politically, have had a stimulating effect on the writing of fiction. Topics which, as we shall see, are especially significant to writers are: the theory of *lesbian continuum* formulated by Adrienne Rich and the debates surrounding it; questions about sex and the nature of lesbian relationships; and the controversial position of the female bisexual.

Rich's discussion of *lesbian continuum* occurs in her essay *Compulsory Heterosexuality and Lesbian Existence* (1980). Commenting on the way that 'lesbian existence has been written out of history or catalogued under disease',[25] Rich defines heterosexuality as an institution and lists the various methods (sexual, social and economic) which patriarchal culture adopts to recruit women into heterosexual relations. Describing lesbianism as a form of resistance to male power, she introduces the term *lesbian continuum*, defining it as follows:

> I mean the term *lesbian continuum* to include a range – through each woman's life and throughout history – of woman-identified experience; not simply the fact that a woman has had or consciously desired genital sexual experience with another woman. If we expand it to embrace many more forms of primary intensity between and among women, including the sharing of a rich inner life, the bonding against male tyranny, the giving and receiving of practical and political support . . . we begin to grasp breadths of female history and psychology which have lain out of reach as a consequence of limited, mostly clinical definitions of 'lesbianism'. (p. 20)

Rich's concept of *lesbian continuum* has generated a significant degree of controversy and debate. Critics accuse it of being reductionist. They complain that, by including experiences of woman-bonding and feminist camaraderie in *lesbian continuum*, Rich neglects the sexual component of lesbianism. They point out that she conflates the terms *lesbian*, *female* and *feminist*, failing to distinguish between them. *Lesbian continuum* has also been attacked as ahistorical since it underestimates the fact that the lesbian identity as we know it today is very much a twentieth-century construct.[26] However, the concept has also been greeted with praise. Jacquelyn N. Zita, whose views I endorse, draws attention to the valuable political function which it performs. It challenges 'the constant erasure of past lesbian existence' and 'defines lesbianism as it exists under patriarchy as a part of a politics of woman-centred resistance'.[27] Another advantage

---

[25]*Compulsory Heterosexuality and Lesbian Existence* (London, Onlywomen Press, 1981), p. 20.
[26]See Elizabeth Wilson, 'I'll climb the stairway to heaven', in *Sex and Love*, pp. 186–8; and Ann Ferguson, 'Patriarchy, sexual identity, and the sexual revolution', in Nannerl O. Keohane, Michelle Z. Rosaldo, and Barbara C. Gelpi, eds., *Feminist Theory: A Critique of Ideology* (Brighton, Harvester, 1982), pp. 147–61.
[27]Zita, 'Historical amnesia and the lesbian continuum', in Keohane *et al.*, eds., *Feminist Theory*, pp. 168, 170.

which the concept possesses is that it helps to heal the rifts existing between lesbian and hetero feminists, drawing attention to the common interests and goals which they share.

Whatever its shortcomings as a theoretical tool, *lesbian continuum* and the debates which it has produced have had an invigorating and beneficial effect on fiction. By stressing the value of women's community and interpreting the word *lesbian* in the widest possible manner, it has encouraged writers to move away from the narrow focus of the novels of the early 70s on a single female character intent on differentiating herself from her peers. It prompts them to focus attention instead on a *group of women*, exploring the affinities and differences they reveal. The debates surrounding the concept have also inspired writers to take a historical approach to lesbianism, comparing and contrasting constructs of lesbian identity and experience taken from different periods. Two writers whose works illustrate the influence of these ideas are Caeia March and the London-based black writer, Barbara Burford.

March in *Three Ply Yarn* (1986) ambitiously seeks to explore both 'the historical' and 'the personal' facets of *lesbian continuum*. Centring the novel on Dee, Lotte and Esther, three women with working-class backgrounds, she examines the relationships which they form with one another and with families and friends. Emphasis is placed on the way that constructs of lesbianism differ from era to era. Dee and Dora first meet one another as evacuees in the Second World War. Cuddling in bed, enjoying 'the comfort and the kisses',[28] they regard their relationship in a purely personal light, and even lack a language to describe it. The advent of the Lesbian Feminist Movement in the 1970s introduces a political perspective. This, while possessing the advantantage of making lesbians visible to one another, becomes at times a source of discord and division. March's novel, though admirable in the new ground which it explores, is not entirely successful. The complexities of the narrative confuse the reader and the transcription of dialect is, on occasion, tedious.

Burford, in contrast to March, concentrates attention on the purely 'personal' aspect of *lesbian continuum*. Her story *The Threshing Floor* (1986) gives a sensitive account of lesbian bereavement. The topic is an important one which writers treat all too rarely. Burford describes the psychological progress made by Hannah, a black woman who is mourning the death of her white lover Jenny, from a state of introverted grief to a re-involvement in work and the forming of a new relationship. Emphasis is placed on the different kinds of connections she forms with the women in her life, including lovers, friends and work-mates. The *lesbian continuum* is shown to encompass, in the words of Rich, a wide 'range of woman-identified experience'. Like March, Burford also explores female divisions and feuds.

The criticism directed at Rich's theory of *lesbian continuum* that, by defining lesbianism primarily in terms of woman-bonding and feminist

[28]*Three Ply Yarn* (London, Women's Press, 1986), p. 2.

camaraderie, it neglects the sexual element in lesbian relationships has also been levelled, in fact, at the feminist theorization of lesbianism as a whole. Critics complain that feminist theorists, reacting against the narrowly sexual definition of lesbianism formulated by male sexologists, have now gone too far in the opposite direction. Presenting 'anger [at patriarchal oppression] rather than eros as the wellspring of lesbianism',[29] they ignore the sexual component altogether. As Ann Snitow and her co-authors point out, this gives rise to a curious contradiction. Although 'Lesbian-Feminism proceeded initially from the insistence of women's liberation on a woman's right to be *sexual*, the strongly political character which the Movement has acquired has led paradoxically to the promotion of 'a desexualized image of lesbianism'.[30] This image, and the censorship (external and internalized) in which it often results, have had an inhibiting and puritanical effect on lesbian writing. The American writer Joan Nestle, decrying what she sees as the repressive effect of the Feminist Anti-pornography Movement and the attack on butch–femme role play, complains of attempts made by feminists to silence 'leather and butch and femme Lesbians, transsexuals, Lesbian prostitutes and sex workers, *writers of explicit sexual stories*' (my italics).[31] Elizabeth Wilson similarly laments the fact that, in their concern to present lesbianism in a positive light and make it appear socially respectable, writers have failed to address 'the darker and more poignant elements of sexual desire, the many ambiguities of sexual attraction'.[32] She sees the current interest in sado-masochistic sex among a small minority of lesbians as, in part, a reaction against this desexualized, sanitized image of lesbianism.

It is understandable, of course, that the majority of writers of fiction are unwilling to focus explicitly on the themes of lesbian sexual practice and desire. The pressures exerted by the dominant heterosexual culture make the authentic representation of lesbian sex in writing, art and film very difficult indeed to achieve. 'The language of Lesbian eroticism', as Duncker rightly observes, 'remains problematic partly because images of Lesbian sex have been so abused within male pornography, and partly because [since sexual discourse has been the province of male sexologists], simply, there are no words'.[33]

Nonetheless, complex though these problems certainly are, a number of contemporary writers are making a successful attempt to surmount them. Lesley Thomson's novel *Seven Miles from Sydney* (1983) and Aileen La Tourette's *Nuns and Mothers* (1984) focus convincingly on the realms of lesbian desire and sexual practice. The two topics also find expression in the lesbian feminist thriller. In fact, Mary Wings's *She Came Too Late*

---

[29]Ann Snitow, Christine Stansell, and Sharon Thompson, eds., *Desire: The Politics of Sexuality* (London, Virago, 1984), p. 25.

[30]*Desire: The Politics of Sexuality*, p. 21.

[31]*A Restricted Country* (New York, Firebrand, 1987), p. 149.

[32]'I'll climb the stairway to heaven', p. 194.

[33]'Writing lesbian', p. 41. See the essays on 'Women and erotica' by Linda Semple and Rose Collis in *Spare Rib*, 191 (June 1988), 6–12.

(1986), one of the most successful examples of the genre, has even been described as 'a pubic hair curler'![34] The format of the thriller, as I illustrate elsewhere,[35] makes a space for a sexualized image of lesbianism and allows for a focus on the transgressive aspects of sexual desire in a way that other, more 'establishment' kinds of fiction do not. This no doubt helps to explain the exceptional popularity which the genre has achieved.

Problems, however, do continue to confront the writer of lesbian fiction. One of the most pressing, as indicated above, is the rift discernible between the political dimension of lesbianism, on the one hand, and the sexual, erotic dimension on the other. Writers who treat the one area generally avoid treating the other. For example, La Tourette, whose approach is predominantly psychoanalytic, focuses on the personal, erotic aspect, whereas Piercy and Anna Wilson, whose perspectives are radical feminist, focus primarily on the political. A genre which is starting to unite the two dimensions is fantasy and science fiction. An example is Anna Livia's novel *Bulldozer Rising* (1988).

Linked to the debate about sex and desire, and the problems it raises, is the vexed question of the nature of lesbian relationships. Are they, as cultural feminists such as Mary Daly suggest, inherently more caring, sensitive and gentle than their heterosexual counterparts, and less fraught by tensions and imbalances of power?[36] Or are they equally prone to conflicts and power-struggles, though ones of a different kind? Theorists writing in the early 70s tended to take the former view. They presented lesbian relations in an idealized light, treating them as morally superior. In the 80s, however, they are likely to take a more realistic approach, scrutinizing problems and areas of stress. A similar shift of emphasis is apparent in works of fiction. It is worth pointing out, however, that writers of fiction have seldom portrayed lesbian relations and women's community in as idealized a manner as the theorists. Piercy's *Small Changes* (1972) and, more especially, *The High Cost of Living* (1978) and Michèle Roberts's *A Piece of the Night* (1978), while affirming the value of lesbian feminist community, simultaneously give a clear-sighted analysis of its flaws, conflicts and imbalances of power. Andrea Dworkin, Lesley Thomson and Elizabeth Wilson, writing in the 80s, place an even stronger and, to my mind, more disturbing emphasis on female antagonisms and power-struggles.

Another topic which helps us to comprehend the different stances which writers adopt in works of fiction, is *the debate about the significance of bisexuality and the position of the female bisexual*.[37] The writer's

---

[34]See Duncker, 'Writing lesbian', p. 41. Sheba Feminist Publishers will be producing the first UK anthology of lesbian erotic fiction in late 1988.

[35]See my essay on the Lesbian Feminist Thriller in Elaine Hobby and Chris White, eds., *What Lesbians Do In Books* (Manchester University Press), forthcoming.

[36]*Gyn/Ecology: The Metaethics of Radical Feminism* (USA, 1978; London, Women's Press, 1979).

[37]See Marianna Valverde's essay in *Sex, Power and Politics* (Toronto, Women's Press, 1985), pp. 109–20.

attitude to the topic, like the theorist's, depends to a degree on whether the position she takes is 'psychoanalytic' or 'radical feminist'. A psychoanalytic approach, in accepting the idea of the fractured self and the contradictory aspects of sexual desire, tends to idealize the figure of the bisexual, treating her as a symbol of the free play of multiple identities and heterogeneous desires. La Tourette in *Nuns and Mothers* (1984) and the French writer Hélène Cixous (*La jeune Née*, 1975) both adopt this perspective. A radical feminist approach, in contrast, since it values lesbianism as a form of political resistance to patriarchy, regards the bisexual in an unsympathetic light. It portrays her at worst as a traitor who, by taking advantage of the social/financial privileges and protection which men offer, deserts her sisters; and at the best as a sort of 'failed' lesbian, a weak and untrustworthy individual easily recruited into heterosexual relations. Nancy Toder's *Choices* (1980) and Barbara Wilson's *Ambitious Women* (1982) represent different versions of this approach.

Of the two approaches, the psychoanalytic one is, in my opinion, preferable. It has the advantage of taking the position of the bisexual seriously, crediting her with a subjectivity and a point of view. Neither, however, is really satisfactory. The psychoanalytic, as is generally the case, underestimates the importance of the social and political dimensions of experience. The radical feminist, again as usual, ignores the psychological complexities of the construction of the female subject and the contradictions of sexual desire. It is to be hoped that in the future writers will recognize the problematic aspects of these approaches and, exploring their tensions and contradictions, give a more complex and convincing representation of the bisexual's situation.

4 Comic and Satiric Fiction: Anna Livia, Joanna Russ, Suniti Namjoshi

A feature which helps account for the vitality and diversity of contemporary lesbian fiction is the willingness of writers to experiment with a variety of different genres. The use they make of popular forms such as the thriller, the historical, gothic and comic novel, as well as being entertaining, is deliberately subversive in effect. It re-fashions, from a lesbian feminist perspective, forms and motifs belonging to the dominant heterosexual, phallocratic culture, parodying their stances and attitudes.

The comic novel, the particular genre on which I choose to focus here, has received little attention from critics. Many readers may in fact be surprised to hear that it exists. Lesbian feminists are not noted, on the whole, for their sense of humour. On the contrary, they are often regarded – with a degree of justification as I illustrated in the previous section – as a glumly tight-lipped, puritanical bunch, more interested in politics than in pleasure. However, whereas one strand of the fiction which they have produced, represented by the works of writers such as Azpadu, Gubb and Anna Wilson, certainly does merit the adjective 'austere', another strand illustrates the very opposite. Writers such as Kate Hall, Anna Livia, Suniti Namjoshi and Joanna Russ, use strategies of wit and humour in a way which may justly be described as 'carnivalesque'. Inverting heterosexual norms and conventions, they present to the reader, to quote the Russian critic Mikhail Bakhtin, 'a world inside out'. In their humorous treatment of sexual attitudes and codes of conduct, 'they liberate us from the prevailing point of view of the world, from conventions and established truths' and 'offer the chance to have a new outlook on the world . . . and to enter a completely new order of things'.[38] It is interesting to note that the subversive aspect of lesbian feminist humour is not restricted to the realm of writing but extends to that of art. Examples include the cartoons of Cath Jackson and the magnificently inventive series of *Stop the Clause* cards designed by Kate Charlsworth, Angela Spark and Cath Tate (see plate).

Radical feminist and lesbian feminist humour in writing sometimes takes the form of word-play and linguistic wit. Joreen, for example, in her satiric squib 'The Bitch Manifesto' (1970) inverts the derogatory meaning of the term *bitch*, interpreting it in a celebratory manner. She identifies *bitch* with attributes of strength, independence and self-assertiveness – ones which, in a patriarchal culture, women are not supposed to possess and, if they do, men see as threatening. This explains why, she demonstrates, the word functions in contemporary society as a term of abuse.[39]

Word-play also features in the title of Anna Livia's *Relatively Norma* (1982), signalling to the reader the satiric focus of the novel. The hero Minnie, identifying as lesbian feminist and living in London, is portrayed paying a visit to her family in Australia where they have recently immigrated. She discovers during her stay Down Under that concepts of normality are strictly 'relative'. Her lesbian identity, which she bravely determines to divulge, strikes the reader as a mere mild eccentricity in contrast to the bizarre self-revelations which her mother and two sisters, who identify as hetero, have to make. The chief butt of Livia's satire is the absurdities of heterosexual norms and conventions. However, she also playfully ridicules lesbian feminist codes of conduct and fashions in dress. In both this novel and her subsequently published *Accommodation Offered* (1985) she punctures the realist surface of the text with references to *deus ex machina* and supernatural machinery. The humour in the latter novel, though too academic and precious for my taste, links her writing to traditions of the mock heroic.

Another motif which appears in a number of lesbian comic novels, one which merits attention here, is the satiric exposé of the follies and affectations of the conventions of heterosexual courtship and romance. Novels as different in tone as Lisa Alther's *Other Women* (1984), Anne Leaton's *Good Friends, Just* (1983) and Joanna Russ's *The Female Man* (1975) all successfully exploit this motif. All three works contain episodes in which the lesbian feminist protagonist inadvertently becomes involved in a scene

[38]*Rabelais and His World*, trans. Helene Iswolsky (USA, MIT Press, 1965), pp. 11, 34.
[39]*Radical Feminism*, ed. Anne Koedt, Ellen Levine, Anita Rapone (New York, Quadrangle, 1973), pp. 50–9.

'How dare they presume. . .' by Cath Jackson, 1986

'I've rung Lesbian Line' by Angela Spark and Cath Tate, 1988.

Satiric treatment of heterosexual conventions in cartoons by contemporary artists (reproduced by permission of Cath Jackson and Cath Tate)

of hetero courtship – and finds herself the unwilling object of male sexual attentions and 'chatting up' routines. Humour, sometimes of a hilarious kind, arises from the discrepancy between the protagonist's independent and articulate behaviour, and the roles of sex object and silent doll which the male assigns to her. Complex reversals of power also take place. He thinks that he is manipulating and dominating her but, in actual fact, she sees through his manoeuvres and buoyantly controls the situation.

A striking feature of many of the novels mentioned here is the stylistic inventiveness which they display. Writers such as Ellen Galford, Anna Livia and Joanna Russ, by introducing elements of fantasy and the absurd, advertise both the fictionality of the text and its ideological focus. One of the most talented exponents of anti-realist devices is the Indian writer Suniti Namjoshi. In *Feminist Fables* (1981) she wittily re-tells from a lesbian feminist perspective a series of fables and fairy tales. In *The Conversations of Cow* (1985), unexpectedly combining motifs from Hindu mythology with ideas from lesbian feminism, she explores a theme of particular interest to women in the process of acquiring a feminist consciousness – transformations of role and identity. The eponymous Cow guides the astonished narrator through a series of fantastic transformations ranging from the animal to the supernatural.

5 Representations of lesbianism in the novels of Erica Jong, Fay Weldon, Margaret Atwood and Angela Carter

The fact that during the past ten years an increasing number of women who write from a heterosexual perspective have started to introduce into their fiction representations of lesbian characters and relationships is not necessarily an event to be welcomed. In the media and the popular press lesbianism is often associated with pornography, with the result that writers sometimes 'use Lesbian material to spice their narratives'.[40] An especially offensive example of this is Erica Jong. In *How To Save Your Own Life* (1977) Jong portrays her heroine Isadora, in pursuit of sensation, as having an affair with the exotic Rosanna Howard. Jong tastelessly exploits the episodes of love-making between the two figures as a source of titillation and prurient humour. Rosanna, clad in satin jeans, rhinestone-studded T-shirt, black lipstick and the predictable musk oil, functions as a blatant sex symbol. It is interesting that, whereas in the first half of this century the lesbian was generally portrayed as masculine and dowdy, in the fiction inspired by the 60s' Sexual Revolution she is assigned the image of whore. Both images are, of course, equally oppressive.

Other contemporary women writers, however, including Margaret Atwood, Angela Carter and Fay Weldon, treat the theme of lesbianism in a more serious and intelligent manner. If, as Zimmerman convincingly argues, there is 'an important dialectic between how the lesbian articulates

[40]Duncker, 'Writing Lesbian', p. 38.

and views herself and how she is articulated and objectified by others',[41] then the representations of the topic in the works of these writers certainly merit critical attention.

Weldon's portrayals are, in my opinion, the most interesting and thought-provoking of the three. The contradictions they reveal illustrates with remarkable clarity the contrary meanings which contemporary society attributes to the sign *lesbian*. The sign has become, in the 70s and 80s, a hub of conflicting intellectual and ideological interpretations, with sexologists, right-wing moralists, feminists and merchants of porn all struggling to appropriate it and make their particular definition the dominant one.

In *Female Friends* (1975), a relatively early novel, Weldon approaches lesbianism from a phallocratic perspective, exploring the contradictory significances which it assumes in the male imagination. On the one hand, as is apparent from the episodes in which the despotic Oliver tries to prevent his wife Chloe from seeing her women friends by accusing her of being a dyke, the word *lesbian* uttered as a taunt functions as (to quote the New York group Radicalesbians), 'the label, the condition that holds women in line'.[42] Men use it as a form of scare-tactics to stop women behaving independently and achieving solidarity with one another. On the other hand, as *Female Friends* also illustrates, the word *lesbian* functions on a quite different level as the focus of a voyeuristic fantasy-scenario, one which is paradoxically both pleasurable and threatening. This is evident from the episode in which Oliver tries to manipulate his wife Chloe and his mistress Françoise into having sex together. When, having vainly tried to resist his persuasions, the two women succumb and reluctantly start to fondle and embrace, Oliver suddenly loses his nerve. Terrified that they might start to enjoy the experiment and, by concentrating on one another, break free of his control, he hastily intervenes and ·separates them.

In the novels which she published subsequently Weldon changes her stance and approaches lesbianism from a female point of view. Her representations of the topic are, however, by no means stable but reveal fascinating shifts and contradictions. She oscillates between celebrating the figure of the lesbian as a symbol of female independence and liberation, and regarding her contemptuously from a heterosexist viewpoint as marginal, exploited and naive. *Praxis* (1978) illustrates the former approach. The devastating indictment of patriarchal power and male supremacy which the novel contains culminates appropriately in the daughter of the female hero rejecting the company of men and identifying as lesbian feminist. *The Life and Loves of a She-Devil* (1983), in contrast, illustrates the latter approach. Relations between women are represented in a cynical light. Lesbian love is presented as a tool of manipulation, a means for one woman to use another in her sexual pursuit of a man. This is

---

41'What has never been', p. 193.
42'The woman identified woman' (1970), in Koedt *et al.*, eds., *Radical Feminism*, p. 241.

the way Ruth Patchett, the eponymous She-Devil, uses poor, naive Nurse Hopkins, inveigling her into a love-affair as a step towards regaining the love of her faithless husband Bobbo. Yet, although Weldon's representation of lesbianism in the novel is, on the whole, negative, it none the less contains moments of acute insight. For example, her perceptive analysis of the mixed flaws and advantages of the lesbian feminist farming commune which provides Ruth with temporary refuge is very similar to the representations of lesbian feminist community to be found in lesbian novels such as Piercy's *The High Cost of Living* (1978) and Barbara Wilson's *Ambitious Women* (1982).

Atwood's and Carter's treatment of the topic of lesbianism is more recent than Weldon's. It is also blander and more idealized. The narrative strategies which Atwood and Carter employ in their representations reveal, in fact, certain interesting similarities. Atwood in *The Handmaid's Tale* (1985) and Carter in *Nights at the Circus* (1984), centring their texts on a heterosexual female figure whose subjectivity is the focus of attention, relegate the figure of the lesbian to a peripheral and largely symbolic role. Atwood's portrayal of Moira, the lesbian feminist who leads the resistance movement against the oppressive Gilead regime, and Carter's representation of Mignon and the Princess of Abyssinia, reflect the feminist theorization of lesbianism as a form of resistance to patriarchal power. They may be criticized on the grounds that, as well as being somewhat superficial, they foreground the political dimension of lesbianism at the expense of the personal and social. However, as a barometer of public opinion they give cause for optimism since they illustrate the notably strong impact which lesbian feminist ideas are starting to make on the fiction of the dominant culture.

6 Conclusion

Certain features of contemporary lesbian feminist fiction, such as its representation of sexual relations between women, and its exposé, by either serious or satirically comic methods, of the oppressive facets of heterosexual conventions and structures, are distinctive and unique. They illustrate the specificity of this kind of fiction. Other themes which it treats relate it, on the contrary, to women's fiction as a whole. These themes include: motherhood, relations between mothers and daughters, women's community, and the oppressive effects of the patriarchal family and of male violence. They are popular with both heterosexual and lesbian women writing in the 70s and 80s. Questions of a theoretical nature about 'role-models' and the idealized representation of relations between women, which lesbian fiction raises, also form a common link between lesbian and heterosexual writers. Moreover, the rift between the political and erotic dimensions of lesbianism, and the conflict between radical feminist and psychoanalytic approaches to feminism which it reflects, constitute, in fact, a version of the rift between 'political' and 'personal' aspects of women's experience which, as I argue elsewhere,[43] is one of the most serious problems facing women writers today.

It is, of course, fascinating to ponder the direction which lesbian feminist fiction will take in the future. The sign *lesbian* is, in the 1980s, the pivot of conflicting ideologies, and the outcome of the struggle is by no means clear. Alternative possibilities are thus available for conjecture. Will the assimilation of lesbian feminist themes into women's fiction in general which, as we saw from the discussion of Atwood's, Carter's and Weldon's novels in Section 5, is already starting to take place, have the effect of making lesbian feminist fiction as a specific mode redundant and cause it, having served its political purpose, eventually to disappear? Judging from the present oppressive political climate in the UK and USA, such an event is highly unlikely – as a short-term prospect, at any rate. A more urgent question for British readers at this particular moment is, what will be the effects on lesbian fiction of the homophobic climate represented by Clause 28 (now Section 28 of the Local Government Act) and its supporters?[44] Will the Clause, by cutting off financial resources from the lesbian community and weakening its fragile social network of centres and help-lines, deter lesbians from writing and publishing fiction? Or will it, as in fact appears more likely, provoke a strong and positive reaction from writers, motivating them to treat with fresh vigour the themes of the oppressive nature of institutionalized heterosexuality and lesbian acts of resistance to it? Lesbian writers have shown themselves capable of responding speedily and effectively to events in the political sphere. This is illustrated by Nicky Edwards's *Mud* (1986), which debates lesbian feminist views of Greenham Common and The Women's Peace Movement, and Jan Clausen's *Sinking Stealing* (1985) which explores issues of lesbian custody and 'father right'. Writers will respond, it is to be hoped, in a similarly dynamic manner to Clause 28. If so, in a few years time critics may perhaps be discussing the complexities of works of fiction which treat a hitherto unexplored theme – the repercussions of *The Clause*.

[43]See Chapters 6 and 7 of my book *Contemporary Women's Fiction: Narrative Practice and Feminist Theory* (Hemel-Hempstead, Harvester-Wheatsheaf, 1989).
[44]For Clause 28 see n. 16 above.

Note

I have taken my examples from very recent science fiction – published within the last five to ten years – written in English by women, most of it published by The Women's Press in their Science Fiction imprint. I have not concentrated on any single text or author, partly because my essay is a sketch of some pointers towards a theory of feminist SF, but more importantly because I wanted to think feminist SF as an intertextuality before thinking it as a collection of discrete texts. The short story has a particularly important place in SF and I have not hesitated to give it equal weight to novels. I have also avoided taking too many of my examples from the best known writers so as to avoid at least some of the distortions inherent in a 'canonical' approach.

There is not much critical writing about women's SF overall, let alone from a feminist standpoint. Sarah Lefanu's *In the Chinks of the World Machine*[1] is the only full-length study of the subject, and as such is indispensable. There are many good things in the book, and it is an excellent survey of the field, complete with a bibliography. Since it covers rather different ground, and is written from a different theoretical standpoint, I hope my much shorter effort will make productive reading alongside it. The SF writer Joanna Russ is another indispensible source on feminist SF, with her witty satires, including *The Clichés from Outer Space (Despatches)*[2], *How to Suppress Women's Writing*[3] and 'The Image of Women in Science Fiction'[4].

In an essay this short, there has not been space to explain where some of my frameworks and terminology are coming from. I'm sorry if this makes it more difficult or, worse, less clear. In terms of general feminist critical theory, my approach is much conditioned by French writers, especially Julia Kristeva. There is a very good broad outline in Toril Moi's *Sexual/Textual Politics*[5] and the reader will find useful directions, should she want them, in her suggestions for further reading (Moi 182–3). It makes a big difference to me, though, that my personal route to that theory was through an intense and formative study of the poet, Mallarmé; *'Par avance ainsi tu vis . . .'*

[1]Sarah Lefanu, *In the Chinks of the World Machine* (London, The Women's Press, 1988).
[2]Joanna Russ, *The Clichés from Outer Space*, in Jen Green and Sarah Lefanu, eds., *Despatches from the Frontiers of the Female Mind* (London, The Women's Press, 1985) *subsequently: Despatches).*
[3]Joanna Russ, *How to Suppress Women's Writing* (London, The Women's Press, 1984).
[4]Joanna Russ, *The Image of Women in Science Fiction*, in S. Cornillon, ed., *Images of Women in Fiction: Feminist Perspectives* (Ohio, BGU Popular Press, 1972).
[5]Toril Moi, *Sexual/Textual Politics* (London, Methuen, 1985).

4

The Liberation of Utopia
or
Note why feminist Science Fiction is a means to the end
of the possibility
that feminist SF in the Ideal Literary Form

Penny Florence

The forms of women's writing evidence a growth in consciousness that means the end of literary genre as 'we' know it.

D-notice[6] Notice-d
genre genre-d gen-d-re gen-d-er gender

Why am I writing about/in a genre-d subject
because I have no alternative at present
when I hate alternatives

Looking forward to the end of gender as we know it.

The forms of contemporary women's writing world-wide do not, taken together, evidence the binary thinking that underlies current cultural constructs of gen-d-re.[7] We are far, as yet, from a global framework within which to approach specific cultural forms. So we are stuck for now with the contradictions of needing to maintain a clear sense of genre-d-differentiation in order to understand the present and the past, when we need to abolish it in order to envision the future; an example not only of the present uneven state of cultural theory, but also of the clashes that recur between feminist strategy and theory/principle. Which is all right. One of the aims of radical criticism is to make itself redundant.

Another example of the theoretical difficulties over strategic and abstract criticism is the slippage when discussing 're-presentation/ representation'. In dominant literary terms, women and/or what is female

Thanks to Elaine Hawkins; a brilliant reader. And to Sarha & Elly.

[6]D-Notice: patriarchal censorship device, used to stop publication in Britain of material considered to be against the interests of national 'defence'.
[7]'gendre' in French means 'son-in-law'.

has been for so long so many men's/male male projections, and few places worse than masculine SF. In terms of society, differently so, and in a dynamic with the same. Theorizing any genre touches somewhere on a relationship with 'the real' extra-textually, even if only by negatives. Realism gets very tricky! It generates so many intrickacies that its validity is called into question. Almost. It may well be that what is imaginable bears a profound relation to what is already imagined to exist, and, crucially, how; what worlds lie hidden in those depths!

But we inherit the patriarchal mental topography.[8] So feminist understanding can (at the moment and up to a point) be furthered through obsolescent genre-d criticism which seeks to describe the forms currently adopted by women involved in cultural production both as writers and as publishers. SF is a self-conscious genre overall, and in addition to films and writing has its own sub-culture of magazines and comics; I'm looking forward with great anticipation to feminist texts in the potentially revolutionary intersemiotic field of the grown-up comic book. Many feminist SF writers situate themselves in relation to this sub-culture, and the Women's Press clearly follow this strategy by initiating their separate SF imprint. There are thus good reasons for looking at feminist SF as a genre. The crucial matter is not necessarily the definition per se – though it can be – it is how definition is used, both to reflect back on to and to change the social and political framework/s within which the texts are produced, as well as the cultural.

Theorizing literature is like SF insofar as it hypothesizes what might be out of what is, both actually and culturally; a present–future dynamic which doesn't have to be limited by the existing shape of mental constructs – as culturally manifest – in any given society, though it has to aim to construct strands of the future overall shape. The most visibly privileged, about whom we can anyway understand little in isolation, don't have to Command our Attention. If we treat them in isolation – though they think themselves the overall – we can merely accede to their values. Joanna Russ rightly points out in her chapter on aesthetics (Russ, *How to Suppress* p. 111–12) that the wholesale cultural omission of women equals distortion; it's not a matter of allowing our work 'back' into accepted criteria and definitions, hitherto 'incomplete'. They are 'distorted through and through'. To try to 're-insert' women or 'the female' is to face the same limitation as 'reversal' type fiction, like Esmé Dodderidge's *The New Gulliver*,[9] in which a descendant of Swift's Gulliver finds himself in Capovolta where gender roles are reversed. Though such scenarios can expose the present, they reproduce the same

[8](A book on Science Fiction opens with the words, 'The idea of literature is unthinkable without the conception of genres, or conventional literary forms.' Given the way that SF places the possible in tension with the actual, it is all the more surprising that the writer of this extraordinary statement should be a critic of SF – and in context it is clear that there are no hidden philosophical or semantic depths to the remark. The idea is unthinkable without the conception, is it? Metalanguage gone berserk! Let's do without the lot and just have the literature. Better still, let's just have writing.)

[9]Esmé Dodderidge, *The New Gulliver* (London, The Women's Press, 1988).

structural restrictions as the present in imagining the future or re-imagining the past. One way out of this would be to take matters forward into the revolution and beyond; but I have yet to see a reversal narrative that goes this far.

If I want to write about feminist SF I may be stuck with genre for now. The drive outside runs deep into Other dimensions, as in feminist SF itself, which is why I'm writing about it (. . . listen to the music some-where else and celebrate a potential far greater than a mere genre whose salient characteristics hitherto were conflict, fembots and techno/logical hardware. A predictable simplification of patriarchal pens. Ill/logically).[10]

Con-stellated '-isms' Beyond the Stars
Feminist SF, Post or Modern -ism, Masculine Fantasy and Real Realism.

Let us take a trip and walk the knife edge between recuperation and furthering the revolution of the disrupting Subject.

> There used to be an odd, popular and erroneous idea that the sun revolved around the earth.
> This has been replaced by an even odder, equally popular, and equally erroneous idea that the earth goes around the sun. . . .
> *what does the motion of the earth really look like from the centre of the entire universe, say,* . . . the only answer is:
> that it doesn't.
> Because there isn't.
> (Russ *How to Suppress* p. 121)

Maybe it has its uses to think feminist SF in relation to masculine discourses of post and modern-ism; but then we need to avoid the entropic cop-out in which interpreters seem to seek rest as they, oddly, find all the shifts, interruptions and disjunctions monotonously monologous and incapacitating.

Is the position of the Subject in feminist SF. An example.

The I-in-the-text[10] is not as narcissistic; any exploration of the Self in relation to the world gives way to the impact of worlds on the Self. Or where it is the Self that the narrative foregrounds, there is still an outward impulse, towards other beings, other worlds. 'I' comes up against 'you' or 'it' rather than 'not-I'. The feminist SF Self, while exploring an often meta-physical universe, is not locked in ontological isolation. The relationship between the ontological Subject and the body is also innovative (see below).

Equally the textual-I, the linguistic Subject is active in a world of shifting signifiers rather than adrift in a world of floating signifiers. The I-in-the-text adopts varying positions in relation to the textual and extra-textual real. Her exploration is less into 'what is real' than into 'what the real is'.

---

[10]See Mary Ann Carrs, *The Eye in the Text* (Princeton, 1981).

Clearly this begins to evidence a different dynamic between the text overall and the 'real', or between textual and extra-textual reality than that of most modernist discourses. Though in the abstract I'd rather not construct my thoughts in this way, I'm going to narrow down my de-finition of feminist SF to a comparison with fantasy. This is not because I necessarily want to privilege a relationship between feminist SF and fantasy over other discourses, but because there is already an assumed or connotative relationship I want to comment on.

Fantasy is often linked with SF both popularly and in critical literature. Sara Lefanu continues in this vein when she argues that Rosemary Jackson should have included SF in her excellent study *Fantasy. The Literature of Subversion*[11] and transfers some of her analysis to SF (*Chinks* pp. 22–3). Sara Lefanu's aim is largely to claim for feminist SF the subversive function/s that Rosemary Jackson elaborates and I share that aim. Some of the confusion arises, as Sara Lefanu rightly says, because of the general looseness of the term 'fantasy'. But Rosemary Jackson is very clear and useful in her definition of both structure/s and themes. Following her map makes it apparent that feminist SF, at least in my definition, cannot be subsumed under fantasy; much of what I have already said would have to be excluded.

Feminist SF is not a fantasy discourse. Maybe the distinction is epistemological. Unfortunately, Rosemary Jackson chose not to deal explicitly with either feminism or gender, so she doesn't help us distinguish between masculine fantasy and feminist fantasy, if such a thing exists. In that it begins from a position of otherness from the dominant, and in its subversive impulsion, feminist discourses have more of a link with masculine fantasy than with other masculine discourses. But feminist SF has structural and thematic features that differentiate it from fantasy.

I want to take this further by adopting some of Rosemary Jackson's terms. According to her location of fantastic narrative as between the poles of the mimetic and the marvellous (Jackson *Fantasy* pp. 31–2) – not that I like being between poles – feminist SF would traverse the space/s between the mimetic and the marvellous close to fantasy, but shifting more towards the mimetic in several respects. As in the fantastic (or indeed any modernist discourse) the break between signifier and signified occurs, occasioning shifting relations between levels and forms of 'the real', whether material or linguistic.

Often feminist SF narrative does have reflexive elements, becoming self-commentating in some sense, but it tends less towards an enclosed language-system than fantasy, as in Lannah Battley's *Cyclops* (*Despatches* 74–9). The text is reflexive in that language and the construction of literature form the basis of the overall narrative and of the secondary narrative within it. Many SF texts involve a manuscript, newly discovered,

---

[11]Rosemary Jackson, *Fantasy, The Literature of Subversion* (London and New York, Methuen, 1981) *subsequently: Fantasy*). You will have noticed Mary Daly's Touching Powers among the tracks in my language-relation. *Pure Lust* (London, Women's Press, 1984).

and the rest of the narrative is structured around its contents, the conditions of its discovery and its implications. This is true of *Cyclops*, in which the secondary narrative (the MS) clearly prefigures what might happen again. Nella Nelby, linguist-translator (did she *have* to be 'tall, slim, dark and beautiful'?) is carrying her MS through a hostile environment that clearly threatens its survival (and, consequently, hers). The MS is a wittily ironic re-telling of a story by Homer, who is 'really' Homa. But Homa's story comes down to her framed and re-told by males; it is narrated through the log of the Captain of a spaceship and an ancient account by one Aeneas, Homa's brother. Aeneas' account is of events witnessed by himself and his sister, who later became a famous storyteller. The event retells the Homeric Cyclops as the landing of a spaceship, the one-eyed monsters being men in spacesuits. The irony operates layer upon layer, and the various versions of the tale – including the one the reader brings to it, assuming a knowledge of Homer – disturb unitary interpretations.

Though Aeneas has been translated by Nella Nelby, her textual function is not unequivocally to provide the dominant voice with the 'right' version, since the layers of the narrative call the possibility of 'right' versions into question. So does the pilot-narrator's scepticism. As in fantasy, the comfort of a unified vision and voice, or unity between vision and voice, is denied. But the multiplication and layering of signifieds within the text does not enmesh either the textual Subject/s or the reader. The story pivots, not on the cultural play in itself, but on Nella's discovery *through* the two documents that Earth could not have been the 'cradle of humanity'. The signified is not the text.

Even if power relations between men and women seem little changed in the future Space Station bar where Nella meets the narrator – another narrative voice; she is a pilot, at that, like the Captain – and Nella fears the suppression of her discovery by her male professorial boss (the rewriting of her story), the notion that the cradle of humanity is elsewhere opens the narrative on to the possibility of wholly different power and meaning rather than dissolution or non-meaning. As the narrator says of conversation, it is 'an improvement on staring into space.' (*Cyclops Despatches* p. 92)

What this exemplifies is a shift in feminist SF more towards the notional slippage-point between language and 'the real', or between signifier and signified, than to the zero point of non-meaning.

Another sign of this is humour and its relative prevalence (see also below). The cultural play in *Cyclops* is ironic and darkly comic. Though there are joke-structures in fantasy, humour is quite rare and few narratives are funny.

Contemporary feminist writers in English do not, on the whole, write fantasy. Even where we do, or where our writing has prominent fantasy elements, the crucial reality-orientation remains. The reasons for this will be complex; but one important factor is broadly socio-political. The free play of signifiers costs too much. Feminist SF writers know that our oppression is inextricably bound up with 'the real', not in some simplistic or indeed purely material sense – though most women suffer too much in material terms to disregard it, even if we're not committed to materialist thinking – but in the sense that whoever defines the real holds power. In Octavia Butler's *Kindred*[12], Dana's ability to deal with the transference between time-zones grows out of her insistence on the reality of events and her practical actions to deal with them. 'Rufus and his parents had still not quite settled back and become the "dream" Kevin wanted them to be.' (Butler *Kindred* p. 18) As she negotiates the 'other' world, her reference points are her grasp of historical fact, and it is the nature/s of Black historical realities in relation to the present and its white reality-constructs that are the thematic and structural signified of the book.

What, then of the closer relation to the mimetic in feminist SF that I'm suggesting? I'm not, of course, saying that SF is closer to realism or naturalism than to fantasy. The point is to move towards reconstructing the basis of these classifications. Thus though what may be named 'realist' elements are appropriated, they are used to different ends. For example 'character', the great backbone of the bourgeois novel, may seem more realist in SF than it does in fantasy, but it is radically altered by its ambivalence both on the level of signification and of narrative structure. The whole construct of 'character' is interrogated rather than remaining in focus or structurally pivotal. Equally where 'interior monologue' occurs (into which 'character' perhaps collapsed as bourgeois masculine individualism entered its ultimate phase) it cannot be read as part of the same signifying process – let alone as signifying the same. In fact, some notion of 'the collective' has resurfaced, both thematically and structurally; as in popular myth, the narrative Subject signifies to the reader because it is part of a broader notion of subjectivity and of meaning. Feminist SF stories cross and recross the boundaries between conventions and form/s, and in this, too, they innovate.

This is so in feminist SF use of allegory – in contradistinction to fantasy where the structural hesitations and breaks with the real do not allow allegorical interpretation.

Josephine Saxton's *Big Operation on Altair Three* (*Despatches* pp. 9–14) is an excellent example of feminist SF allegory which makes several satisfying sideswipes at patriarchy. It's only a sketch because it's only around 1500 words; but what interests me as radical in the story is how she makes the creation of an advertising image signify female castration. The idea, that the sexual sell disempowers women, is familiar enough. But she brings it right within the body and/of the narrative. The narrator is an advertising 'continuity and stage-manager's aide' having a mid-career crisis, and the twist in the tale derives from the medium of Altairean adverts: holograds which work so well as adverts because they can't be faked. The advert is for a car so smooth you could perform an operation on the backseat. The operation is a hysterectomy, and the model

---

[12]Octavia E. Butler, *Kindred* (London, The Women's Press, 1988).

is pregnant. She wants a child, but needs her career. What is being done in advertising is not only a matter of appearance and/or psychological oppression; it is physically real. This takes the physical and economic oppression of women to its logical and sterile conclusion. We can see the hideous continuity between patriarchal image-making and the appalling existence of the snuff movie. The holograd-text signifies what the present real is, textually and extra-textually. Mutilation by metaphor. The signified is displaced and complex, but not fluid or uncertain.

TheMa-trix,
Some Tricky Themes (by no means exhaustive).

    Matrix: womb, a place or medium in which something is 'bred', produced or developed, a place or point of origin or growth, the substance situated between animal or vegetable cells, the rock mass surrounding or adhering to things embedded in the earth. Etc. (OED)

TheMatrix: structural theme subversive of patriarchal values. Not necessarily explicit. There may be several component themes in a theMatrix, and the reader can, by a shift of her concentration between themes, discover varying overlapping revelations between theMatricks.

Gender-power is a major theMatrix.

    The nature/s and sources of the power-general-power con-figurations are a central concern of feminist SF. I can't think of a single narrative that does not somewhere touch on the lies and dementia of patriarchy's fascination with power-over and its fundamentally competitive motivation/s. It is explicit in Sally M. Gearhardt's *The Wanderground*,[13] and Joan Slonczewski's *A Door into Ocean*[14] (see also below).

    As a theme, gender-power is prominent enough to make examples slightly arbitrary. However, it is expressed in ways as far apart as Sandi Hall's *The Godmothers*,[15] where feminist networks span past and future, and in the present take on big communications business, and Lisa Tuttle's *Wives (A Spaceship built of Stone* pp. 25–34)[16] which grimly brings out gender-power as a source of horizontal violence on a colonized female planet.

    The component theme of gender, separately expressed, is less common, indicating the current inseparability of power from the social construction of gender. Men are never central and rarely even equal, and they are often marginalized. Males can have the role of a learner, like Spinel in *A Door into Ocean*. Occasionally they are deliberately eliminated, as in Caroline Forbes's *London Fields*, where a chromosomal mutation resulted in boy-children dying. When the women were threatened by the reappearance of

[13]Sally M. Gearhardt, *The Wanderground* (London, The Women's Press, 1985).
[14]Joan Slonczewski, *A Door into Ocean* (London, The Women's Press, 1987).
[15]Sandi Hall, *The Godmothers* (London, The Women's Press, 1982).
[16]Lisa Tuttle, *A Spaceship Built of Stone* (London, The Women's Press, 1987).

some males, they finally had to face either their own destruction or that of the men.

Sex is also comparatively minor as a theme when compared with masculine literature – in which it is a dominant (*sic*) – especially (good) heterosex. In relation to fantasy there is little sexual angst, at whatever level of symbolization. Not that feminist SF narratives are sexless – far from it, and many feature lesbian sexual harmony. Heterosex sidles in sometimes when a female body passes through a male state. (Contrast the 'utopia' of Gilman's *Herland*,[17] written in 1915, where the women are without sexual feeling. Until the male invaders arrive, that is. Sex is the most dated aspect of the book.) Rhoda Lerman's *The Book of the Night*,[18] in which sexuality is virtually a theMatrix, is in this and other respects in a class of its own. But 'sexuality' here is understood productively in genre-d terms, as it is in Joanna Russ. In feminist SF marriage is virtually non-existent as a theme. It functions powerfully in *Kindred* where Dana's marriage to a sympathetic white man allows into the narrative a problematized nexus of meanings around race and gender and violence in different historical conditions. One nice irony occurs where she has to call her white husband 'Master' when she is among her ancestors who have been forced into slavery. This is not a matter of liberal or even linguistic niceties; it is one of survival. It is all the more important because she loves him, and is capable of loving her white ancestor, even at the moment when she has to choose between his life and hers.

Thematically reproduction and childbearing, though not very prominent, are as common as sociological motherhood. The most fully elaborated on liberal motherhood is perhaps Mitchison's *Memoirs of a Spacewoman*[19] written in the 1960s. Pearlie McNeill's *The Awakening* (*Despatches* pp. 150–63) is a more recent example. So, to some extent, is Suzy McKee Charnas's *Motherlines*).[20]

Genre-d Re/production is, however, another major theMatrix.

Pregnatress: A (feminine) agent of power that brings to birth.
'For the Pregnatress of Time is a Model or Plat-form of the Eternal Pregnatress.' (OED)

The continuation of the species is frequently seen to in feminist SF by means of parthenogenesis.

As Ros Coward points out (*Female Desire* p. 241),[21] males are more reproductive in their sexuality than females, because orgasm and reproduction are indissolubly linked for them. For us they are not.

[17]Charlotte Perkins Gilman, *Herland* (London, The Women's Press, 1986) (Written 1915).
[18]Rhoda Lerman, *The Book of the Night* (London, The Women's Press, 1986).
[19]Naomi Mitchison, *Memoirs of a Spacewoman* (London, The Women's Press, 1985).
[20]Suzy McKee Charnas, *Motherlines* (London, Gollancz, 1980).
[21]Rosalind Coward, *Female Desire* (London, Paladin, 1984).

Having decentred phallicism, feminist SF broadens conception of female creativity.

Genre-d Re/production is part of feminist rethinking of sado-science. Carol Emshwiller's *Carmen Dog*[22] has motherhood as a component theme in its hilarious satire of patriarchal sado-science. The males try to ignore what is happening and set up an Academy of Motherhood. They are inevitably overtaken by events, as women participate with females of all species in an evolutionary melee, which eventually begins to bring the males round. 'By now, in a manner of speaking, all men have lost their mothers. Even if the mothers live where they have always lived, they are greyer or greener than expected or more moustachioed. They slide down the bannisters, fall asleep on the Persian rug in front of the fireplace. . . . Others do not encounter their mothers except on outings to the zoo' (p. 109–10).

SCIENCE:
. . . Lie has been added upon lie and it has been called science.
(FICTION:
No entry. Of course.)
TRUTH:
affirmation is repeated two times, on the third it becomes a scientific truth.

> (Monique Wittig and Sande Zeig.
> *Lesbian Peoples. Materials for a dictionary*)[23]

Sado-science is often a component theme of Genre-d Re/production, as is to be expected, since it is in uncreative tension with it. Both *The Wanderground* and *A Door into Ocean* affirm female creativity through biophilic technology, organically generated. There is, even so, not much 'techno-wonder'. Contemporary anti-life hardware begins to seem old-fashioned.

Communo-language is a TheMatrix

All three of these narratives involve some fabulous element of biophilic communication, especially *Carmen Dog*. Jaks in Doris Piserchia's *Star Rider*[24] have a symbiotic relationship with their canine mounts, and together they have evolved way beyond humans.

Feminist science explores fictions of mind expansion, telepathy, telekinesis. Many feminists know a fair bit about psychic evolution at first hand. We also know about experiencing language as a block; to communication, expression, pleasure in signification, you name it. Feminist SF writers have to exorcize the 'Thing in the Typewriter', like Joanna Russ in

[22]Carol Emshwiller, *Carmen Dog* (London, The Women's Press, 1988).
[23]Monique Wittig and Sande Zeig, *Lesbian Peoples. Materials for a Dictionary* (London, Virago, 1980).
[24]Doris Piserchia, *Star Rider* (London, The Women's Press, 1987).

her hilarious encounters in *The Clichés from Outer Space* (*Despatches* pp. 27–34), where 'fulgous luminescence streamed from old copies of *Conquer Absolutely Everything* and *The Sexist From Canopus*' (p. 28).

So Lisa Tuttle's narrator writes in *The Cure* (*Spaceship* p. 123–34), 'Would you have told me that the virus was language?

A virus carried in the genes, waiting to be born, infiltrating other cells in the brain, taking them over one after another, using the cell machinery to its own purpose' (133). And in her widely resonating (class, gender, race; none explicit) story *The Other Kind* (*Spaceship* p. 165–82) the tell-tale scar showing the removal of the vocal chords reveals the grim truth about the mutilation of humans into Ederrans.

Exploring language and perception, Naomi Mitchison's experi-mentor says to the writer in *Words* (*Despatches* p. 164–74), '''I think you must have the experience yourself before you write any more.''' (p. 172) The experi-mentor dies and the technician fears it's not meant. (The story has a reference point in Huxley's mind-expanding inquiries through mescalin, herstorically interesting for its co-incidence with the re-emergence of feminism in the 1960s.)

(See below for more on this theMatrix in relation to Suzette Haden Elgin in her novels *Native Tongue* and *The Judas Rose*[25], as well as in *A First Dictionary and grammar of Láadan*.[26])

Suniti Namjoshi wittily scrambles the lot in her satirical narrative *Conversations of Cow*,[27] which I am appropriating as feminist SF, partly because white feminist SF is still culturally highly specific when it comes to Terran fictional traditions, and Namjoshi makes Canada collide with India. The dinner conversation, mischievously initiated by B/Bhadravati, and ostensibly about whether men are really maladjusted Martians, slips between race, gender, species by means of Namjoshi's linguistic manoeuvres. Next day, the goddess-cow 'is unquestionably a Martian' (p. 96).

> 'B!' I insist.
> 'What? Oh.' She turns down the volume. 'It's all right,' she says, 'identity is fluid. Haven't you heard of transmigration? And you call yourself a good Brahmin?'
> I don't, as a matter of fact, but I let that pass.
> 'But, B, aren't you really a lesbian cow?'
> 'Well, I don't know,' she says. 'That seems rather exotic . . . What's wrong with being a white man?' (p. 32)

Textually, of course.

TheMatrix: I/eye, the Body!
(Watch out! Vag-eye-na Dentata)

[25]Suzette Haden Elgin, *Native Tongue* (London, The Women's Press, 1985). *The Judas Rose* (London, The Women's Press, 1988).
[26]Suzette Haden Elgin, *A First Grammar and Dictionary of Láadan* (Madison, The Society for the Furtherance and Study of Fantasy and Science Fiction, 1988).
[27]Suniti Namjoshi, *The Conversations of Cow* (London, The Women's Press, 1985).

B/Bhadravati's fluid identity is a great linguistic advantage. Overlapping with Communo-language is the theMatrix of the multiple Self, with language as a vital component. There is as yet nothing in feminist SF written in English to compare with Monique wittig's *Les guérillères*,[28] whose form-language and/or linguistic body fights the border patrols between the semiotic and the symbolic, without the aid of a Voice. Our SF english body-language-body traces her eyedenti-ties along interweaving differant (*sic*) paths from those of Wittig or Cixous' plural Voice.[29]

Mary Daly and Jane Caputi's *First New Intergalactic Wickedary of the English Language*[30] compares with Wittig and Zeig's *Lesbian Peoples* in semantic time-travel.

. What else of the bodies of our multiple SF Self as she/s/he shifts between autonomy, fabulous animal-friendly trans-formations and incorporeality? *The Book of the Night*, *I, Vampire*,[31] *Conversations of Cow* all refuse to be limited by body or species. These physical transformations are the manifestation of multiple selves rather than of psychic fragmentation, whether or not physically manifest. (Jekyll and Hyde are basically psychic transformations, signified in the physical.) They create new paradigms within which such female forbiddens as autonomous pleasure, desire, power and violence dis-embody new signifieds. Can textual desire in Jody Scott's *Passing for Human*[32] and *I, Vampire* traverse violence while maintaining anti-violent desire? In the middle of terrible carnage, the vampire experiences death as a laboratory mouse. The anthropologist Rysemian in her Virginia Woolf body yells, 'Forget your "humanism" if this is what it means' (*I, Vampire* p. 192). What does this textual violence signify? For sure it is no Sadean dynamic. Active and direct violence is a great female forbidden. Is a volcano violent?

In *Kindred* Dana explains to Kevin the way the impersonal violence of injustice traps the liberal pacifist (pp. 50–1) into violence. Finding herself up against slavery she faces the same reflected violence as the ANC in its opposition to apartheid, or the attacked woman in the presence of a rapist. Lisa Tuttle, in *Wives* and Caroline Forbes in *Snake*, *Equal Rights* and *London Fields*[33] dare to transgress the violent boundary line.

Female heroism, where it occurs in feminist SF, co-notes these multiples rather than a mere reversal of the heroes' role.

Feminist SF is signifiant. Yes. Signifiant.

Feminist SF signifies something Other than contemporary masculine fantasies. A significant theMatrick difference between feminist SF and

[28]Monique Wittig, *Les Guérillères*, Trans D. LeVay, (London, The Women's Press, 1979).
[29]See examples of texts by Hélène Cixous and Luce Irigaray in Marks and De Courtivron, (eds.) *New French Feminisms* (Brighton, Harvester, 1981).
[30]Mary Daly with Jane Caputi, *Websters' New Intergalactic Wickedary of the English Language* (London, The Women's Press, 1988).
[31]Jody Scott, *I, Vampire* (London, The Women's Press, 1986).
[32]Jody Scott, *Passing for Human* (London, The Women's Press, 1986).
[33]Caroline Forbes, *The Needle on Full* (London, Onlywomen Press, 1985).

masculine fantasy – this time one of ab-sense – is the comparative paucity of themes of vision and/or scopic structures. There is less narcissism. The transitional world is not through a looking glass. It is predicated less on uncertainty than on possibility.

Fantasy overall may be subversive; yet here, too, there is a hierarchy of values and visibility. Masculine writing and masculine SF in particular is notoriously backward with its juvenile projective-fantasy woman-image. Somewhere, not easily accessible, this has to do with power.

TheMatic Inter/text/mission. Lettered Litter,
Past and Future, literary, literal.

And so to past and future. Feminist SF is prophesy. Words that spell, drawing on ancient wisdom to effect changes that seemed impossible.

Looking back, the rise of feminist SF would have been predictable when we'd read it.

> FUTURE:
> 'Let me tell you
> this, someone in
> some future time
> will think of us'
> (Sappho, *Poems* Lesbos, Iron Age).
> (Wittig and Zeig, *Lesbian Peoples* p. 59)

Dream memories of flying darting through my mind like fish through phosphorescent, Aegean water. Like ships through incandescent space.

In the near future a streetwise vampire-ette from the twelfth century meets Virgina Woolf in the Ladies and falls in love with her. Thus *Orlando*[33] is projected forward into Scott's SF narrative. These are the closing words of *I, Vampire*,

> 'How do I know you won't run out on me? ''How do I even know this is real?''
> Then that slow, green-eyed smile, of the Virginia Woolf I knew long ago.
> ''Trust me,'' she says.' (p. 206)

In *Orlando* Woolf's critique of 'Literary History' (especially hilarious in relation to the nineteenth century) is inseparable from her narrative, and so is her exploration of the tension between the Self and any given historical moment. In both regards, it is truly radical narrative. Interwoven as they are, they afford such insight into the way culture interacts with the individual in the construction of human possibility. By having *Orlando* change sex as s/he romps from the Elizabethan to the modern age, the insight goes further, into the construction of the gendered self, both in society and in literature. *Orlando*[34] and *A Room of One's Own*[35] written at the same time. As now.

Futher exploration of two theMatricks: 1 Gender-power. 2 Language.

1 Gender-power.

> But what I'm also sharing with you is this thought: The Universe responds.
>
> (Alice Walker *Living by the Word* p. 192)[36]

Until feminist women began to write SF there was very little SF that either textually or thematically tried radically to reconstruct power or power relations.

Much masculine SF has been about war, the colonization of Space, petty hierarchy written large across constellations. There may well be an impulse towards something called Good, a belief among the writers that their 'heroes' were participating in some mythic, eternal battle between the bad/good old polarized absolutes. Even where something like modernist doubt rendered the pattern more sophisticated, the changes were surface.

Masculine SF writers understand enough to know that SF frees you in some sense to think yourself outside the present political and social (dis)order. But there seems little evidence that they are able to enter into that freedom in any structural sense, partly because they are not able to image their incapacity. It is very hard indeed to imagine difference from within. Feminist women have since the beginning of patriarchy understood this radical truth. But it is only recently that we have begun as a mass movement to imagine entry into freedom.

The question, 'What would happen if . . .' is one of the recurrent bases of SF. It is a question that is as interesting in the manner as well as the matter of its answer. It has both retro- and trans-gressive potential.

In masculine film, this strain has been particularly virulent in its attack on alternative values, perverting any progressive potential into McCarthyite paranoia. The aliens' threat is set against an idealized small-town wholesomeness, usually as expressed in some variant of the nuclear family, and with the men motivated by the need to protect their apple-pie women. *The Invasion of the Body Snatchers* is an example.

Feminist SF does not often foreground or evidence the conservative game of projecting the idea of threat onto outsiders and then playing out its destruction. If any given narrative is about threat, then it is usually more complex than the projection game. In *The Wanderground*, for example, the evolution of the hill women is threatened by the old order that still persists in the city. This may clearly be read in terms of multiculturalism, the dynamic between the dominant – here marginalized – and alternatives. In other words, the threat is not that aliens might invade

[34]Virginia Woolf, *Orlando* (London, Grafton, 1985). (Written in 1928).
[35]Virginia Woolf, *A Room of One's Own* (London, Penguin, 1977).
[36]Alice Walker, *Living by the Word* (London, The Women's Press, 1988).

the established order; nor is it simply the opposite. It is that the established order might overcome or re-possess the new, which, far from appearing from outer space, developed out of inner space. Nor is this inner space purely individual; it is in the process of being collectively evolved. In contradistinction to *The Invasion of the Bodysnatchers*, the narrative seeks to change the ground rules so that the nature of power both collective and individual is altered and brought within. It seeks empowerment, not disempowering.

The threat of chaos in masculine SF can equally be introjected, which is in some ways more interesting because it is not simplistically escapist. In *Forbidden Planet*, supposedly based on Shakespeare's *The Tempest*, the terrible and alien power is discovered to come from the unconscious. Victory is enacted as through projection, however. Like the forms and textual energies of masculine fantasy, this is expressive of patriarchy.

We on the Other hand revel in the idea that our minds have within them energies whose release might bring about the end of patriarchy. Our textual energy is not expressive of patriarchal hier-achey.

Textual Pleasure-politics

'Wish-fulfilment' in feminist SF is crucially different from escapism in that its drive is ex-centric. It moves towards transgression, not conformity, and it maintains a structural link with what the real is, while the escapist link is only surface. While feminist SF may draw on all the delights of SF and other traditionally popular escapist forms, its narrative and thematic desire is not for escapism. Traditional popular forms have been appropriated, defused, reduced to become compatible with desire-less-femininity, which still obtains no matter how many heroines and sybaritic female rulers stalk a story. Such galactic soap opera no longer manifests mythic freedoms and is incapable of communicating, expressing or signifying any desire of political and social change.

Pleasure as a source of revolutionary desire
Revolutionary desire as a source of pleasure

(including where a text is not either thematically or explicitly for revolution)

is one way into differentiating between SF romances and feminist SF. Romance is essentially (*sic*) obsessional. Its pleasure is in a containing circularity which returns to the point of departure, but now completed or 'ideal'. The source of satisfaction is external to the Self or to the deep structure of the form (narrative, language, manifestation of authorial voice, etc). Often it claims a spurious relation to myth because it has faery or recurrent trappings that are superficially taken to be signifiers of myth. Obsessional repetition is mistaken for archetypal structure. The desire for transcendence is preferred over transgression, or the strenuous and ex-centric engagement with the structures of repression/oppression.

Pleasure is in some idea of perfected reality ('achieved' through 'victory', 'recovery', 'return', 'arrival' and so on) rather than in freedom.

A feature of feminist SF desire for entry into freedom is the creation of narratives that explore alternatives to power struggles. I do not mean that there is no conflict in the narrative structure or thematics. I mean that playing out obsessional conflict-victory scenarios is not the source of pleasure. Where conflict and/or its resolution is a source of pleasure, it is often either separate from power or signifies the desire for reconciliation rather than victory.

A Door into Ocean and *The Wanderground* are two such radical imaginings of power difference. Both imagine a female world of ecological harmony whose technology is far in advance of contemporary sado-scientific hardware. Both try to open their power to others, in the full knowledge that they risk destruction by those who use power-over. *A Door into Ocean* structures its exploration around pacifism. The aquatic planet, Shora, is coherently and beautifully imagined; the bio-science of the Sharers is convincing. So it is comparatively straightforward to understand what the relationship between the textual and extra-textual real is. *The Wanderground* is more bound to the Earth, though not Earth-bound, and its science more internalized. Because it is set on Earth, it posits a direct relationship with extra-textual reality. In a world dominated by patriarchal rationalism it can be demanding for a reader to know on what level to read tales of telekinesis and mentally-propelled flying. To recognize what the real is. Which is part of the point.

TheMatrix 2
Language
The Big Space
        Ship
   Censor

> Can you *really* become a sorcerer and get your own way a lot, and be happy, successful, and ethical? Yes. This is a solemn promise I'm making you now. What do you think psychic evolution is all about?
>   Jody Scott's Virginia Woolf-Benaroya
>   (*I, Vampire* p. 206)

As we have seen, Feminist SF takes women into forbidden realms. Active agency, autonomous power, the creation/adaptation of physical worlds, exploration and so forth are all in some sense transgressive for women in contemporary 'developed' cultures. To imagine them for ourselves under present conditions, women have a great deal of internal and external censorship to overcome.

This is a reason why there is a lot of humour in feminist SF. (Less in fetishist SF. Which is not funny). Papa Freud is good on jokes, if not on laughs. The joke form, and laughter, are ways to bypass censorship;

psycho-linguistic routes from the unconscious to the conscious.[37] Not that jokes and humour are the same thing. Joke structures abound in *The Book of the Night*. but it isn't funny. Sister St Laure's game of chess in Zoe Fairbairn's hilarious *Relics* (*Despatches* pp. 175–89) is altogether far funnier than Lewis Carroll's Alice's. These structures are part of the covert language/s, covert form/s of feminist SF, though of course they're not exclusive to it. The same applies to narrative structures like the short story with the twist.

Roll up, ladies, step right this way! See Jane Palmer's Diana, (*The Planet Dweller*,[38] Joanna Russ's Alyx (*The Adventures of Alyx*),[39] Jody Scott's Benaroya and Sterling O'Blivion (*I, Vampire*), and while you're looking the other way, dis-cover that you've made the switch. If you resist, that's okay, but stay with it. It's about getting round the rules. Resistance; patriarchy quells it by turning it back on us. And don't swallow that stuff about repression being the condition of civilization and art. There's repression and repression. Then there's suppression. (Conscientious parent-thesis: there is, of course, much, much more to be said here as elsewhere in this essay about theoretical frameworks. But for reasons of Space, abbreviated pointers will have to do.)

I experienced quite powerful resistance when I first read *Orlando* and *I, Vampire*. I was initially irritated by the whimsy in *Orlando*, the sheer pleasure in words and in description for its own sake. I failed to see at first how political this pleasure is; or rather, I have believed in the abstract principle for some time, but did not recognize it in action when I saw it. In the end I felt like a child who has been cajoled by a favourite adult into good humour, despite my efforts to remain sulky. I felt very uncomfortable and I became unsure where the source of my resistance was. Until I let go. It was an instructive reading-dynamic.

What language, in our new worlds? How shall we speak? How shall we speak our being, our being speak? Few stories, yet, shape this question directly. In what ways will we extend, ex-trick-ate linguistic philosophy, re-knew the question, what is it? Language, that is. Indirectly of/f course in many ways. In the narrative of one such as Pooch/Pucci, dog on the way up the evolutionary scale to becoming woman, her continuity being that she is female. Oh. She isn't one. Meaningless to say 'one such'. In the narratives (*Carmen Dog*, *I, Vampire*, *The book of the Night*, perhaps Joanna Russ's *The Female Man*)[40] language is in play because identity is multiplied, problematized or Other-wise destabilized, thus disturbing the relation between the voice and the utterance. I-in-language cannot

---

[37]See especially Sigmund Freud, *Jokes and their Relation to the Unconscious* (London, Pelican, 1978).

[38]Jane Palmer, *The Planet Dweller* (London, The Women's Press, 1985); also *The Watcher* (London, The Women's Press, 1987).

[39]Joanna Russ, *The Adventures of Alyx* (London, The Women's Press, 1985); also many others including *The Female Man* (London, The Women's Press, 1985).

[40]Arthur Rimbaud. Letter to Paul Demeny, 15 March 1871. (His celebrated "Lettre du Voyant".)

remain unreconstructed if I is in process. I is not the modernist I/eye, not fragmented, patriarchal ego. Rather s/he is in constant process in interaction. With what patriarchy regards as external.

What is this process, then? Outside meaning. Or not. *The Book of the Night* seems dedifferentiated, pre-Oedipal. The Subject, the voice, has no body and no chronology, rethinking our de-finition of language out of consecutive development. With identity in play, crossing the Symbolic line, out?

Language on the borderline with chant, telepathy, animal-communication, telekinesis, an expanded sense of language, pre-utteral. In what form is the transferred idea? If it is a shape, is it language? If it is communication . . . 'a means of communication' is clearly inadequate as a de-finition of language, misleading, even.

> As Ijeme opened to her, she was assaulted by a cacophony of feelings, tastes, colours, pictures, sounds, odours . . . Pain leapt in sharp blasts through her body. Streaks of rage, hurt, madness surged through her long bones. Fear screamed in her softself. . . . Ursula inhaled deeply. Aloud she whispered, 'The beginning, Ijeme. Make a beginning. Come up on it easily.'
>
> Ijeme relaxed. Ursula took the opportunity to shortstretch to Krueva. 'I've dropped the monitor,' she said.
>
> 'I have it,' came back. 'Go ahead.'
>
> (Gearhart, *The Wanderground* p. 67)

. . . with consciousness

'Woman will discover part of the unknown! Will her world of ideas be different from ours? She will discover things strange and unfathomable . . .'[40]

> Josie sang.
>
> It was a dream-song more than dolphin speech, utterly strange and yet somehow familiar. And as she listened, Susannah began to understand what it meant. . . .
>
> She was aware now of other presences, other intelligences. Not merely in the dark sea around her, but much, much farther away. She could neither see them nor hear them, yet she knew they were there, she *felt* them, a non-tactile, yet definite sensation, which she understood was commonplace for dolphins.
>
> (Tuttle, *From a Sinking Ship, Despatches* p. 148)

A sense, sure, that language has been brutalized, that women possess greater readiness to open to the potential . . . but of what? contact with other beings, language itself, something repressed in women, specifically female utterance/understanding/communication? Most of the stories written in English are not language-specific. Often it's a rejection of arid rationality, as in *From a Sinking Ship*, with language as a symptom. The narrative incorporates language thematically, even theMatrickally, but is not structured on it.

In Suzette Haden Elgin's *Native Tongue* and *The Judas Rose* the women are developing a secret language, Láadan. It is USA, the twenty-third century. As men have started to make contact with alien worlds (or think they have, though we are to discover that theirs was not the initiative) the need for speakers of alien languages has produced an élite group, the linguists of the Lines. Their lives are totally dominated from babyhood by the political need for them to learn and translate languages. Though they participate in this prestigious work, the women are apparently more subjugated than most women are today. But they have a secret project for the transformation of reality. It is to develop a language, Láadan, to express the perceptions of women. It has a cover-language, Langlish, whose function is to deflect patriarchal suspicion. Langlish is deliberately defective, to accord with the perceptions of the men. Language is thus central to the politics and narrative sequence, and passages centre on fictionalized discussions of language and linguistics. The radical restructuring of language is a vital part of the women's strategy for survival.

Elgin's emphasis is on playing out the political implications of dominance and control through language, and the subversion of that power through linguistic innovation, especially the precious Encoding, 'A word for a perception that has never been known before.' (*Native Tongue* p. 158)

Elgin is interested in why SF had not sought to deal with the hypothesis 'that women are not superior to men (Matriarchy) or interchangeable with and equal to men (Androgyny) but rather entirely *different* from men.' She proposes that it might be because 'the only language available to women *excluded* the third reality' (*Láadan* p. 4). She therefore began writing the novels and developing the language.

I have a regret, though, in the separation between Láadan and the novels. The novels are formally and linguistically conventional in some ways; for example, though they incorporate different narrative voices, from fictional scientific papers, changes in narrator, to Nazareth Chornyak's diaries, the notion of Voice remains radically unchallenged. Láadan has no radical structural function.

We need to see the effect of an 'Encoding', of events or the narrative pivoting on a change in perception. Without this it is difficult to gain a sense of what her 'third reality' might be, her sense of how women might be different – according to her own reasoning, you can't do it within the bounds of conventional English.

Two features of Láadan are particularly interesting as feminist SF language: its 'state of consciousness morphemes' and its 'evidence morphemes', (*Láadan* pp. 131–2) both of which expand information on the relation of the speaker to the utterance. The former is emotive/affective and the latter epistemological. It's not that they are like the Encodings – signifying a totally new perception – but that they introduce as basic to sentence-structure information about the speaker at the moment of utterance. Thus their omission would be aberrant and would carry meaning. Láadan, therefore, is not structured primarily on a subjective–objective divide between speaker and language, potentially a radical linguistic shift. Elgin has only to bring her language – fiction together. Only!

Words.

It's a matter of logic. No, I don't mean Logic, I mean logic. The inner dynamic that every second reinvents probability. No accident, naturally. That logic, the word, comes from and leads into the word. The Greek language may be had wisdoms we lost, 'logos' meaning
both
'word' and 'reason'.
The words we have and the way we reason in symbiosis, making and remaking us, in the conspiratorial game against Logos and Logic.

The words we have arrange themselves, sucking at our footsteps with nightmare resonance while our musculature develops and we equalize the struggle. Then, just look back to see, a-mazing! the con-notative lianas turn unbidden to Ariadne's thread and know for the first time our history, what it is to recognize the thread, not the maze, whose invention is the point of the game.

Note

Alice Walker is a poet, novelist and essayist. She was born in Eatonton, Georgia, in 1944; she attended Spelman College in Atlanta 1961–63 and got her BA at Sarah Lawrence College, New York in 1965. In 1967 she married a civil rights attorney; they were divorced in 1977. She has one child, a daughter.

Writing

Once, 1968; *The Third Life of Grange Copeland*, 1970; *In Love And Trouble*, 1973; *Revolutionary Petunias and Other Poems*, 1973; *The Life of Thomas Lodge*, 1974; *Langston Hughes, American Poet*, 1974; *Meridian*, 1976; *Good Night, Willie Lee, I'll See You in the Morning*, 1979; *I Love Myself When I Am Laughing . . . and then Again When I Am Looking Mean and Impressive, a Zora Neal Hurston Reader*, 1979 (editor); *You Can't Keep A Good Woman Down*, 1981; *The Color Purple*, 1982; *In Search Of Our Mothers' Gardens and other essays*, 1983; *Living By The Word*, 1988.

Alice Walker is also consulting editor to the feminist monthly *Ms*, and the black political quarterly *Freedomways*. She won the Pulitzer Prize for fiction in 1983 for *The Color Purple*;

Criticism on Walker

'An Essay on Alice Walker', Mary Helen Washington, and 'Alice Walker: The Diary of An African Nun', Chester J. Fontenot, in *Sturdy Black Bridges*, eds., Roseann P. Bell, Bettye J. Parker, and Beverly Guy-Sheftall, Anchor Press, (1979);

The Southern Review, Summer 1985: special issue on 'Afro-American Writing';

Black Women Writers, ed., Mari Evans, Pluto Press 1985;

5

Fear of the Happy Ending: *The Color Purple*, Reading and Racism

Alison Light

One of the many emotions I felt after reading this book was shame. Before I had forgotten or put aside my obligations as a woman, most of all as a black woman. Being wrapped up in myself I had forgotten the shit my sisters had to live through and even die for to put me where I am today: a Black woman able to think for myself, work for myself and plan my future. (Review of *The Color Purple*, Gerry. *Spare Rib*, No. 135, October 1983).

Novels which change lives

This piece grows out of an earlier contribution to a collective presentation entitled, 'Problems of the Progressive Text', given at the sixth Literature/Teaching/Politics conference in 1985.[1] As lecturers in higher education we chose to discuss the specific delights and demands of teaching or studying those texts which appear to be overtly aligned with a left-wing politics, or whose radical reputation has gone before them, as it were. Alice Walker's *The Color Purple* (1982) seemed a good route into some of these issues since it ties together the major strands of a politics of difference – those of race, class and gender – in a contemporary bestseller by a black American feminist. Walker's story is the first-person narrative of Celie, a poor black girl in the Deep South between the wars; she relates, in a series of letters, the process of her eventual triumph over the most brutal forms of exploitation, her gradual recovery of her racial past and, via lesbianism, her claiming of an affirmatory sexuality. The novel, published here by The Women's Press, took the feminist world by storm even before it won the Pulitzer Prize in 1983. It has now been made into a blockbuster Hollywood film by the director, Steven Spielberg (he of *Jaws*

[1]LTP is a national network of teachers and students who hold an annual conference and produce a journal. The 1985 papers are available (£1.25) from Helen Taylor, Department of Humanities, Bristol Polytechnic. I would like to thank the other members of the Sussex group, and especially Rachel Bowlby, for their help with this piece.

and *ET* fame).[2] This tremendous take-off of a 'minority' text, however, not only highlights the problems of black writers being lionized by the dominant white culture; it raises also some crucial questions about the reading and reception of black writing by those of us, who, as white teachers and students, place or find such texts on the syllabus of 'English'. On the Left there has long been a deep and resourceful vein of 'countercriticism', criticism which reads 'classic' texts, the literary canon, against the grain, pointing up their complicity with dominant ideas and values and their refusal, however tortured, to admit the full range of cultural and social difference. Thus to teach a text like Walker's which speaks to and from those who are normally *absent* from the literary heritage of English, marginalized or oppressed groups, and in particular black women, sets us a different pedagogic and political agenda. *The Color Purple* is more about good subjects than bad objects; it closes with achievement and happiness, harmony and celebration – not topics which are easily accommodated by those left analyses whose emphasis is finally upon struggle, strife and conflict.

In fact my own piece began from just such a nagging doubt about the pleasure of the text. How do we – as teachers – criticize a text which so many feminists, including myself, have felt to be about ourselves in powerfully involving and politicizing ways? Being on the side of the angels, such a novel brings forcefully home the fraught question of the influence and effect(ivity) of 'literature'. Do novels change lives, and if so, what (if any) is the job of criticism in relation to such experiences? How can the processes which the individual undergoes in reading be understood as part of that wider, collective struggle called politics? Further, what is the place of the pleasures of such a text – identification, affirmation, celebration – in political discourse and engagement?

These are some of the questions which I want to pursue here. To ask what goes on in the gap between reading and action is one way of trying to connect a cultural studies with a cultural politics, with what goes on *outside* the classroom. It is to refuse to polarize either 'culture' or 'politics' in a familiar opposition which designates the one as purely academic or aesthetic, and the other as divorced from the making of representations and their reception.[3] Instead we need to ask how the structuring of pleasures and anxieties in the practices of reading and writing help to maintain or disrupt our notions of our 'selves' in those other modes of our existence; what kinds of subjectivities are formed and offered by different texts and what are the political parameters and perimeters of our readings; what do they mean for different groups at different times in history and the culture?

Such questions take on an especially urgent form in relation to black culture when we ask them as white people in the 1980s. For how are we to

---

[2]For discussion of the film see Alice Walker's *Living By The Word* (London, 1988) and Andrea Stuart's coincidentally entitled '*The Color Purple*: In Defence of Happy Endings', in *The Female Gaze* ed. L. Gamman and M. Marshment (London 1988).

[3]See 'Culture and politics', Janet Batsleer *et al.*, *Rewriting English* (London 1985).

understand our own 'identification' and solidarity whilst still acknowledging the political reality of difference? What indeed are we doing as white readers and white teachers when we read the black text? How are the meanings of our readings to be situated within an understanding of the history and formation of racial subjectivities? And how far do the writing and reading practices of what is revealingly called 'English' shore up and reproduce precisely, Englishness, a sense of cultural difference which depends in part on a notion of racial superiority and a history of imperial power?

The pleasures of reading and the power of racism, the connections between our supposedly private fantasies and our so-called public politics – this is an enormous area, and I shall do little more than skate across its surface. As was made clear by black delegates at the LTP conference, it is our own ignorance as white academics which has made for some pretty thin ice in places. Yet ironically, it is the passionate hopefulness of a text like *The Color Purple* which may at least help us to get our skates on. For Alice Walker's novel remains for me a profoundly inspiring and contradictory text because it is finally *utopian*: it is a fantastic success story, offering its readers an imaginary resolution of political and personal conflicts. It is the meanings and difficulties of this utopianism, how it might direct our readings and mobilize us politically, which I want to explore further.

Problems of Identification

> You got to fight. You got to fight. But I don't know how to fight. All I know how to do is stay alive.[4]

I co-taught *The Color Purple* recently on an adult education course, to a group of about ten women, all white and mostly under thirty, although one woman was in her sixties, and only about half the group were graduates. After reading short stories (Kate Chopin, Katherine Mansfield) and extracts on 'women and writing' we chose *The Color Purple* as the only complete novel read, in the hopes that it would bring together our earlier discussions of race, class and sexual politics. Importantly, and perhaps typically, we were not looking at the text in the context of other black writing, nor even of American literature, but in the context of contemporary feminism. Nevertheless as tutors we were surprised that the discussion did not lead into the issue of racism, and at the ways in which it did not.

Our readings began instead from a position of identification rather than of difference. Many students, like myself, had found the novel deeply moving on first reading, and had been exhilarated by its ending. The opening passages of Celie's brutal treatment, in which she, as teller of her tale, is never ultimately left degraded or without dignity, and her finding of sexual pleasure or social peace – we all talked about the power and

---

[4]*The Color Purple*, (London 1983), p. 17.

appeal of such writing in terms of recognizing, identifying with, and desiring such affirmation as women, white, working-class, middle-class, feminist or not. We felt strongly drawn into the novel because of its structure of Celie's articulation of her life. Yet it was staggering how quickly the discussion became negative when we began to 'criticize'. The shift from re-telling the pleasure of reading to analyzing its meanings was severe and dramatic. I noted down at the time that 'the book threw up the issues of its language and of Celie's development – who it was for – and of its possible romanticism. I felt people were being very heavy about the happy ending, as though it were necessarily a bad thing.'

I am still intrigued by that last comment – 'as though it were *necessarily* a bad thing'. Why were we so afraid of the happy ending and what does it mean for a group of white students to see as 'romantic' the empowering of an impoverished, beaten, raped and abused Southern black woman? Ironically, whilst we were involved in the novel's project as women, our critical terms for theorizing the questions of social and sexual conflict in a woman's life seemed to lead us into a disavowal of the importance of that process. We could only describe Celie's enrichment in a series of negative -isms: romanticism, idealism, sentimentalism all smacked of dismissiveness. It seemed that as feminists we could never be satisfied with being satisfied; the novel's appeal to the possibility of an achievable, social and sexual transformation of your life seemed both deeply pleasurable and deeply suspect.

There were several issues at stake in this disjuncture. It might be that the problem was simply one of reading, of the strategies of English which brought with it an emphasis upon character and moral growth ('Celie's development'), and through whose distorting lens we had read the story and re-focused it as an image of self-fulfilment and liberal humanist values, without realizing our own short-sightedness. This slippage from pleasure to displeasure could be seen as a function of English and/or Englishness – a refusal to engage with difference, all those discourses which make the text quite 'foreign' to our own culture. Alternatively, there seemed to be a special problem with the structure of the text itself, its first-person narrative which invited the mechanism of identification and needed it in order to be read. In both cases we are brought up against the complex question of politicization, either proceeding from the unifying claim to solidarity or from the fictional process of identifying, which leads us to wonder what part the formation of such 'identities' as woman, or black woman, might play in the generation of, and involvement with, any political discourse.

Is it English?

> The real question, however, it appears to me, is not whether poor people will adopt the middle-class mentality once they are well fed; rather, it is whether they will ever be well fed enough to be able to choose whatever mentality they think will suit them.[5]

[5] Alice Walker, *In Search of Our Mother's Gardens*, (London 1984), p. 126.

Critics of the text, including some of my colleagues in the LTP presentation, have pointed out various reasons why *The Color Purple* is particularly vulnerable to the ravages of English. Unlike elsewhere in her work (in *Meridian* for example), Walker is not primarily concerned here with black struggle against white racism but with experience within the black community, within families and sexual relationships. This foregrounding of 'the private sphere' has made it possible for the question of difference, racial, sexual, social, to be ignored and effaced as a conflictual and political force and to be reformulated in the rhetoric of a liberal humanism (of which English is one discourse) as a repository of essential and eternal truths about a universal human condition. Celie's story in such a reading becomes a kind of latter-day 'Bildungsroman', her coming to power an embourgeoisment accompanied by the necessary modicums of moral wisdom and self-knowledge. Thus *The Washington Post*, heading the British edition, can call Walker's novel 'a fable for the modern world', reducing or transforming into myth the actuality of the social historical conditions and ideologies around which the text is constituted. Universalizing the specificity of the tale (the words 'black' and 'lesbian' do not appear on the cover of the The Women's Press edition), reproducing an invisibility to which those who are defined as 'other' are consigned by the dominant culture, such homogenizing makes the text more manageable, more marketable. Difference which is potentially alienating, frightening and challenging, is written out in favour of a transhistorical truism: as the advertising trailer for the film puts it, 'It's about life. It's about love. It's about us.'

Recent critical theories, notably within marxism and feminism have made the exposure of this rhetoric of liberal humanism a prime target, and have revealed the ideological positions which have lurked beneath the appeal to equality, liberty and fraternity (*sic*). The claim of the white bourgeois male to full subjecthood has often depended historically and socially upon the relegation and exclusion of all others from just this status: the dark continent, the great unwashed, the second sex, all these others are pushed to the margins of humanity, sometimes, as in the racist theories of the nineteenth century, even denied such humanity.

But these naturalizations of the political in favour of the eternal drama of the humanist self are not the only potentially racist response. Ironically, those of us for whom this critique appears a political priority can be as much dominated by liberal humanism in our rejection of its terms as in any complicity with them. To reduce Walker's text to these discourses in order to 'criticize' it – a reading, which as white educated subjects we can well afford – is equally a way of holding on to a cultural supremacy, of denying and incorporating difference: an attempt at colonization. My own first reading, for example, saw Walker's visionary ending as akin to 'the synthetic and religiose American familialism of "The Waltons"'.[6] This cheap joke (which got me a laugh at the conference) betrays not just my own ignorance but a complicated travesty both of the actual history of

[6] *LTP Conference Papers*, (Bristol 1985), p. 130.

white Americans (as opposed to the normative and conservative marketing of it on TV), and of the very different relation which black familialism has had to capitalism given the history of slavery and of racism itself, especially in the South. Similarly, (mis)reading the question of spirituality in the novel, wearing the cultural blinkers of English Protestantism, is to be equally ideologically blinded by our own cultural discourses; such misrecognitions can easily slide into a refusal to accept the very different meanings and possibilities which 'religion' has had for black strugggle.[7]

English, then, moves in mysterious ways. At its most obvious it shores up the racist response of one student who literally could not read the text because its language was 'primitive', 'badly written': it simply wasn't English, in all senses of the word. More tricky is the colonization of the text via the naturalizing aesthetic of lit. crit. which collapses its cultural specificity into moral value, emptied of any social or political referent: a 'consummately well written novel' enthused the *New York Times Book Review*, whilst the US *Tribune* praised its 'sweetness of tone . . . the sweep and daring of its literary ambition'.[8] Both responses efface the material and political conditions within which black language emerged as a *weapon* against, as well as a consequence of, slavery, and as a means of creating and maintaining a separate and inviolable community for black people in the face of white oppression.[9] Yet those of us who reject the interpretation of Celie's story as yet another journey into bourgeois bliss must find ways of affirming black power and achievement; we can hardly want only fictions in which black protagonists remain powerless – we have had those for centuries. For without such acknowledgment a familiar double-bind operates whereby the black subject is robbed of history and status either by being incorporated and ignored by the dominant social order or by being made visible *only* as victim, a helpless sufferer condemned to pain. Whether difference is therefore denied altogether, or whether it is (often simultaneously) insisted upon only as lack and failure, both strategies work to subordinate black people. This has long been part of our English inheritance, though such strategies have taken on new historical forms since the war in our dealings with 'decolonialization'.[10] *The Color Purple* is vividly at odds with the myth that 'freedom and whiteness [are] the same destination'.[11]

Clearly, for white academics, part of the problem is that *The Color Purple* is not about 'us' at all. Nothing is harder than for those who trade in knowledge to admit ignorance. What is even more threatening is to feel that those outside of 'our' dominant culture do have a knowledge and strength of their own precisely *because* of being outside. Not only is it

[7]See, for example, Alan Sinfield's discussion in the LTP 1985 papers.
[8]Quoted on the back cover of The Women's Press 1983 edition.
[9]See B. Bryan, S. Dadzie and S. Scafe, *The Heart of the Race: Black Women's Lives in Britain* (London 1985), especially Chapter 5.
[10]See Centre for Contemporary Cultural Studies' analysis *The Empire Strikes Back: Race and Racism in 70s Britain*, (London 1982).
[11]Walker, *In Search*, p. 291.

often the case that only those who take privilege and comfort for granted are able to be dismissive about the struggle to leave poverty and hardship behind; it is also such people who are unable to learn that different lives produce their own equally important forms of knowledge and community – knowledge, from which they are by definition excluded. Wanting *The Color Purple* (as I did) to lead into a discussion of racism is certainly easier than seeing myself as marginal to its concerns. Thus any real engagement with racial difference in the text (and in our politics) has to be far more dialectical than any simple model of 'otherness' and its recuperation or appropriation (embourgeoisment) within the dominant culture, might propose. It means in part giving up the power of naming and of assuming knowledge of someone else's struggle, accepting that there are things which we cannot share, and initiatives which we cannot create. Otherwise, as Stuart Hall and Martin Jacques have argued.

> our model of society is that the only things worth getting involved with are our things; others are not capable of creating movements and currents which deserve our support, enthusiasm and intervention. This is a very patronizing view of the world.[12]

And when white readers refuse to listen to the black voice, accusing it instead of some kind of ventriloquism, such patronization is deeply racist.

There are many inroads to be made still into the territory of 'English', ways of fragmenting that impulse to homogenize and thereby control the diverse subjects and subjectivites which come within its boundaries. Cora Kaplan has pointed to some of the strategies of re-education which the white British reader might need in order to situate *The Color Purple* more properly in the historical, social and textual relations from which it emerged.[13] But for this process to be anything more than a textual encounter of the academic kind, we have also to press hard upon our first 'naive' readings which will tell us more about our own relation to difference, the assumptions with which we start and which structure our pleasures and anxieties as white readers. We need to return to our 'selves' not in order to wallow in guilt but because such selves are historically and socially produced. In doing so, however, it is clear that deconstructing 'English' is only part of the story since, as my own course insisted, no text can be read or written solely as addressing one form of difference; the structures of racial, sexual and class difference intersect and often contradict each other, offering a range of positions to the reader, never simply a unitary or unified one. It is to the positive possibility of these identifications which do not deny difference, but work in tandem with them, that I want now to return.

[12]'People Aid', *Marxism Today*, July 1986.
[13]'Keeping the color in *The Color Purple* (LTP Bristol 1985); see also, for further reading, the debates in *Feminist Review* no. 17 (1984), no. 20(1985) and 23 (1986).

The politics of utopianism

I'm so happy, I got love, I got work, I got money, friends and time.[14]

I have argued that *The Color Purple* appeals especially to readers of *all* kinds because it is utopian in its form: Celie gets it all at the end of the story, and through her we are offered this dream of full achievement, of a world in which all conflicts and contradictions are resolved. Whilst I have maintained that such fictions *mean* very differently for different groups in the culture, nevertheless there is a bottom level at which *The Color Purple* keys into a far more diffuse desire for personal and social changes, what Carolyn Steedman has called 'historically much older articulations – the subjective and political expressions of radicalism'.[15] The desires for a world in which all people might have love, work, friends, money and time, underpin political theories like socialism and feminism: an appeal to the possibility of amelioration, of 'progress', which is no less potent or mobilizing for being an imaginary vision, a happy ending still to come.

Yet it is the power and persuasiveness of these desires which the left has so frequently found problematic, from the debates around Owenite socialism to the politics of the peace movement.[16] Part of the response – that fear of the happy ending – has been a definition of radical politics which sees itself as one half of a binary opposition (left as opposed to right), and conceives its job as one solely of critique from underneath the dominant culture, as it were. In this definition the day of *not* having to be on the left never comes. This structural definition, however, offers little or insufficient insight into why people join and remain within political struggles, unless one assumes a rampant or global masochism. At its worst such a position becomes a moralistic kill-joyism which finds all pleasures in political engagement guilty ones, and indeed can see the question of pleasure itself as ideologically unsound. Running through such uneasiness is ironically a strong thread of empiricism, an insistence on the world 'out there' as separable and separate from the world 'in here' and a one-way model of determination. Such a model insists upon a divisive opposition which wrenches apart the field of 'the political' from that of personal or subjective space. The recalcitrant psyche, thus nominated, cannot then keep up with the revolutionary political/public Joneses and must be dismissed or denigrated, either as outside of social or cultural change and determined by that 'outside', or as irredeemably interior – 'confessional', 'sentimental', 'romantic', 'private', 'personal' – depending on your century. Feminism alone, in its long dialogue with socialist theory, has pointed to the androcentricity implicit and produced in the making of these spheres. For clearly such demarcations of knowledge and power have political effects, working through and speaking through, for example, the meanings given to sexual difference.

---

[14]*The Color Purple*, p. 183.
[15]*Landscape For A Good Woman*, (London 1986), p. 14.
[16]See, for example, Barbara Taylor, *Eve and The New Jerusalem: Socialism and Feminism in the Nineteenth Century*, (London 1983).

Thus a novel like *The Color Purple* can be popular with a whole range of women readers, cutting across the specificity of its black history, in its concern with family, emotionality, sexual relations and fantasy life. Walker herself has noted the operation of such collusive divisions of psychic and social existence in reproducing the inequalities of gender *and* race:

> black writing has suffered because even black critics have assumed that a book that deals with the relationships between members of a black family – or between a man and a woman – is less important than one that has white people as primary antagonists. The consequence of this is that many of our books by 'major' writers (always male) tell us little about the culture, history, or future, imagination, fantasies, and so on, of black people, and a lot about isolated (often improbable) or limited encounters with a non-specific white world.[17]

What is crucial in our understanding of the 'utopian' appeal of the text is not to reinstate subjectivity at the expense of 'the social' but to begin to dissolve those polarities, seeing the structures and site of subjectivity as exactly (equally) social and historical, equally the site of the operations of power. Terms like 'sentimental' and 'idealistic' are not themselves transparent descriptions of knowledge or response. They carry with them cultural prescriptions and assumptions and have themselves to be historicized. Not coincidentally both women's and black writing have been accused of 'emotionalism'. We need to ask why this *is* an accusation. Who is calling whom sentimental, when, and with what effect?

So to call *The Color Purple* 'utopian' is the beginning of an analysis, not the end of it. Words like this signal the insistent presence of the demands of subjectivity – of how sexual and racial differences come to be lived and felt in the act of living – as being a pressure in excess of what is 'realistically' on offer in a culture. Fiction, like fantasy, is the place of this excess. It re-informs and re-imagines the scene of its production, the unconscious as well as conscious desires which social relations cannot or will not fulfil. In other words, these questions of the 'effects' of reading, of the mobilizing of desires and pleasures in the activity of reading, are questions about fictionality itself; the processes of reading and writing occupy *simultaneously* intimate and public (because linguistic) space, space where desire and history intersect in the subjects of those practices (writers, readers, 'characters') and where new subjectivities can be formed. Such subjectivities are shown to be constantly negotiated, constantly fragmented and contradicted by the differences (racial, sexual, class-base) which they simultaneously try to unify and encompass. These 'identities' are broken up as soon as they are forged, seeming only to remain stable at the novel's point of closure – the happy ending – but this is the point at which the disjuncture between 'fiction' and 'life' is

[17]Walker, *In Search*, p. 261.

most apparent, where you shut the book and go off to face another fragmenting day.

All fictions are utopian – though some more than others; the worry about how politically mobilizing fiction can be is a worry about the tension within the act of representation itself. Subjects, in texts as in life, are constituted and re-constituted around those cultural interpretations of, or meanings given to, difference, which always threaten to disrupt the security of defining one'self' solely or fully as, for example, a woman, a black person. Literary texts, and pre-eminently novels, take subjectivity as their material, but to argue that any reader is either fully positioned by a novel or can ever fully resist its strategies is to underestimate the contradictory process at the heart of linguistic representation: a process in which subjects, even as they gesture toward that idealized and coherent 'I' who will be marvellously coping, miraculously loving and loved, run headlong into the de-stabilizing actuality of what it means to be 'woman', 'black', 'poor' and so on, in the world.

If *The Color Purple* allows readers to speak their rage or their delight because of its appeal to a unified self, that appeal is precisely fictional, or fictitious, appealing because there is not and cannot be – other than in fictions – a safe and sealed place in which to find or be such a self. This self can be recognized both as an effect of language and of the attempt to heal the split demanded in the act of representation. It has also to be acknowledged, nevertheless, as a fiction which keeps us sane and active. For without such momentary fixings of the flux of subjectivity, the illusion of being a powerful and coherent agent in the world, how would we get out there and do things – how indeed can we have a political theory of action and responsibility? If we do not accept the force and temporary necessity of such identifications, textually and socially, are we not condemned to a theory of being which leaves us stranded in a quicksand of discursivity, fascinated but finally immobilized by 'the play of difference', fragmented always and totally, unable not just to act politically (to see and know ourselves collectively), but to act at all? Perhaps it is not that we need to act as though we believe utopian achievements are possible – that like Celie we really will get it all; rather it seems that we need to believe in such utopias in order to act, in order to survive as human beings, making our own texts and histories in the face of the divisions and conflicts in our psychic/social existences which determine and fragment us. As Juliet Mitchell has written,

> We all live within ideology, both the general ideology of all human society and the specific ideologies of our times. It may well be the case that the humanist ideology is in itself only the liberal side of the capitalistic, free-enterprise coin – but we cannot escape it: must live ourselves (indeed, be ourselves) within its meanings while we are in such a society.[18]

---

[18]*Women: The Longest Revolution* (London 1984), p. 247.

To ignore the power of the fictional 'I', however much it is a figment of humanist ideology, is to risk denying the need which we have to believe that we are at the centre of our lives, a motivating need felt strongly too by those who have been oppressed by, and want to challenge the forms of this society. It is to risk robbing subjects of the chance to construct alternative histories of the world and of its power-relations, and of their politicizing visions of the future – however much we must insist on the ultimate fictionality of these accounts. For where would political struggle against oppression, against misery, be without such human narratives? The narratives may be inventions, but the suffering people cause one another, and the pleasure they are capable of giving each other, exist and continue to exist.

Unhappy Ending?

> It is the misfortune (but also perhaps the voluptuous pleasure) of language not to be able to authenticate itself. . . . language is, by nature, fictional.[19]

Fictions are fickle and cannot alone guarantee the political directions which our identifications might take. Reading the black text as a white reader, even as a feminist or a socialist reader, does not guarantee reading as an anti-racist. On the other hand, in terms of teaching and of political solidarity there will also be readers who strongly object to having what is the moment of their politicization 'de-constructed'. The problem is how not to undermine the strategic importance of that solidarity – wherever it appears – whilst remaining open to difference, critical of any final fixing of the meanings and forms of the political. Texts like *The Color Purple* are important because they signal the tension between the necessary rhetoric of desire for identification, the importance of an imaginary unified subjectivity in the process of politicization – the tension between *that* enabling dream and the forms which such 'selves' might take in our daily lives. For fixings can all too easily become fixed, a refusal of difference and a re-instatement of new but equally authoritarian power-structures. Such absolutism is a danger for any politics. Identifying ourselves as 'woman', 'black', 'working-class' can only be staging-posts on the 'road to revolution'; they cannot be places where we want to settle indefinitely. Neither the process of politicization nor that of social change can be so simply or reassuringly 'progressive'. Stable moments of solidarity may give us the energy to move on but it is the tension between solidarity and difference which creates political urgency, and it is the dialectical relation between our knowledge and our ignorance of others which keeps a political movement moving.

Finally then, for white academics, challenging English means inevitably untacking the subjectivities in which we have dressed our selves for a long

---

[19]Roland Barthes, *Camera Lucida* (London 1984), p. 85.

time. It hurts to discover that so many of our investments – literally economic, as well as social and personal – are going bankrupt. For women like myself, who made the move from the working-classes via books and a liberal education, it is intensely painful, as well as hard, to continue to attack the positions which have only just conceded me a foothold in the dominant culture. I suspect, however, that if we cannot give up that power and those securities peaceably and in co-operation, then we will lose them in any case on much stonier ground in future struggles, when solidarity and difference will become exclusive alternatives, and black and white a violently polarized opposition. If we want to attack the more reactionary forms of our culture it is perhaps the televisual, filmic and electronic ones which are shaping the subjectivities of the next generation of white, middle-class children which we need to address most of all.

As was once said, the same capitalist forms which have enslaved people will also provide the means for their breaking those chains. So when we criticize the essential reductiveness of humanist fictions, we need nevertheless to channel their democratizing potential – an impulse without which both socialism and feminism are inert. Not to do that, and to dismiss the powerful optimism and collective historical significance of a text like *The Color Purple* is to throw the baby out with the bathwater. Which is not just anti-humanist, but inhumane.

Note

Life and Works

Grace Paley was born in New York in 1922, the daughter of Jewish immigrants who arrived from Russia at the turn of the century and settled in the poor quarter of Lower East Side Manhattan. Her mother worked in sweatshops while her father struggled to become a doctor.

She grew up amidst the rich ethnic and cultural mix of the Bronx, learning Yiddish and Russian – as well as English – from her parents and exulting in the lively, noisy streetlife which we see and hear in her stories and which she still loves although she now divides her year between New York and Vermont.

She dropped out of full-time education at the age of seventeen, willingly enticed into conversations she encountered en route to the classroom.

She has always been a pacifist and has been active for many years in the anti-nuclear, anti-militaristic and women's movements. Her political activities have taken her from neighbourhood issues to travelling around the world, including Hanoi in 1969 and Moscow in 1973. In 1961, she helped organize the Greenwich Village Peace Centre, serving as secretary and in 1966 she spent six days in jail for her part in a sit-down protest against military force. When I spoke to her in November 1985, she had recently returned from Nicaragua and El Salvador.

She is continually in demand for readings, lectures and guest professorships and she often uses the readings at universities and community centres as opportunities to talk about the people and political situations she has encountered on her travels.

She has a daughter and a son and is a woman of many roles not least of which is that of most interested grandmother. She is an extremely busy person and the rareness of her publications make them all the more precious.

Her first collection of short stories, *The Little Disturbances of Man*, appeared in 1959, when she was thirty-seven. Since then she has published *Enormous Changes at the Last Minute* (1974) and *Later the Same Day* (1985). She has also published one collection of poetry, *Leaning Forward* (1985).

Bibliography

Blanche Gelfant, 'Grace Paley: Fragments for a Portrait in Collage', *New England Review*, 3 (1980), pp. 276–93.

Cora Kaplan, 'Grace Paley Talking with Cora Kaplan' in Mary Chamberlain, ed., *Writing Lives* (Virago, 1988).

Hermione, Lee, ed., *The Secret Self: Short Stories by Women* (J.M. Dent & Sons, 1985). Included in the collection is the story, 'The Loudest Voice' from Grace Paley's first collection.

Grace Paley, *The Little Disturbances of Man* (Virago, 1980).

Grace Paley, *Enormous Changes at the Last Minute* (Virago, 1979).

Grace Paley, *Later the Same Day* (Virago, 1985).

Grace Paley, *Leaning Forward* (Maine, Granite Press, 1985).

Grace Paley, Introduction, in Barbara Deeming, *Prisons That Could Not Hold* (San Francisco, Spinsters' Ink, 1985).

6

Listening and Telling in Counterpoint : a conversation with Grace Paley

Rosemary O'Sullivan

Grace Paley's stories deal with life's disturbances and changes, big and little, often with hilarious irony. They affirm the need for adaptability, for intelligent, humane social change, for common sense, for informed realism and for the 'heart felt brains' of Faith's children.[1] In the words of this, her most recurring character, 'If it's truth and honour you want to refine . . . Make no images; imitate no God'.[2]

Her stories mock idealism and consoling generalizations, empiricism without creative vision and a sense of history which lacks respect for detail. Her characters are both practical realists and romantics who are 'interested in man as a person'.[3]

Grace Paley's characters have a tender and sensual interest in other people; *she* is clearly interested in her characters whose lives and relationships change and develop throughout the pages of the three collections. In 'Enormous Changes at the Last Minute', the title story for the second collection, Dennis asserts that 'the mind *is* an astonishing, long-living, erotic thing'. His lover Alexandra, however, wonders, 'What is the life expectancy of the mind?'[4] – such is the cynical optimism of the voice of Grace Paley.

When I first came upon Grace Paley's stories, I was immediately impressed by her distinctive voice – cynical and sentimental, tragic and comic, wise-cracking and sombre – and her compressed, elliptical style. The woman behind the voice, I imagined, must be a formidable blend of the learned and the streetwise, the mature feminist and the experienced political campaigner.

I had the chance to meet her when she came to Newcastle upon Tyne as part of the city's literary festival in November 1985. I was expecting a sharp, possibly abrasive, no-nonsense tone of a shrewd observer of people and a very busy woman, much sought after for interviews, preparing

[1]Grace Paley, 'Faith in a Tree', *Enormous Changes at the Last Minute* (London, Virago, 1979), p. 100.
[2]Paley, *Enormous Changes* p. 86.
[3]Paley, *Enormous Changes*, p. 113.
[4]Paley, *Enormous Changes*, p. 121.

herself for a public reading that very evening. The person I met up with in a cosily tiny but impersonal hotel room in the twilight of a November afternoon was anything but intimidating and abrasive, though lively and shrewd she certainly was. She struck me initially as a homely (in the English sense), sprightly, grandmother figure, small and unassuming with wispy, silvery hair – an impression belied by her alert, humorous eyes and her continual chewing of gum. She was a woman without airs, who gave the impression that she would be at home anywhere and yet who was intrigued by all the little differences of detail she encountered, thoughtful and unwilling to pass over anything too quickly. Inevitably we ended up talking about children. . . .

RO'S   I'd like to start with something from your earlier two collections.[5] I took a quotation from 'The Immigrant Story', 'I believe I see the world as clearly as you do . . . Rosiness is not a worse windowpane than gloomy gray when viewing the world'.[6] I'd just like to ask you about that – how much that is your attitude, what you feel that attitude develops from, and how much you think perhaps it's a woman's attitude rather than a man's.

GP   Well I don't know whether it's a woman's attitude rather than a man's. I think it probably comes from my attitude, or not my attitude so much but as a person who maybe because of children has to look forward – maybe that's part of it. But a lot of it is just disposition – you know? And she says in the beginning of the story, 'I was raised in the sunlight of upward mobility' – so there's something in that. Also, some of it, a lot of it, has to do with not only your particular household because any household will throw out gloomy people and cheery people – sometimes things have to do with the period of history, of time in which you came into grown-upness, not maturity but into young womanhood. Sō that has something to do with it.

RO'S   Yes but it's also to do with your continual undermining of generalization and theory. You seem to be very much anti-jargon, anti-theory.

GP   Yes, you can say that again. That's true.

RO'S   Do you feel it's also part of the fact of you having grown up female?

GP   Oh I think so, I think so now. I wouldn't have thought so much earlier. But I do think so now. I think we need to be, we are more specific and somehow more grounded in lots of ways, and I think we need to be, you know, just to get through the day – we really have to, *have to* and we have to know what's happened. We can't deal with not knowing what's happening in the day or in the school or in the system or in a life.

[5]Grace Paley, *The Little Disturbances of Man* (London, Virago, 1980).
[6]Paley, *Enormous Changes*, p. 174.

RO'S But it is also to do with your own attitude towards institution-alized learning. Apparently you're self-taught or something like that?

GP I'm not – I am, except that if I had taught myself something, I'd call myself self-taught. I haven't taught myself too much. I did finish my schooling when I was about sixteen or seventeen and that was it.

RO'S And did you decide that for yourself?

GP I can't say I decided – I simply ceased to go. One day I came up to the classroom and I left it – I walked away before I walked in the door, that's all.

I think in general in my life, I've done most of the things I want to do without really arguing about it too much. Sometimes it's made trouble for me, but not before I did it, just afterwards. But I have done lots of things . . .

I like your question very much, you know, about rosiness and that . . . it's a good one so even though I don't answer it right now, I'll think about it.

RO'S It just seems to me to sum up so much about your kind of realistic optimism – you're very realistic about life's little tragedies but also there's the Faith character who has a kind of acceptance of things, wanting to see things not quite rosy but at least to see the good as well . . .

GP Well I do remember when I was a kid, when I was in my teens or twenties or whatever, it wasn't that I was happy, because nobody's happy in their teens. There are a few people you meet who say, 'Oh did I have a good time!' but I wasn't happy then. There was an awful lot of 'classy unhappiness' – I don't know whether that translates into English from American but it was a kind of aesthe-tic gloominess. I was already writing poetry and stuff and this made me feel I could hardly be a poet because despite being unhappy, I was not dark.

RO'S I was going to ask about that too because I had read that you started off writing poetry – how you got onto writing short stories and how you write.

GP Well that has a lot to do with women – the fact that I wrote stories. I wrote poetry for a long time and I still do. I have a book just out as a matter of fact. It's called *Leaning Forward.*[7] I wrote poetry and then I had kids and I kept writing poetry but at a cer-tain time in my life, which I really think was my middle thirties, I realized that I wasn't able to do in poetry what I wanted to do – to deal with people, characters, humour and the things that were worrying me.

What had begun to worry me was really the lives of women, the women around me more or less – not even so much my own but

[7]Grace Paley, *Leaning Forward* (Maine, Granite Press, 1985).

my own too – and the kind of consciousness without my calling it feminism because I really was kind of dumb, I couldn't know that's what it was but something like that.

When you're writing it's because something is bugging you, something's really pestering your mind and hounding you. You have to deal with it because writing is an expression, but more than that. It's cerebral in the sense that you begin to teach yourself to think in fiction.

So all this stuff about the lives of the women was bothering me a lot and that's really what drove me into story-telling. Not that lots of people don't do it in poetry – they do – but I couldn't. I didn't have the means. As a poet, I was much too literary.

RO'S   And you like to write with people's voices, don't you?

GP   It's really that, that's another point. I once said it long ago and then I forgot about it but it's true. You tend to find your own voice if you really listen to lots of voices. If you're able to take in lots of voices you find your own because then you're able to have one just like everybody else.

RO'S   Well, in relation to what you said about being 'dumb' about feminism, I felt that 'The Long-Distance Runner'[8] seems to raise something – as if it's quite aware that it's placing itself within a feminist background. It seemed to me that Mrs Luddy, the black, working-class woman who says to Faith, 'Girl you don't know nothing', is pointing to the disparity between theory and actually living your life.

You seem to be continually pointing to that, the disparity between theory and people just living their lives through. On the one hand, through theory or activism we can try to get more control over our lives and society in general and on the other hand there are these terrible tragedies, where we have no control. It's particularly highlighted by people's lack of control over their children's fate.

I thought in your last collection, *Later the Same Day*[9] that those two things are rather more in parallel than overlapping as they seem to be in the earlier two collections . . .

To return to feminism, in the very last story, 'Listening', suddenly you have the lesbian, Cassie, accusing Faith of never telling *her* story, '. . . where the hell is my woman and woman, woman-loving life in all this?'.[10] I wondered if that was answering some criticism from women.

GP   No, no nobody criticized it at all, but after I wrote it, I'd friends who said, 'I really meant to ask you that, Grace.' Nobody had ever said a word to me. I have lots of very close friends who are gay but they never said a word to me. We all worked together in so many

[8]Paley, *Enormous Changes* p. 177.
[9]Grace Paley, *Later the Same Day* (London, Virago, 1985).
[10]Paley, *Same Day*, p. 210.

things, we've done a lot of things together, been very close. So I haven't really thought of it, you know. A lot of those women happen to be women with kids so my relation to them is less sexual than as people in my own age group. As I got to know younger and younger people, it began to occur to me.

I didn't know I was going to do that, by the way. When I began that story, I had no idea. It was called, 'Listening' and I was thinking about this. As I came to the end I said, 'Oh my god, I wasn't listening.' I didn't plan it at all. It began with listening to two men talk, leaflets and a soldier . . .

RO'S   But it is quite a strong ending, isn't it? Although so many of your stories show women working well together, with a lot of love for each other, it's true that they are always going off with men, fancying men all the time, that's always there. The very last words of this story – and therefore of the whole collection – are Cassie's to Faith, '. . . I promise you, I won't forgive you . . . From now on, I'll watch you like a hawk. I do not forgive you.' I found that quite strange – how do you feel about that yourself? You obviously wanted to write that.

GP   Well, I'm just telling you exactly as it happened. I couldn't be more clear than that. You see, I was going to have a bunch of stories called, 'The Story Hearer' and there is one in there with that title and then there's the old man with the black grandson – that's called 'Telling'. The orginial thing was 'Telling' but . . . I read aloud a lot, I believe in it, religiously, and I noticed when I read it that it was a man talking so I had to call it 'Zagrowsky Tells'. That's the only reason I changed if from 'Telling'. And then this last one, 'Listening' – again I realized I hadn't listened, that's all. It's as simple as that. So it was really a self-criticism, in a way but people did afterwards say to me, 'Gee, we really meant to ask you that, Grace.'

RO'S   It's not that it's lacking, it's just a question of emphasis. There is one thing I would like to ask you, though. I noticed in the earlier stories that the relationships that seem to be the most important – in the sense that you actually examine them rather than them being in the background – are the daughter–father and the mother–son relationships. Most of the women have two sons, the mother–daughter relationship is not much in evidence. I, myself, have two sons and I noticed with interest that you have a daughter and a son. I kept wondering, 'Now why has she done that? There must be some reason for it.'

GP   Well one reason is I didn't want it to be me and it isn't me. I lived with my children's father for twenty-two years, we didn't part until then. So you know I'm not that Faith at all – I didn't have her problems or the pleasures of her variety either so it wasn't me. Also, I was afraid that if I did a girl and a boy it would be too much verisimilitude and I wanted to protect my daughter, being the first child. I didn't want anything I wrote to be an imposition on my own children – I used enough of their clever little remarks!

RO'S   What about the daughter–father relationship, though? You pay homage to your father at the beginning of *Enormous Changes at the Last Minute*.[11]

GP   Well, 'A Conversation With My Father'[12] is really a generational conversation. It's a conversation between an old man and a younger woman but it's also a generational discussion. At the same time, it's historical in the sense that he's an immigrant basically and he comes from a culture where there's no possibility of change. He's not wrong and she's not right – it's just historical. She says, yes they can change and, sure you could change in the United States in '69 or '70, '72 or '74, or whenever it was – I think that book came out in '74. You could have one career and then change but there were still a few places in your life where you couldn't. So those things always have to be read historically rather than psychologically. It's not a generational argument in the Freudian sense but in an historical sense – and it's also a discussion about literature. I used to argue with my father a lot about things like that.

RO'S   But in 'Faith in the Afternoon' and even in 'Enormous Changes at the Last Minute',[13] you've got the father in there.

GP   Well, my folks never lived in an old age home.

RO'S   Well, I wasn't suggesting that it's stemming from your own experience but I'm interested in the difference between that and the latest collection, where I noticed that Faith goes to visit her mother *and* her father – and she ends up running away from her father.[14]

GP   My mother died when I was about twenty . . . There are a couple of little things about my mother – there's a very short story in there . . .[15]

RO'S   Yes, I noticed in this book that there are very short stories which I really like. That's new isn't it, to do such a short story?

GP   There were a couple of things like it in *Enormous Changes* There was a story called 'Living' which was two pages. But these are really short.[16] The critics in the States didn't like them.

[11]Paley, *Enormous Changes*, acknowledgements at the beginning of the collection: 'Everyone in this book is imagined into life except the father. No matter what story he has to live in, he's my father, I, Goodside, MD, artist and storyteller. GP.'
[12]Paley, *Enormous Changes*, p. 159.
[13]Paley, *Enormous Changes*, p. 29 and p. 117.
[14]Paley, 'Dreamer in a Dead Language', *Same Day*, p. 11.
[15]Paley, 'Mother', *Same Day*, p. 111.
[16]'Mother' is one and a half pages. Another with the ironically over-long title, 'In This Country, But in Another Language, My Aunt Refuses to Marry the Man Everyone Wants Her To' is just over one page, as is, 'A Man Told Me the Story of His Life'.

RO'S   Ah, I did like those, actually.

GP   Me too.

RO'S   It's interesting that you said you liked reading aloud. I read somewhere that you 'write' aloud.

GP   Yeah, I tend to read it aloud before I'm through. When I don't do that I just don't seem to get it right, that's all.

RO'S   But also obviously it lends itself to your use of voices or at least the voices come across well. Do you write again and again?

GP   Oh, I rewrite and rewrite and rewrite.

RO'S   So what is it that makes you feel that it's just right, it's ready?

GP   Well, I go after two things. Sound is one thing but it's not the thing I go after first although I'm reading it aloud. Mostly it's meaning. It's hard for me – I'm sure there are people who can write and say right off what they mean but for some reason, I can't. It takes me a while. I'll write something and I'll look at it and I'll say, 'Gee it looks nice but that's not what I meant to say at all. That's really not it at all you know. It's not *true.*' You know, I teach so . . . I think about it in terms of lies – that some things are lies – and I go through it really for lies. And the lies can be very trivial like saying something is very tall when it's just tall – or it could be much more complicated. It could be a real live character or some way of just showing off. People do. I always use this example – writing something that I know my husband will like or my daughter. She's strict.

RO'S   But your style is very compressed, isn't it?

GP   I think it's from the poetry. That's my school.

RO'S   Well, to switch for a moment to your politics then – to the politics of your writing and the politics of your own experience. Apparently you're very busy and very much involved in politics. You say that your writing takes you a long time. If you're that ruthless with it, getting it right, taking a long time over it, do you find that there are patches of life when you don't do any writing and then times when you're writing a lot? Is that how you work?

GP   Yeah, pretty much. The point at which I had a bunch of stories and needed two or three more to finish a book, I'd work very hard. But after a book, after one of these three books I slow down quite a bit. It's as though you go onto something else and you don't know what your plans are, you don't know what your mind is doing, because you really want to investigate different things, think about them, different forms. It's all interesting so it's pretty slow. It's just as well because I have lots of other things to do, I don't want to write all the time. I tend to look at life in a very round way – I want to do most of it and I seem to have less time now coming up so I try to do as much as I can. I do worry a lot about the world – I have a grandchild now so I have to really.

RO'S   When you say that you see things in a 'very round' way, I definitely felt that was a theme which I liked as well as the form – particularly of the earlier two collections. I particularly love your story, 'Faith in a Tree'[17] – the way there are so many different voices coming in, many conversations going on simultaneously, one character replying to questions which have only been muttered in the private musings of another, with the overall effect of overlapping lives . . .

GP   I liked writing that story a lot.

RO'S   But I felt there was a change in the later stories, do you feel that yourself? They seem to be much more like what you said about 'Listening', that it seems to meander more, pop into one conversation and then another.

GP   Well, I became interested in having things more open at the end. Not that one works better than the other – I don't have a preference but it's an interesting idea for things not to be tied up at the end, sort of open as though to something else, maybe yes and maybe no. But I like that possibility for a while anyway – see what happens.

RO'S   And do you see each story, then, as being a new beginning? I think Hermione Lee in her introduction to the collection, *The Secret Self*[18] describes the short story as a liberating form, particularly for women when there isn't much time available. Each one is a new start.[19] But also for you it seems important that there are so many overlapping characters.

GP   Well, I just don't lose interest in those people. It's true I want to start again but at the same time I'm really interested – like Ruthy has suddenly appeared[20] and has *really* begun to absorb me a great deal and I've written a couple of things. And I have Edie in mind too, I want to do things with her. She's a teacher and I just think of those people as women. It's not even character that I'm all that interested in, it's just that certain lives – well I want to see what happens to them. Ruthie has certain things happening to her now so I just don't lose interest. On the other hand, I don't want to write a novel, I don't see why I should. I think most novels should be short stories – they're far too long.

RO'S   But the short story has a kind of symbolic impact doesn't it? And also the twist in the tail. You said you like things more open now but in fact there's often a twist at the end isn't there? 'Life' is just like that – always unexpected and unpredictable and yet there's

---

[17]Paley, *Enormous Changes*, p. 75.

[18]Hermione Lee, ed., *The Secret Self: Short Stories by Women* (London, J.M. Dent & Sons, 1985).

[19]Lee, *Secret Self*, pp. vii–viii. She is drawing on quotations from short story writers, Elizabeth Bowen and Eudora Welty amongst others.

[20]Paley, *Same Day*. Ruth appears in 'Somewhere Else', p. 45, 'Ruthy and Edie', p. 115 and 'The Expensive Moment', p. 179.

still always the predictable aspect of that very unpredictability. It's as though you have a liking for a character, a feel for someone, for some kind of identity such that you don't see them as a fully developed character, but you'll pick them up again and again, in different ways, at different times? Is that how you feel about it? You don't think of them as symbolic, a type of person or a type of life?

GP   I tend not to think psychologically. I have this kind of opposition to it somehow and I don't know why but I do.

RO'S   You're always very tongue-in-cheek – 'all you little psycho-analysed people'.[21]

GP   Wise-guy remarks I make – what my father used to call my 'wise-guy remarks'.

RO'S   How do you put your stories together because they definitely seem to cohere as a collection? Are they arranged chronologically as they have been written?

GP   No, no. Actually the last couple of stories are among the last but the first story, 'Love',[22] I wrote some time in the middle of this whole collection. It was about eighth.

RO'S   So how do you put a collection together?

GP   Well, I don't know exactly. It's really a funny business how you do it. I think I like to put first one that people can get into pretty quick but I don't really think of it quite that way. I really couldn't tell you. I just know that I keep shifting it around and shifting it around and then I hand it to a couple of people and say, 'What do you think of this order?' and they say, 'Oh, that's good but why don't you do that?' and I say, 'Why?' But I don't have a specific thing. It just seemed that the last part, the last few stories seemed to me to be right at the end. Or I could be wrong . . .

RO'S   Well . . . I'd like to move onto something more general now. It's obvious that you have an increasing awareness – almost a tender-ness – of the way children's lives can go terribly wrong and how little control we have over that.

GP   It's good you brought that up. It's important, very important. It's very important for a woman because women – women of my generation especially, I'm sure here as much as in the States, maybe there more – have the whole responsibility for what happens to children dumped on us. I mean psychologically, I don't even mean when someone says, 'Well, you're in charge.' But what happens is really the mother's fault and so forth. The fact of the matter is, it's a terrible burden for women. Of course, I'm older than you and I see what a cost it's been to friends of mine whose kids have been in a lot of trouble and have gone to psychologists and psychiatrists and who have been told it was their fault really – it infuriates me.

It's one of those things that absolutely makes me angrier than almost anything because we don't raise our children, hardly, even if we're home every day at two o'clock or three o'clock when they get home from school – even if we kept them home all day. I mean the children are really raised by the society in which we live and we're pressed by it so that the ways in which we are pressed, they are too. Certainly I didn't raise my kids to grow up right into the period of the very long and horrible war of the United States – the Vietnam war. I didn't raise them to grow up in a period of terrible drugs and so forth. That's what they have to deal with, as well as life in general.

So I just feel women have to understand that. Of course we have – everybody has, I have – responsibility to your children, you know, if they were here, to be decent to them but it's really the society that has tremendous responsibility to its kids and has got to see to it that they survive and that it's decent.

RO'S   It also fits in – does it? – with your cynicism about theory or right answers, particularly political theory. Left politics did tend to leave out mothers and children – generally it was very sexist wasn't it?

GP   It was sexist but it really was not more sexist than its moment in history.

RO'S   Well, that's right. Not to attribute guilt or blame but you do learn that whatever theory you commit yourself to or try to become active with, when you're involved with children it is politically very enlightening. You realize that you are very powerless in fact because, as you say, the children are the living proof of what society does to a person.

GP   Yeah and even when society doesn't mean it. I take my grand-daughter to school. I look at her in her classroom and she seems such a little noble creature, you know, her little chin is out, she's so brave amongst all these people who are her size and are equally brave, looking at each other, scaredly.

RO'S   You always refer humorously to parents' pride in their children. I like all those things you say and about the way children are so brilliant and sensitive and so on in the eyes of their parents – and, in a way, in reality. All potential.

GP   Yeah, they are really great beginners. They begin us again and again. I feel 'begun' by her. In a way we all have a citizenly responsibility to the world as far as our children are concerned and I do have a theory. I do have a very strong feminist feeling, that patriarchal attitudes have done terrible damage from the beginning of our own civilization and I think war comes from that. I think the raising of sons is a very serious business, right now.

RO'S   Yes. You say in 'Listening' that every boy child for hundreds of generations has been raised to be a soldier. That is a problem, isn't it? It's a problem also for women who are bringing up girls to be strong – finding ways in which to be strong is quite hard isn't it?

GP   I think the women's movement, in my country at least, has really had a good effect. All those people don't want to admit it but I think it has changed a lot of the boys of my son's generation who are really young men – not boys any more. I think it's done them a lot of good in their ability to deal with their own children, to spend time with them and not feel diminished.

RO'S   I did notice that in your earlier stories you have the men always going – coming and going, coming and going. The woman is always left, trapped with the child – the source of her fulfilment but also of her imprisonment. Whereas, in the later stories you do have fathers bouncing their children – perhaps losing their temper but collecting their children from school, that sort of thing. That's obviously something you see that has changed.

GP   Well, I think that's happened, yes.

RO'S   Perhaps lastly, could I ask you how you about a development I see in your writing? One of the things I've been thinking about is the political development in your stories, particularly in relation to change. In the first collection, change is a fact of life, a given, there's always something around the corner and that is part of the form of your stories. Then, in the second collection it seems to be more that *qualitative* change is possible. In 'Northeast Playground', the older woman is saying, 'Yes, it was like that for me too' but the younger women say, 'No, it's different now'.[23]

GP   Yes, and they kick her out.

RO'S   Yes, 'Beat it.'

GP   It's interesting for me that you could even see that story. It's not only a New York story, that 'Northeast Playground' but it's really a corner of New York. It's really a *corner* of one of the play-grounds, it's so local. You see that's what happens with things that are very specific sometimes – you really get it. Very specific but you say, 'Yep, that's the way it is in the corner of *my* playground?'

RO'S   Right, but it's absolutely true – isn't it? – , just that attitude, the way she tries to reassure them so learnedly that bringing up children was fundamentally the same for her although details may have changed and they dismiss her. It's that kind of urging of qualitative change which I liked. Would you say that that's part of your politics, that notion that real change is possible and also that the politics of personal life is important?

GP   Oh yeah, well I think for us as women, you know that is politics. Okay, the statement. 'the personal is political' – it really *is* for women because our lives are so dependent on social feelings. I just

[23]Paley, 'Northeast Playground', *Enormous Changes*, p. 147–8, paraphrase.

think of my mother and her life. My personal life is so different and that was my political life, in a sense, in which I made those changes.

RO'S   In 'The Expensive Moment'[24] you have the Chinese woman, Xie Feng, and Faith, finally getting down to discussing and comparing their lives, and they say how they weren't sure how to bring up their children, of what was the best way to help them – did they do the right thing? They agree that that was the most agonizing part of their life – you obviously feel that is central.

GP   I had that discussion with a Chinese woman. That was really sad. She came to see me and we talked a lot. I had been to China long before. She'd really had a rough time because she had been sent to the countryside. And yet, when we sat down to talk that's what we talked about – how to raise the children.

[24]Paley, 'The Expensive Moment', *Same Day*, p. 179.

Note

Alison Lurie was born in Chicago, Illinois on 3 September 1926, and was educated at Radcliffe College, Cambridge, Massachusetts where she majored in English history and literature, and wrote a thesis on the relations between the sexes in Jacobean comedy. From 1968 to the present she has been a professor at Cornell University, where she teaches courses in Creative Writing and in Children's Literature, on which topic she has written a variety of critical essays. The recipient of the Pulitzer Prize in 1985, Lurie has published eight novels, together with a memoir, works for children, short stories, and a social history of costume.

Novels
Love and Friendship (Heinemann, 1962; New York, Macmillan, 1962).
The Nowhere City (Heinemann, 1965; New York, Coward McCann, 1966).
Imaginary Friends (Heinemann; New York, Coward McCann, 1967).
Real People (New York, Random House, 1969; Heinemann, 1970).
The War Between the Tates (New York, Random House, 1974; Heinemann, 1974).
Only Children (New York, Random House, 1979; Heinemann, 1979).
Foreign Affairs (New York, Random House, 1984; Michael Joseph, 1985).
The Truth About Lorin Jones (Michael Joseph; Boston, Little Brown, 1988).

Other
V.R. Lang. A Memoir, Privately Printed 1959, and in V.R. Lang, *Poems and Plays* (New York, Random House, 1975).
The Heavenly Zoo:Legends and Tales of the Stars, for children (Eel Pie, 1979; New York, Farrar Straus, 1980).
Clever Gretchen and Other Forgotten Folktales, for children (New York, Crowell, 1980; Heinemann, 1980).
Fabulous Beasts, for children (New York, Farrar Straus 1981; Cape, 1981).
The Language of Clothes (New York, Random House, 1981; Heinemann, 1982).
Ms. collection: Radcliffe College Library, Cambridge, Massachusetts.

Secondary Criticism
Michael S. Helfand, 'The Dialectic of Self and Community in Alison Lurie's *The War Between the Tates*', *Perspectives on Contemporary Literature* 3, 2 (1977), pp. 65–70.

Interviews
David Jackson, 'An Interview with Alison Lurie', *Shenandoah* 31, iv (1980), pp. 15–27.
Martha Satz, 'A Kind of Detachment: An Interview with Alison Lurie', *Southwest Review* 71 (1986), pp. 194–202.

7

The Revenge of the Trance Maiden: Intertextuality and Alison Lurie

Judie Newman

As intertextuality is an extremely capacious term,[1] some working definitions seem to be in order. Most readers will be familiar with the term, as coined by Julia Kristeva, as founded upon the proposition that 'every text builds itself as a mosaic of quotations, every text is absorption and transformation of another text.'[2] At its narrowest, this has been taken to limit the applicability of the term to parody, mere allusion, source criticism, and casual generic resemblances. More commonly, however, the intertext of a given story may be defined as the set of plots, characters, images and conventions which it calls to mind for a given reader. In other words, it is not merely another text to which a work alludes, but to a totality, creating a general sense of a work of art which interacts with an entire tradition. The relationship obtaining between two (or more) texts is therefore between the texts as structured wholes. One can of course go one step further (following Kristeva's lead) and define a 'text' as a system of signs, whether in literary works, spoken languages, non-verbal sign systems, or symbolic systems.[3] Thus, Kristeva proceeds to define intertextuality as the transposition of one or several systems of signs into another. In its furthest expansion, therefore, intertextuality may incorporate all sorts of social phenomena. We may wish to consider that paradigmatic plots abound, not just in literary culture, but also in general culture. The term 'intertextuality' can describe this sense of life as repeating a previously heard story, of life predestined by the notions that shape our consciousness. In this way 'real life' may be structured according to

---

[1]For two clear theoretical accounts see Laurent Jenny, 'The strategy of form', in Tzvetan Todorov, ed., *French Literary Theory Today* (Cambridge University Press, 1982) pp. 34–64; and Jeanine Parisier Plottel and Hanna Charney, eds., 'Intertextuality: New Perspectives in Criticism', *New York Literary Forum*, 2 (1978). For an excellent demonstration of ways of working with intertextuality see John Hannay, *The Intertextuality of Fate*, (Columbia, University of Missouri Press, 1986).
[2]*New York Literary Forum* 2 (1978), p. xiv, a translation of 'Tout texte se construit comme mosaïque de citations, tout texte est absorption et transformation d'un autre texte.' Julia Kristeva, *Sémiotike, recherches pour une sémanalyse* (Paris, Seuil, 1969) p. 146.
[3]Julia Kristeva, *La revolution du langage poétique* (Paris, Seuil, 1974).

patterns familiar from literary culture – just as literary culture may be structured according to patterns familiar from 'real life'. It follows that the sources underlying human actions may come from other domains of reality, as much as from everyday life situations – from proverbs, folklore, fiction, music, television commercials. As Susan Stewart expresses it in her intertextual study of folklore and literature: 'our neighbourhoods are full of Madame Bovarys, Cinderellas. Ebenezer Scrooges, Constantine Levins and wise fools, as much as fictions are full of people from our neighbourhoods.'[4]

Intertextuality, then, offers an interactive model of art. Human experience may generate literature – but such experience has already been filtered through forms of artistic organization. Women's writing seems particularly sensitive to the ways in which female acculturation and socialization are promoted by such 'texts' as folklore, myth, fairy tales, movies, and other sources of exemplary representations. Alison Lurie's retelling of classic fairy tales in her 1980 volume, *Clever Gretchen and Other Forgotten Folktales*[5] may be said to be an activity consonant with this perception of the ways in which art can affect life. The tales are deliberately selected from the body of available folklore, in order to reconstitute a tradition, and to promote images of women as brave, clever and resourceful, able to defeat giants, answer riddles and outwit the devil – rather than as passively waiting for their prince to come. Lurie's semiotic expertise has also never been in doubt. Her 1981 volume *The Language of Clothes*, a serious examination of the history and interpretation of costume, begins from the premise that one set of signs is translatable into another, that clothing may be envisaged as a sign system, and that human beings communicate in the language of dress. Importantly, Lurie emphasizes here the notion of interaction between sets of signs (clothing and social context) in terms of situational participation and involvement.

> According to Erving Goffman, the concept of 'proper dress' is totally dependent on situation. To wear the costume considered 'proper' for a situation acts as a sign of involvement in it, and the person whose clothes do not conform to these standards is likely to be more or less subtly excluded from participation. When other signs of deep involvement are present, rules about proper dress may be waived.[6]

Erving Goffman is not being invoked casually at this point. The internal evidence of *Imaginary Friends* reveals a fairly close acquaintanceship on Lurie's part with his ideas. In this connection two of Goffman's notions are of special significance, firstly that of the relation of self to role, and secondly that of 'frame analysis'. In the first, Goffman's most distinctive line of thought has been to adopt a dramaturgical approach to social

[4]Susan Stewart, *Nonsense: Aspects of Intertextuality In Folklore and Literature* (Baltimore, Johns Hopkins, 1979) p. 26.
[5]Alison Lurie, *Clever Gretchen and Other Forgotten Folktales* (London, Heinemann, 1980).
[6]Alison Lurie, *The Language of Clothes* (New York, Random House, 1981) p. 13. The point is made by Erving Goffman in *Encounters* (Indianapolis, Bobbs-Merrill, 1961) pp. 145–6.

interaction, emphasizing particularly the discrepancies between the self-image which the actor presents to others in interactive process ('the presentation self') and his underlying private attitudes. Goffman's studies[7] of such diverse groups as salesmen, hotel workers, surgical teams, games players, mental patients, argue for pervasive role playing in social situations, suggesting that the individual is always acting within a fiction, a text, which is socially evolved. In this model, the autonomous bourgeois individual subject becomes more of a 'holding company' for a set of not relevantly connected selves. Some roles can be independently validated (Goffman cites that of law student), others cannot. (Goffman cites the claim to be a true believer, or a friend – two important points of contact with *Imaginary Friends*.[8]) The reality of such claims will depend upon the establishment by group members of a shared conception of the horizon or frame of a situation, of shared symbolic systems. Thus, in Goffman's view, reality is sponsored by the team. In addition, coming on to our second point, Goffman's sociological employment of frame analysis as a metaphor for the organization of experience has been applied to literary theory.[9] Intertextuality is the recognition of a frame, a context that allows the reader (of literature) or the actor (in a social situation) to orient him/herself, to distinguish 'text' from 'context', and to make sense of what would otherwise appear senseless. Just as a book offers a comprehensible *new* experience only because the reader has a framework of familiar points of contact between the self and the book, so in Goffman's analysis, everyday life depends upon the adumbration of a pattern or model, a conscious degree of role playing within the frame of situation, within the social text. Deciding what degree of involvement is required, mutually sustaining a definition of a situation – these are processes socially organized through rules of relevance and irrelevance, inclusion and exclusion, rules concerning 'what counts' as the reality of the situation. Thus, almost identical actions may be transformed or transcribed by participants from one frame to another, via a systematic alteration which radically reconstitutes for participants 'what is going on'. An obvious example offered by Goffman is the distinction between fighting, and playing at fighting, in animal or human behaviour.

Imaginary Friends, then, draws upon Goffman's theories in order both to proceed intertextually *and* to thematize intertextuality. At first, the novel appears to be intertextual in a fairly limited literary sense. Lurie's decision to name her 'trance maiden' Verena, after the inspired orator of *The Bostonians*, argues for a fairly active intertextual intention, just as the

[7]Erving Goffman is referred to by name in *Imaginary Friends*, (London, Penguin, 1967) p. 275. Major works include *The Presentation of Self in Everyday Life* (1956), *Encounters* (1961), *Asylums* (1961), *Behavior in Public Places* (1963), and *Frame Analysis* (1974). Although the latter postdates *Imaginary Friends* the concept of frame is initially elaborated in *Encounters* (pp. 20, 25, 26).
[8]'Claims to be a friend, a true believer, or a music-lover can be confirmed or disconfirmed only more or less.' *The Presentation of Self in Everyday Life* (London, Penguin, 1967), p. 53.
[9]*New York Literary Forum*, 2 (1978), p. xix.

cult group, the Seekers, which Verena leads, shares its name with a similar religious group in Edith Wharton's *Hudson River Bracketed*. Nor are these merely casual allusions. Both Marius Bewley[10] and more recently Howard Kerr[11] have identified a structured intertext, a common pattern, surrounding the figure of the trance maiden in nineteenth-century American literature. Representative novels – Hawthorne's *The Blithedale Romance* (1852), Howells's *The Undiscovered Country* (1880) and Henry James's *The Bostonians* (1886) – focus upon such elements as the connection of an entranced female with some kind of Utopian social enterprise, her exploitation by a ruthless mesmerist, her romance with a sceptical male, and her eventual rescue from mediumistic servitude, through the love of a good man. This is a topos with a fairly obvious normative patriarchal content, generally involving a woman who is as passive as Sleeping Beauty in her trance, the silencing of the female, the excision of her Utopian or progressive connections, and her resocialization within the safe categories of home and matrimony. Priscilla, the Veiled Lady of *The Blithedale Romance*, may stand as emblematic of the patriarchal view of woman – totally under male control, veiled to deny her physicality, an idol obscurely in contact with spiritual mysteries, and yet exposed to prurient commercial exploitation. Priscilla's rescue by Hollingsworth marks the end of the Utopian experiment at Blithedale, and is connected with the extinction of feminist Zenobia. Similarly, in Howells's *The Undiscovered Country*, spiritualist Dr Boynton uses his daughter Egeria as his spellbound medium, until she is liberated from his clutches by Ford, a sceptical amateur scientist. (Shakers supply the Utopian community in the novel.) Howells also implies a precise correlation between Egeria's mediumistic gifts and the repression of her sexuality. At one point, mere geographical proximity to Ford (who is simply visiting the same location) is enough to inhibit her to the extent that her powers fail her completely.

As Kerr points out, the extreme example of the passivity of the trance maiden occurs in Henry James's 'Professor Fargo' (1874) an anti-spiritualist satire, in which she is actually deaf and dumb. More subtly, in *The Bostonians*, James characterizes his heroine's passivity in terms of the acculturated female desire to placate and conciliate. Basil Ransom, the sceptical rough wooer of the novel, understands Verena Tarrant's gift as a speaker as simply a willingness to please, which leads her to utter the sentiments of others without compromising her own innocence. (Because they are sexually suppressed, trance maidens are always apparently innocent although they may spring from a corrupt or 'low' milieu.) For Basil, the nature of these sentiments is consequent upon the person to whom Verena stands closest, at any point, in a relation of dependency. She thus passes

---

[10]Marius Bewley, *The Complex Fate* (London, Chatto & Windus, 1952).
[11]Howard Kerr, *Mediums and Spirit Rappers and Roaring Radicals: Spiritualism in American Literature 1850–1900* (Urbana, University of Illinois Press, 1972).
[12]Alison Lurie, *Imaginary Friends* (London, Penguin, 1967). Page references which follow quotations in parentheses refer to this edition of the novel.

easily from the control of her father (ex-member of the 'Cayuga' Utopian experiment, now a mesmeric healer) to that of feminist Olive Chancellor, and thence after prolonged sexual and ideological warfare into the arms of Ransom. Like Howells, James also suggests that Verena's inspired self springs from a buried or displaced capacity for passion, and he indicates a sexual basis for her gifts – as well as for Olive's behaviour.

The reader who turns from James to *Imaginary Friends* will discover that all the elements of the intertext of the trance maiden are firmly in place. Verena Roberts resides appropriately on West *Hawthorne* Street, in the imaginary small town of Sophis, which is located in an area of Upper New York State which was a locus for religious fringe groups in the nineteenth century. It is close to the spot where Joseph Smith met the Angel Moroni, and where the Oneida community flourished. As the narrator comments, Verena 'was right in the local tradition, only about a hundred years too late.' (p. 30)[12] Although Verena's spirit messages, received via automatic writing, emanate from extraterrestrial beings, notably Ro of the planet Varna, this is not much more than a variant on established tradition, the result of the fact that 'science now dominated the culture to the point where people were sitting round a table conjuring up ectoplasmic rayguns and little green men, instead of ladies in white veils.' (p. 14). Verena also remains firmly in the tradition of American Utopianism, her cult, at least in part, a disguised attack on the affluent society. Conspicuous consumption is roundly denounced as excessive attachment to 'material clingings'; Cosmic Love is invoked, and the belief system excludes evil in favour of a vision of the universe as imbued with spirit light and benevolent power. Like her predecessors, Verena is young and virginal, resides in a distinctly lower-class milieu and initially features as passively pliant, providing her interlocutors with what they want to hear, quieting anxieties, sympathizing with problems, and generally providing 'uplift'. One cult member, Ken, figures as the sceptical young wooer, excluded from the Seekers when he denounces their beliefs, and subsequently kept at bay by Elsie Novar, Verena's aunt, who is using Verena, in a fashion not unlike Olive Chancellor, to promote her own emotional needs. In the dénouement the lusty Ken elopes with Verena, who abandons the Seekers in favour of matrimony.

It would be a mistake, however, to envisage *this* Verena as sinking into passivity. *Imaginary Friends* gives us the revenge of the trance maiden in no uncertain terms. As events develop Verena progresses from passively catering to her audience, towards actively attacking their cultural norms. At the close, far from being silenced, she has expanded her career to that of radical orator. A photograph in *The New York Times* shows her protesting vigorously at a political demonstration. Two 'texts' (systems of signs) are actually involved here, and it is the interaction between the two which generates the ironies of the novel. When Tom McMann and Roger Zimmern, two social scientists, set up a small group interaction study of the Seekers, they use the methods favoured by Goffman: participant observation, role-playing, and non-directive techniques. The transcrip-

tion of the literary intertext into the social text (and vice versa) foregrounds
the whole notion of intertextuality. In addition to their literary intertext,
the Seekers are also modelled on an actual group investigated by social
scientists in the 1950s and documented by Leon Festinger and others in
When Prophecy Fails.[13] Festinger and his colleagues were studying the
behaviour of individuals in groups which made specific prophesies,
looking for evidence of increased commitment following disconfirmation
of belief (on the model of such historical groups as the Anabaptists,
Millerites, and the followers of Sabbatai Zevi and of Montanus.) Alerted
by press reports they investigated the activities of Marian Keech, a fifty-
year-old housewife, who declared herself in contact with beings from the
planet 'Clarion' and prophesied the destruction of 'Lake City' by flood on
21 December. (The sociologists' report omits the actual year and conceals
real identities and locations beneath pseudonyms.) Mrs Keech had
initially received messages by automatic writing, and then became
involved with a group called 'The Seekers' operating some 200 miles away.
Originally a group of college students, meeting in a Protestant church to
discuss religious and ethical matters, the Seekers were swayed by their
pastor's enthusiasm for flying saucers, and eventually developed an
eclectic belief system of their own. Some went as far as to resign from their
jobs and give away all their possessions in the anticipation of imminent
world cataclysm, from which they personally expected to be saved by
flying saucers. If anything, Lurie's fictional text appears decidedly *less*
sensational and fantastic than the events chronicled by Festinger.[14] In
addition to the intertextual doubling of referents in the case of the
Seekers, Lurie also thematizes the operations of reading and writing
involved in the production of a text, by establishing a continuing analogy
between the elaboration of a fiction, and that of the belief system of a
small group. Since the establishment of the 'social text' itself involves
interactive techniques, Lurie thus effectively sets up a *mise en abyme* or
infinite regressus, in which the novel offers both a sociology of the sociologists, and a metafictional fiction. As a result, its scope expands into a

[13]Leon Festinger, Henry W. Riecken and Stanley Schachter, *When Prophecy Fails*
(Minneapolis, University of Minnesota Press, 1956). Special thanks to Professor Malcolm
Bradbury for comments on this source, made at the initial delivery of the present paper at the
British Association for American Studies Conference in 1988.
[14]In common with Lurie's group the historical Seekers frowned on meat-eating, engaged in
meetings of exceptionally long duration, during which they discussed messages received from
outer space, suffered from a leadership struggle between two women, and developed a
clothing taboo. (Metal on the person was suddenly forbidden, leading to the frenzied
removal of trouser zippers, shoe eyelets, belts and undergarments.) When prophecy failed,
Mrs Keech explained that the group had spread so much spiritual light that God had saved
the world after all. Unlike Lurie's group, their story attracted national publicity and was
headline news for a week in the press and media, culminating in complaints to the police
about their activities, threats of incarceration in mental hospitals, and flight. Like McMann
and Zimmern, the historical sociologists, posing as ordinary group members and proceeding
in a non-directive fashion, found it increasingly difficult to remain neutral, and often
unwittingly reinforced the group's beliefs.

discussion of the manner in which cultural norms are established and inscribed, deviance and difference defined.

The doubling of intertexts is indicated from the beginning in Verena's residence on *West* Hawthorne Street, which evokes the starting point of small group study in the United States – Elton Mayo's pioneering researches at the Hawthorne Western Electric Plant in the 1930s.[15] The methods of sociological analysis – the various conceptual frames on offer – are then themselves introduced in terms of literary genres, as texts and titles. As an empirical, descriptive sociologist, Tom McMann favours the type of social diagnosis based on accumulations of case histories, known generically to the younger generation as 'Nuts and Sluts'. (William Foot Whyte's *Street Corner Society*, a study of street gangs in an Italian slum, is cited as a typical example of the genre.) Similarly the diagrammatic Parsonians feature as 'Boxes and Arrows'; those favouring statistical analysis are involved in 'The Numbers Racket'. Dazzled by the prospect of collaborating as co-author with the famous McMann, Roger finds titles floating 'mirage-like' before his eyes. 'Anomie in a Small Town Setting' is one such; 'We and It: Role Conflict in a Belief Group' is another, as Roger sets to work labelling and framing before the study has even begun. For Roger, the 'real' is his career as a social scientist. The Sophis study is cut off and set apart; it does not 'count' in the same way as his real life. Thus, when approaching Sophis for the first time, Roger describes the landscape of hills, barns and cows as having 'all the pastoral props' (p. 15). Putting up at Ovid's motel, he notes a paint-by-numbers picture, which 'represented Art. Literature was represented by an old copy of the Post' (p. 16), rather as if he were stepping onto a stage set. The impression is reinforced by Roger's own role play. Following good sociological principles he conceals his professional identity beneath a cover story, the fiction that he is carrying out public opinion survey work. As McMann argues, to obtain unbiased data 'You had to filter your presentation.' (p. 17) In short, as the later Roger wryly remarks, 'with the excuse that we were seeking truth, we were proposing to lie ourselves blind to the Truth Seekers.' (p. 18)

On first encountering the Seekers, however, Roger finds that his methods rebound upon him. Rather than settling down to observe Verena, he finds himself the focus of observation, as Verena scrutinizes his 'aura' and pronounces him 'a complete blank' (p. 26). This unwelcome news is compounded when she obtains a spirit message from Varna for him. The message is merely a series of interlocking loops. For Roger, this experience is profoundly disquieting: 'No possible statement is as uncanny as one you can't read at all.' (p. 29) He is cheered, however, when the term 'automatic writing' occurs to him. Roger is considerably more secure with a long word between him and phenomena, preferably a

---

[15]F.J. Roethlisberger and William J. Dickson, *Management and the Worker* (Cambridge, Mass., Harvard University Press, 1939). As director of the project, Elton Mayo launched the Western Electric Research Program in 1927, working with Roethlisberger and Dickson, and carrying out research at the Hawthorne Works in Chicago, which demonstrated the importance of social-psychological dynamics, operating in groups in the real world.

word which labels and positions a text within a frame of assumptions. Verena is almost as adept, however, at framing Roger within hers, as her next message suggests. Roger, attempting to suppress a fit of laughter, finds himself silently praying to the totemic deities of his brand of sociology – Max Weber, C.Wright Mills, and Machiavelli. Verena promptly produces the message 'Makes Favour. See Right Ills. O Make A Veil High', reinscribing his gods within her own textual system. The commonsense explanation is that Roger had unwittingly muttered the names under his breath, and that Verena who has never heard of Max Weber, or Machiavelli, and therefore lacks the right frame to make sense of the utterance, has simply done her best with the verbal system at her disposal. Roger, however, is quite unnerved. As his previous facility with titles indicates, Roger *does* treat the world as a text, but one which he does not expect to operate on him. He believes that he can maintain distance and objectivity, observing the Seekers without being in any way affected by them.

Thus, as a participant-observer, Roger implicitly occupies a readerly role. Indeed, the Seekers' extrapolation of a system of beliefs is overtly equated with the formation of a fiction, by Lurie's concentration on messages generated by automatic writing. Verena's first message from Varna is received when words in another hand are added to a letter which she is composing, quite beyond her conscious volition. It looks like divine intervention, and very much conforms to the popular image of what an author does.[16] In this model, an author creates a narrative by some mystic alchemy or inspiration, and it is made public in a book which the reader passively enjoys, gaining private satisfactions. Similarly the traditional critical process focuses on the author as creator, and translates reader responses into statements about the work and its creator. The reader is thus able to operate without taking full responsibility for his or her own feelings, casting the self into a pseudo-objective role. The same is true of Roger, in his role as non-directive participant observer, aiming to offer as little input as possible to the group, while gaining professional satisfactions from it. As Miles Coverdale to Verena's Veiled Lady, Roger 'frames' the Seekers as if they were a fiction, as if they 'didn't count' as real people. Thus, in the absence of local kinship ties, the group provides an undemanding social life for all its members, which Roger labels an 'imaginary kinship system'. He participates in it, enjoying an evening at the Freeplatzers' as 'almost a social occasion' (p. 65). Of course, for all the other participants, it is a social occasion. Only Roger has framed it as 'group interaction'. Roger also assumes that the Seekers' friendship for him will end with the study (p. 254). But of course, for the Seekers, there *is* no study; they are quite unaware of the frame which Roger has placed around them. Nor is their sense of kinship unreal – whereas, as a friend, Roger is almost as imaginary as Ro of Varna.

[16]See Hugh Crago, 'Cultural Categories and the Criticism of Children's Literature', *Signal*, 30 (1980), pp. 140–50.

The problem of Roger's 'role distance' from the social text is particularly focused in relation to Verena. Roger originally perceives the belief system of the cult as created and authored by Verena. He describes her as 'able to dream for others or to fit them into her own dreams' (p. 45). In fact, however, Verena is co-authoring her text in close collaboration with the group. The Seekers' sessions focus upon the reception, interpretation and elucidation of spirit messages, with each member relating the messages back to his or her own personal framework (popular science in Rufus's case, spiritualism in Catherine's) and emphasizing those aspects of the message which suit them best. In short, via reader input, a text is slowly extrapolated within a shaping culture, interacting with, and being modified by that culture.

Unfortunately Verena's openness to others allows her text to slip from her control, passing for a time at least to Elsie, who wrests control from Verena by enforced sexual suppression. In a hysterical, Salemesque accusatory mode, the group stigmatize Verena as a 'filthy, unclean vessel' (p. 97), polluted and spiritually weakened by proximity to Ken, who is characterized as a 'negative vibrational force' (p. 94) surrounded by a greasy, smoky aura. Verena is forced to abase herself before them, proclaiming 'I am cleaned and made pure' (p. 99) only after prolonged humiliation. Roger and Tom stand passively by, capable only of non-directive comment. On one level, the scene recognizes the ethical problems posed by participant observation as a sociological method. Goffman unwittingly provides a rather good example in *Behavior in Public Places* where he discusses the different classes of involvement obligations within one situation: 'I have seen patients watch passively, from a few feet away, a young male psychotic rape an old defenceless mute man.'[17] Disapproving glances were apparently the most which the patients in the asylum risked. Goffman, himself, also observing, appears to have risked even less. Similarly Roger Zimmern is uncomfortably reminded at this point in the novel of snapshots in *The New York Times* showing prisoners being tortured in Vietnam: 'You couldn't help asking, why didn't the photographer do something? He was right there, wasn't he?' (p. 104). Partly as a result of Roger's refusal to allow his objective observations to be biased by emotional involvement, Verena is now downgraded to the role of symbolic leader, while Elsie reinterprets the messages on her own terms, engineering a sharp shift in the group ethos, from its earlier Transcendental cast, towards a more Manichean, sin-oriented creed. Just as Olive Chancellor exploited Verena Tarrant's style to transmit her own convictions, so Elsie reduces Verena to mechanically rehearsing another's script. Roger describes Verena as 'like a painting in reproduction', 'as if she were imitating herself, or reading from a script she had memorized earlier' (p 105).

The death of this particular author, however, turns out to have been

---

[17]Erving Goffman, *Behavior in Public Places* (Glencoe, Illinois, The Free Press, 1963) p. 207.

very much exaggerated. Verena is able to act in a consciously intertextual fashion herself, and she gains her revenge by adopting the sociologist's own methods. Earlier, when McMann was rumbled as a professor, he had adopted the strategy of over-acting, carrying more books and papers, making ostentatious notes, muttering to himself, and mislaying objects – imitating, not so much a real academic as the popular image of the absentminded professor. Verena plays McMann at his own game, exaggerating the stereotypical role of the trance maiden into parody. In response to the repressive identification of her sexuality with sin, Verena apparently meets the group demand for purity by anorexic self-starvation. Far from internalizing the prohibition against female physicality however, she externalizes it, imposing her own food phobias on the group and evolving a complicated set of dietary taboos, which reduce them all to the intake of the tame rabbit. Verena also exaggerates female pliancy to the point at which her blank gaze, flat voice, and mechanical echoing of Elsie's suggestions suggest to Roger, first the 'waxy flexibility' (p. 115) of incipient schizophrenia, then an uncomfortably close mirroring of his own non-directive techniques. Both Roger and McMann subscribe to the orthodox psychological notion (initiated by William James) that the trance maiden is possessed by an ordinarily quiescent second self, emerging only in states of dissociated consciousness. In this analysis Ro of Varna is actually Verena's subconscious. Verena's revenge is to split the two investigators into fragmented selves. McMann is eventually defined as insane himself, when he becomes convinced that he is Ro of Varna. His partner's fate is also appropriate. Roger, who had constituted Verena as his object of study, finds himself subject to Varnian academic requirements, forced to take notes at meetings, copy messages, memorize prayers and generally embark on an exhaustive course of study in which he is an involuntary D student. As a result he separates himself consciously into 'Clever Zimmern' (his 'real' self, the objective scientist) and 'Stupid Roger' (the role he plays within the group and the person who is also erotically fixated on Verena). Since fragmentation into alternate or suppressed selves is commonly the fate of women in patriarchal culture, where men are unitary characters, it is a peculiarly apt revenge.

One scene specifically emphasizes the problems inherent in labelling behaviour as delusionary on bases of sexual norms. With Ken out of bounds, Verena makes overtures to Roger, when he consults her about the date of 'The Coming', the imminent descent of Ro to earth. Erotic double entendre runs through the scene, with puns on the group's 'desire for the coming' which appear to foreground the repressed sexual bases of their delusionary system. With Verena praying over him, Roger averts his eyes from her heaving breasts to take refuge in the notation of 'neutral sociological details' (p. 143) – knobs on a maple bureau, a mirror reflecting a non-existent waver in the window frame, a framed reproduction. Wavering between spiritual and sexual frames himself, it occurs to him to stop resisting. After all, 'What Verena had always done with her gift was to guess what people wanted and then to give it to them' (p. 143). Indeed, when Verena removes his shirt and jacket, on the grounds that these material clingings are preventing the Varnian vibrations from having 'a chance to penetrate' (p. 143), even Clever Zimmern collapses into Stupid Roger, and seizes her in his manly arms. Of course, on one level, if the reader accepts that Verena is deluded, Roger's scruples are entirely proper. He reflects that, but for the interruption of footsteps outside the door, 'The Junior E [Experimenter] on the Sophis Project (National Institution of Mental Health Grant No. 789 etc.) would have raped his principal S [Subject]' (p. 145). On these 'objective' grounds, he should resist, as a psychiatrist is expected to resist the overtures of a disturbed patient. But who defines Verena as deluded? On less disinterested grounds, for the social study to continue, Verena must remain repressed. In Roger's theory, her dammed-up sexual energy is the source of Ro of Varna. The suspicion lingers that Roger is actively repressing Verena's as well as his own emotions, an impression strengthened by subsequent events.

At the next meeting Verena announces to the group that Ro has prohibited clothing made from natural materials. Only artificial fibres created by pure science are acceptable. Having been unwilling to remove his clothes in private, Roger finds himself forced to disrobe in public. Despite Verena's assertion that 'There is no shame in the True Universe' (p. 160), the other Seekers also show some resistance to total nudity in the front parlour, and are permitted to borrow synthetic garments from the family wardrobe. This poses no great problem for the women, who have both Elsie's and Verena's clothing to choose from, and whose apparel, in any case, tends more towards synthetics, but it is a disaster for the males. When they reappear, Ed is wearing plastic duck waders, McMann an old nylon shirt which suggests an auto salesman in the 50s, Bill baggy paint-streaked slacks, Roger striped pyjamas, which make him look like a comic strip convict, and Rufus swimming trunks and a floral quilt. As they descend the stairs, they are framed in a wall mirror as

> some group from the Theatre of the Absurd, a tall middle-aged duck hunter, a small convict with horn-rimmed glasses, a plump comedian in baggy paint-spotted pants, and a large used car salesman, all led by a skinny lunatic in Dacron socks and a flowered quilt (p. 162).

By the proclamation of new sumptuary laws from Ro, Verena at a stroke deprives the males of their chosen sartorial identity. In the language of clothes, they have been effectively struck dumb. In addition they have been forced to impersonate a dramatic character, a presentation self, quite at variance with their own internal attitudes.

Up to this point Roger has been treating his involvement with the Seekers as one that 'does not count' in real terms, rather as a fiction is traditionally marked off from 'everyday life' on the grounds that its events are reversible, that we can 'take back' their meanings by saying 'it was only a story' or that we can revise their meanings by intertextual transformations and rewritings, so that (to quote Borges) 'every writer creates his own precursors.' Verena, however, decides not to permit this, and insists upon irreversible actions. Roger has to commit his expensive organic tweed jacket to the flames. In addition the manner in which this occurs is carefully staged by Verena so as to re-enact and revise her own preceding humiliations. *She* may be said to be acting intertextually here; the other characters are not granted the same freedom. Thus when the bonfire begins, the room fills with pungent smoke, exposing the whole group to the aura formerly ascribed to Ken – 'as if some particularly strong and unpleasant astral force were present' (p. 165). As the Seekers burn their garments, they proclaim 'I am purified and made free' (p. 166), a variant on the lesson Verena was forced to recite. Roger, on the sidelines, is still constituting himself as an observer. He notes, for example, that since Sissy Freeplatzer spent a long time knitting her woolly sweater, Verena was psychologically astute to leave her 'to the last' (p. 168). But Roger's turn is yet to come – *he* is actually the last to be called upon and such is the power of group consensus that he actually does burn his cherished jacket. While the Seekers have been behaving as if invisible beings (Ro and Mo) were present at their meetings, the two sociologists have been acting as if *they* were invisible, not 'really there' (p. 155), just as readers do. Verena, however, now hauls them bodily into her frame. As Roger comments, it is as if 'someone else, possibly Ro of Varna, was conducting a field study on American sociologists. To him, we were the white rats.' (p. 171). Verena thus enforces the correct degree of involvement on Roger's part, by forcing him into the 'proper clothes' in Goffman's terms, those which express participation in the situation. In Sophis, Roger has to kit himself out from head to toe, in inorganic clothing. The result, he realizes, observing himself re-framed in the motel mirror, is to transform him into 'a small nondescriptly lower-middle-class young man' (p. 174) in Dacron shirt, Orlon sweater and limp slacks, a figure who now matches the motel room perfectly: 'It was Stupid Roger, in his real clothes' (p. 175). Verena's vengeance is thus both a class revenge and a sexual retaliation. The penalty for Roger's pretensions to superior detachment is to be forced into a position where he is entirely controlled. When next he is alone with Verena, he is deterred from *any* sexual responsiveness, inhibited by the knowledge that he is wearing 'blue rayon undershorts decorated with beagles' (p. 178).

It is as well to pause here to anticipate a major qualification. Although the results of Verena's actions constitute a fairly thorough-going revenge, Lurie fosters a productive ambiguity concerning the degree of intentionality involved. When Verena announces the new sumptuary laws, it is noteworthy that she has already donned a new, synthetic robe for the occasion. Roger catches himself thinking, 'She must have *known* what was coming . . . because her old robe . . . was cotton velvet. But of course she knew, what was the matter with me? Was I beginning to believe, like the Seekers, that Ro was a separate entity?' (p. 161). But how far does the author 'know' what is coming next? Verena may be scripting the messages and pulling the plot strings without being consciously aware of her own control. (Messages may be issuing from her subconscious.) Strong hints are also dropped that McMann had advance knowledge of this announcement (he is clad in synthetic trousers) and of the announcement of 'The Coming'. McMann wants to test his hypothesis – that disconfirmation of the group's beliefs will not dissolve the group – and may therefore be prompting Verena with millennial suggestions, abetted by Elsie. Or, of course, all three may be in cahoots. When Roger finds out that Tom has entered the date of the millennial prophecy in the records before that prophecy was uttered, it looks like decisive evidence. Challenged, however, Tom appeals to social norms as the explanation. Given the existence of what Roger describes as 'the ordinary Protestant delusionary system' (p. 33), to which the Seekers broadly adhere, an announcement of the descent to earth of a god in December is strictly in accordance with tradition. Only Roger, who is Jewish, is surprised. In addition, the fictional frame also conditions events. For Roger the Varnians are purely imaginary, mental constructs, and he therefore *knows* that no little green men will put in an appearance. But the reader, especially if well versed in recent feminist science fiction, for example, has no such certainty. Inside the frame of genre, little green men are perfectly permissible. In little, therefore, the novel seems to offer a near perfect model of the various potential theories of how a text is generated. Does it originate in a single author? In that author's conscious or unconscious self? In some sort of collaboration with an Ideal Reader (the reader in his presentation self) or a Common Reader (a member of a group audience whose generic expectations must be respected)? Or is it socially produced in accordance with a well established framework of group norms and assumptions?

These uncertainties are not merely matters of literary interest, as becomes abundantly clear in the denouement. Ambiguities as to who is in control, who is deluded, who sets the norm for the group, extend from the literary into the social text, raising the question of the ways in which cultural hegemony is established, how situational norms are defined, and deviance penalized. At the close of the novel, Verena invents a happy ending for the Seekers, announcing that the Varnians have descended to earth, that they have been incorporated into all the group members equally, and that from now on the Seekers must go forth into the world, to spread the word. When, however, Roger reads the last automatic message from Ro, previously elucidated at length by Verena, he discovers that it consits only of meaningless scrawls. Verena has deliberately engineered the dissolution of both the group and its text, in order to be free to join Ken. For the Seekers, however, the non-appearance of actual Varnians constitutes a fairly radical disconfirmation of their belief system. Tom promptly intervenes, proclaiming the felt presence of spirits within him. Reconstitution of the group is accompanied by a brisk reinterpretation of Ro's last verbal message. 'I am in Man On Earth' becomes 'I am in Tom McMann On Earth'. Or, in Roger's sociologese, 'At approximately 2.20 a.m. on December 5, Ro of Varna was accepted by the group as being incarnated in the senior project researcher.' (p. 231).

An exceptionally non-objective reader, Tom has had a decidedly creative input to the evolution of the group text. As a result of his over-enthusiastic adoption of his new role he ends up in an insane asylum, where he is visited each week by Elsie, intent on fulfilling her desire 'to make it with her god' (p. 280). Unlike Verena, who has transformed her role as trance maiden on her own terms, Tom appears to have been entirely engulfed by his intertext; he is now fully on the inside of the 'Nuts and Sluts' genre. It finally dawns on Roger that this has been threatening from the start. Two small groups have been involved throughout – the Seekers and the sociologists. Roger had been so intent on the activities of the former that he had failed to perceive that every development there was replicated in the group in which he saw himself as having primary membership. McMann's initial choice of subject – the effects of internal opposition within a small group – was occasioned by his own experience of opposition within a small group, his University department. Thus, the evolution of the study has been predestined by events which shaped McMann's own consciousness. Formerly a hero of sociology, McMann has lost out humiliatingly to younger men and is eager to revise and restore his status. The title of one of his essays, 'The Sociologist – Seer or Statistician?', proves entirely proleptic of the generic options available to him. As the Seekers' seer he accrues once more the respect, reverence, even hero-worship once accorded to him within his professional group.

If Verena's escape depended on the use of her intertextual skills to redefine her role, moving out onto a larger stage, and leaving behind something of a dent in the cultural monolith, Tom's subsequent actions reveal the potential hazards of intertextual operations. Tom is also able to switch frames and to transpose systems. First he 'takes back' the meaning of his incarceration, claiming that his madness was only an act, a role assumed originally in order to avoid criminal prosecution, and later perpetuated in order to allow him to undertake the ultimate participant observation study, of the asylum. (This paradigm is imported from Goffman, whose own study *Asylums* was carried out while posing as assistant to the asylum athletic director.) Having therefore established the fictionality of his own 'Nuts and Sluts' intertext, McMann is about to move into 'The Numbers Racket' in a more sinister sense. Earlier in the novel, Roger had expressed unease with the frequency of the sociologists' non-directive repetition of group opinions on the grounds that they were offering too strong a reinforcement: 'If you push quantity too hard, it becomes quality' (p. 61). Visiting McMann, Roger is unnerved by the ordinariness of the asylum, which is reminiscent of a small college or school, perfectly standard in every way. Roger's disquiet, the product of the lack of any obvious distinction between sane and insane, will be familiar to readers acquainted with *either* the sociological literature concerning the political definition of mental illness (Goffman, R.D. Laing, Thomas Szasz), *or* the fictional intertext (*One Flew Over the Cuckoo's Nest*, *Catch 22*, *The Crying of Lot 49*). Roger had previously experienced a similar unease when he first visited West Hawthorne Street: 'The whole place made me uneasy; it was so ordinary, so average, like the mid-point on a distribution which has no positive correlative' (p. 19). In short, in her typical frame house Verena inhabited the norm, and the norm has no real existence; it is merely sponsored by the team, socially defined by the majority. It follows for Roger that 'Madness can be defined as a conception of reality that is not shared by others in your environment' (p. 39). But McMann's conception of reality *is* shared. He has at least half a dozen followers, and is actively planning to expand the Seekers into a mass movement, with himself as their god, drawing on his own professional knowledge of leadership techniques. Nor may he be said to be pretending to be Ro of Varna. If we take the view that identity is socially defined, then McMann *is* Ro of Varna. He has been so constituted by the small group. If thousands more were to follow him, the individual delusion would be reframed, first as a mass delusion, then as a respectable religious movement, its dietary taboos as acceptable as those of any other faith, its compulsory Dacron no more surprising than, for example, obligatory headgear in places of worship. In that case, since Tom would be spending most of his time playing the role of Ro, we would have to say, with Roger, that 'Ro of Varna is insane to believe he is still Thomas McMann, a professor of sociology' (p. 286). Thus, if numbers are on his side, McMann will be able to accomplish an intertextual move himself, from 'Nuts and Sluts' to 'The Numbers Racket', and from statistician back to seer.

Imaginary Friends thus leaves the reader to decide for him – or herself what is the proper degree of involvement, whether in the social or the literary text, which readerly role to adopt and which reality team to sponsor. Roger's objectivity results in the loss of a woman whom he genuinely loved, passed up in favour of a small group interaction study. Tom's view, that the observer, who remains external to events is not so much unbiased as incompetent (since the mental set of the group is what he needs to assume and understand) induces a degree of commitment which results in him actually being committed – to a mental asylum. In Verena's case, intertextuality may subvert literary and social ideologies to radical ends. But Verena's vacant place is swiftly filled by a male god who may prove equally adept at redefining his act, rewriting the past – and thus, potentially, controlling the future.

Note

Julia Kristeva's essay 'Women's Time' in Toril Moi, ed., *The Kristeva Reader* (Oxford, Basil Blackwell, 1986) provides theoretical hints on ways of connecting gender and history which have been fundamental to my thinking in this essay. Her essay was previously published in *Signs* 7 (1981), 13–35 with an important introduction by Alice Jardine. The essays collected in Frieda Johles Forman, ed., *Taking our Time: Feminist Perspectives on Temporality* (Oxford, Pergamon Press, 1989), some of which discuss Kristeva's work, explore the idea of time as a cultural construct. Interesting new theoretical perspectives on history and its relationship to fiction are represented in Robert H. Canary and Henry Kozicki, eds., *The Writing of History: Literary Form and Historical Understanding* (University of Wisconsin Press, 1978). Lyn Pykett's essay, 'The Century's Daughters: Recent Women's Fiction and History', *Critical Quarterly* 29 (1987), 71–7, looks at contemporary women's fiction; Alison Light in 'Feminist Cultural Studies', *Englisch Amerikanische Studien* 1 (1987), 58–72, discusses women's historical novels of the 1950s. The feminist dialogue with deconstruction carried on by Nancy Miller in *Subject to Change* (New York, Columbia UP 1988), Jane Gallop in *Thinking Through the Body* (New York, Columbia UP, 1988) and the contributors to Teresa de Lauretis, ed., *Feminist Studies/Critical Studies* (Bloomington and Indianapolis, Indiana, UP, 1986) has been stimulating and important.

Pat Barker is the author of *Union Street* (Virago, 1982), *Blow Your House Down* Virago, 1984) as well as The Century's Daughter (Virago, 1986).

Beloved (Chatto, 1987) is Toni Morrison's fifth novel. She has previously written *The Bluest Eye* (Chatto 1970), *Sula* (Chatto, 1973), *The Song of Solomon* (Chatto, 1977) *Tar Baby* (Chatto, 1981). There is a bibliography and essays about Morrison in Mari Evans, ed., *Black Women Writers* (Pluto Press, 1983).

8
The Re-Imagining of History in Contemporary Women's Fiction

Linda Anderson

In one of her earliest pieces of writing, her unpublished 'Journal of Mistress Joan Martyn', Virginia Woolf imagined a contemporary woman historian discovering a fifteenth-century woman's journal and thus, through her researches, making present a lost moment of women's history.[1] By focusing on the fifteenth century Woolf both grounds the journal in the specificity of a particular period and suggests that this kind of historical knowledge is probably groundless: according to her narrator and fictional historian Rosamund Meridew, who speaks to us with undercurrents of Woolfian irony, the barrenness of documentation for the social life of the fifteenth century means that the historian, lapsing from 'his sterner art' must be 'content to imagine like any storyteller'.[2] 'Imagining like any storyteller' may be closer than is generally admitted to what the historian does anyway, and if Woolf draws on historical evidence to create her fictional journal, the historian, she implies, characteristically employs the conventions and codes of narrative to tell his/story. The boundaries of genre are open to question and it is precisely in the cracks, the slippage between fact and fiction, that Woolf can begin to sight (site) the possibility of the missing woman.

Part of the point of the piece – and we could say of much of Woolf's writing – is to challenge the route by which masculine thinking arrives at its conclusions. Rosamund Meridew's female quest, her search and research, cannot be undertaken in a straightforward linear fashion: following her intuition she both literally and metaphorically takes a sharp turn to the left to find the Hall which conceals the manuscript; she must also be tactfully oblique in her enquiries of the present owners. Mrs Martyn can tell her virtually nothing – as wife she is subsumed into her husband's family and lost in the forgetfulness that deprives women of their own history – whilst Mr Martyn is only interested in 'grandfathers', commemorated both in ancestral portraits and the factual records of

---

[1] 'Virginia Woolf's *The Journal Of Mistress Joan Martyn*', edited with an Introduction by Susan M. Squier and Louise De Salvo, *Twentieth Century Literature* 25 (1979), 237–69.
[2] 'The Journal of Mistress Joan Martyn', p. 242.

ownership and property. The existence of the journal is anomalous: it can surface only by chance. Stylistically, too, it seems to speak to us from another time, not time as historically conceived, but almost as an opening or a gap in time:

> I pull aside the thick curtains, and search for the first glow in the sky which shows that life is breaking through. And with my cheek leant upon the window pane I like to fancy that I am pressing as closely as can be upon the massy wall of time, which is forever lifting & pulling & letting fresh spaces of life in upon us.[3]

This subjective time, a blazing up of consciousness,[4] exists as a precarious present bearing the pressure of an unknown future; its language seems to border the indefinable and to resist a meaningful teleology. Significantly we are told Joan Martyn dies when she is thirty, like the heroine of Woolf's first novel, *The Voyage Out*, Rachel Vinrace, just before her impending marriage. The death could suggest an impasse: what is the connection between woman's subjectivity and a historical and narrative paradigm that posits marriage as woman's destiny and thus deprives her of existence as a person in her own right? Because, however, our knowledge of Joan Martyn's death *precedes* our reading of the journal the death is not simply, or not only, terminal; refusing the boundary of narrative, the end, the journal speaks to us from the place of the permanently desiring subject; it exceeds its meaning in history, creating a space, an opening beyond the margins of chronological time, which is unimaginable, or which can only exist for the reason that it *is* imagined.

My own thinking about recent historical novels by women has taken this preliminary detour through 'The Journal of Mistress Joan Martyn' because, in its bringing together of history and fiction, it seems to open up important questions, even to function as a succinct and playful allegory, about what it might mean for a woman to 're-imagine history'. Like Rosamund Meridew's, the quest of many recent feminist historians has been to recover women's submerged or unrealized past. What has also happened as a consequence of this recuperative work has been a 'restructuring of the canon',[5] a re-visioning of history, for women cannot simply be added on to history – expanding the boundaries of historical knowledge empirically – without putting under pressure the conceptual limits that excluded them in the first place. The story of wars, nations and dynasties, the tangible public events – so long assumed simply to *be* history – take on a different meaning, a different configuration when we begin to see through them – in both senses – to women's concealed existence in the private sphere of family and home.

Yet the further step which Virginia Woolf imaginatively presages, opening up the generic boundary between history and fiction as a way of

---

[3]*Ibid.*, p. 254.
[4]'The Pastons and Chaucer' in Virginia Woolf, *The Collected Essays* (London, Hogarth Press, 1967) 4 vols., III p. 16.

releasing the woman into a life beyond her conventional confinement within the divisions and paradigms of patriarchal thinking, still seems a very large one. In theory historians have argued that history cannot be given the status and authority of being objective or 'real', determined by past events, standing outside or before its shaping into story. According to this radical critique historical narratives do not reveal meanings that are in some sense already 'there'; rather they construct meaning much as fictional narratives do.[6] By claiming a privileged relationship to the 'real', historical narratives are thus really claiming interpretive power in a world of discourse, a power, which as feminists have gone on to suggest, is indissolubly linked to the repression of difference in both language and culture and the positioning of the (masculine) subject as universal source of meaning.[7] In practice, however, despite their general currency – and the new horizons of meaning they seem to open up – these ideas have by and large resisted translation into the actual writing of historical narratives by women. Why?

One answer, suggested by historian Linda Gordon, is that for the history-writer a certain conception of her sources and her own relationship to them remains binding however much she may want to jettison old myths of history and develop new ones of her own. Historians, unlike Virginia Woolf, are not free to 'make up' their evidence or to ignore it; thoroughness and accuracy remain positive virtues and set some limit to how far history and fiction can be usefully concatenated.

> It is wrong to conclude, as some have, that because there may be no objective truth possible, there are not objective lies. There may be no objective canons of historiography, but there are degrees of accuracy; there are better and worse pieces of history.[8]

Yet these cautionary words, important as they are, cannot be the whole story. The uses women are currently making of fiction, where a greater freedom could be said to exist, to reinscribe a certain conception – myth – of history as 'real', suggests that something more is at stake: a powerful desire for women to exist historically in the world, to be more than textually present.

This is the view that emerges in a recent article by Lyn Pykett where she sees 'a younger generation of women novelists' deliberately opposing the kind of deconstructive undermining of history that has motivated the

[5]See Carroll Smith-Rosenberg, 'Hearing Women's Words: A Feminist Reconstruction of History' in *Disorderly Conduct* (New York and Oxford, OUP, 1985), p. 11.
[6]See for instance Lionel Grossman's 'History and Literature' and Hayden White's 'Historic Text as Literary Artifact' in Robert H. Canary and Henry Kozicki, eds., *The Writing of History: Literary Form and Historical Understanding* (The University of Wisconsin Press, 1978).
[7]See Alice Jardine, 'Introduction of Julia Kristeva's "Women's Time"', *Signs* 7 (1981), 5–12.
[8]'What's New in Women's History' in Teresa de Lauretis, ed., *Feminist Studies-Critical Studies* (Bloomington and Indianapolis, Indiana UP, 1986), p. 22.

experimental writing of male novelists such as John Fowles and J.G. Farrell. Instead of wanting to address the question 'What is History', women novelists, according to Pickett, are 'seeking to recover and reclaim the past on behalf of those who have been silenced and marginalized by history.'[9] But in describing this act of recovery, this bringing into the present, Pykett also covers it with nostalgia, a nostalgia directed less at the past than at certain ways of representing it. Pat Barker's novel, *The Century's Daughter*, is compared eulogistically by her with the nineteenth-century novel. The two narratives of this novel, she opines:

> have a common concern with a human world of shared meanings and values, and together they constitute a closely – observed, lucidly written piece of realism. Like the nineteenth-century social novelists Barker uses realism to confront and explore the individual's experience of family, the local community and the wider society.[10]

Newly liberated into history, women, it could be objected, are stuck in the same old place, contained within the eternal domain of liberal humanist values. The idea that both narratives, despite their splitting between male and female viewpoints and their deliberate juxtaposition of the present with the past, can be seen to flow together into 'a human world of shared meanings and values' perfectly describes the way realism and the ideology it supports can manage to occlude difference through its very gestures towards continuity, coherency and wholeness. Can women, so long excluded, be joined to history so seamlessly? The problem which Pykett's critical language unconsciously demonstrates is that history is not so easily separated from its own representation and that reclaiming the past for women, if the past is the version which we recognize and accept to be real because its 'realism' seems familiar, may mean speaking from within the very values that denied our presence in the first place. It may be that the female subject can take over as the unified autonomous subject of realism only by taking on its ideological legacy as well.[11] But is that what is happening in the novel?

The 'century's daughter' of the title of this novel is Liza Jarrett who is, coincidentally, the same age as the century.[12] Refusing to move from her house which is scheduled for demolition, now the only inhabitant left in the street, Liza is 'a case, a social problem, a stubborn, possibly senile old lady' (p. 6). Her memories, however which are partly recounted to the young social worker Stephen, partly internal reverie, fill her; they both inhabit her and enlarge her emotionally and morally, making her into a 'full' character. Liza, herself, becomes the most enduring creation of working-class women's silent battle against oppression and hardship, a

[9]'The Century's Daughters: Recent Women's Fiction and History', *Critical Quarterly* 29 (1987), 71–7 (p. 75).
[10]*Ibid.*, p. 73.
[11]See Toril Moi, *Sexual/Textual Politics* (London, Methuen, 1985), particularly pp. 45–9.
[12]*The Century's Daughter* (London, Virago, 1986). All further references to the novel are included in the text.

history which passes through her, which her memories help to record, and which she also embodies.

An important symbol in the novel is the old metal box, which has been handed on from mother to daughter for at least three generations. Barker emphasizes its significance through her attention to its decoration, which consists, pointedly enough, of human figures in an enigmatic, but potentially meaningful relationship to each other:

> It was an old metal box . . . painted on the lid and sides with dancing figures, women holding their clasped hands high, dancing in a ring. Behind the women, almost in the shadow of the trees, were two other figures. One was so shrouded in a long robe that neither age nor sex was visible; the other was a young man. The draped figure held something in its hands, but the box-lid was so filmed with dirt that Stephen couldn't see what it was. (p. 7)

At the climax of the novel when Liza is dying, having finally been invaded by a 'faceless' present (p. 266) – the youths who break into her house seem to represent as well as be the offspring of an even more alarming general disregard for the community and its meaning – the patterning of the box both holds her, contains her, and releases its meaning into her consciousness and Stephen's. In a dream Stephen receives the message which he was not able to understand before about his own place in the pattern, in the past, from the androgynous figure, who simultaneously represents both his father and Liza. Liza, having now become the cowled figure as she arranges herself for death, is carried by the rhythmic dance of her memories back to her childhood and her mother calling her home from the streets. At the end of the novel Stephen has become Liza's inheritor: privileged by the knowledge he has acquired of his relation to his own past and by being the empathic recipient of Liza's story, he carries both towards a future which is also imaged, like the ending of Liza's life, as a homecoming:

> Long scars ran through the grass where a vanished street had stood. But all around him, brushing against his chest as he walked through them, grew the tall spires of rose bay willow . . . The wind blew, bending the dead flowers, and from one or two of them seeds began to disperse, drifting down across the wasteland, like wisps of white hair.
> In the shrouded cage, Nelson stirred and stretched his wings.
> 'Howay, son,' Stephen said, opening the car door and putting him inside. 'Soon be home.'
> He glanced back once only and drove away. (p. 284)

The reader can enjoy here the fulfilment of an ending which, by drawing past and future together, seems both complete and coherent. Despite the evidence of urban waste, the context of poverty and neglect which points to decline rather than improvement, the individual himself offers a sense of arrival through the securing of his identity: whatever threat remains in the outside world, it is no longer felt as a danger to the achieved development of the self. Indeed it is his development which now makes the narrative intelligible and the problematic relationship between past and present can be viewed, from this perspective, as a more comforting and comfortable sense of continuity from one life to another, and as growth and maturity within the self. A narrative which has addressed a history inflected through the multiple differences of gender, region and class, has in the end become the familiar story of the journey towards the self.

The reclaiming of the past as memory, as oral history – the realization that in order even to ask 'what our mothers and grandmothers were doing, how they were living' we must turn to sources other than written texts[13] – becomes part of the content and framework of this novel. Recalling her life, Liza Jarrett also gives us the sense of an era as it was lived by working-class women. The private experience of home and family – 'women's sphere' – split off and rendered invisible by (male) historical discourse – is promoted and given the status of historical truth. But that history is inscribed by Barker within a realist novel, a genre which she does not substantially challenge, and which is profoundly implicated in a set of historical meanings of its own. Dignified by her position of centrality, Liza is also installed within a narrative with a positive (historical) destination: the fully integrated and all-knowing self. Thus Liza's memories cannot contradict the relation between past and present as unitary and socially agreed, but instead become absorbed into a larger pattern of continuity. Like the box with its enigmatic pattern which seems to encode some past significance which is only understood later, so the novel offers the past as having a plot, a meaning, which is only fully disclosed when it is integrated into the present. The novel moves *towards* a point of understanding– implying that there is only one way of perceiving and representing the world – which can, by seeming to complete the pattern, stand outside history, and sublate the very differences of epoch, class and gender which have been the novel's supposed theme.

The fear that post-structuralist theory could be disabling for women, making history disappear even before we have had a chance to write ourselves into it, needs to be set against another danger: the constant danger that by using categories and genres which are implicated in patriarchal ideology we are simply re-writing our own oppression. The 'reclaiming of history', the discovery of how our foremothers preceded and even anticipated us, can help to assure us that, despite the evidence, we do in fact exist in the world; yet if we ignore how that existence is textually mediated we end up simply reconstituting 'reality' as it is. The battle between theory and empiricism, textuality and experience, in which feminist thinking is also caught up, can feel as if it leaves little room for fresh negotiations and yet both sides of the debate could be seen as exerting a pressure towards conformity, towards aligning 'truth' on one side or the

---

[13]Julia Swindells, *Victorian Writing and Working Women* (London, Polity Press, 1985), p. 119.

other, which needs to be resisted. One of the paradoxes that we face is that even as post-structuralist theory frees us from paradigms which underwrite the (masculine) subject, it catches us back in theoretical toils in which we can also lose ourselves and thus renews our need to reach beyond texts into the materiality of our lives. Describing her attempt to situate her own thinking about history in an unthought-of space between fact and fiction, Linda Gordon finds that her critical poise is uncomfortably put in question:

> I would like to find a method in between. This in-between would not imply resolution, careful balance of fact and myth, or synthesis of fact and interpretation. My sense of a liminal method is rather a condition of being constantly pulled, usually off balance, sometimes teetering wildly, almost always tense. The tension cannot be released.[14]

Sliding between positions and yet keeping our feet can feel tricky, especially if what we are ultimately trying to do is change the very ground of our thinking.

In an attempt to move forward with all the difficulty that involves, I want to think how, in 're-imagining history', the emphasis could be placed in different ways, shifting, as Linda Gordon describes, between both terms without seeking a resolution: between the resistance and transformation implied by the action of 're-imagining' and a 'history' which has both determined the moment *and* has already been imagined. The view of history which emerges is not as something that exists outside us, that we can position ourselves in relation to once and for all. Rather our knowledge of it is something that we now actively shape, even as we are shaped by it.

It is this important notion of the interrelationship and mutual dependency of the subject and history that Julia Kristeva writes about in her essay 'Women's Time'.[15] There she defines 'historical time', what we think of as History, as 'project, teleology, linear and prospective unfolding; time as departure, progression, and arrival' (p. 192). For Kristeva this temporal linearity also structures language and the (masculine) psyche; it is at the basis of the socio-symbolic contract that we enter into in order to become subjects and it 'rests on its own stumbling block', the sense of an ending or death (p. 192). The time of 'project and history' is what women have struggled to gain access to through feminism by asserting their equality with men. In contrast Kristeva defines another time, monumental or cyclical time; because this sense of time is 'all-encompassing and infinite' the word temporality, according to Kristeva, hardly seems to apply to it at all: it presents itself to us more as a place. This time has traditionally been associated with maternity and with female subjectivity when it is thought

[14]Gordon, 'What's New in Women's History', p. 22.
[15]*Signs*, (1981), pp. 13–35. 'Women's Time' is also included in *The Kristeva Reader*, ed. Toril Moi (Oxford, Basil Blackwell 1986), 187–213. The page numbers in the text are to this version.

about in terms of the maternal, as well as with mysticism. Kristeva offers a connection with a different phase of feminism from that referred to above, one which universalizes or 'globalizes' Woman and which refuses involvement in the political dimension. Feminism in this form has sought to give language to 'the intra-subjective and corporeal experiences left mute by culture in the past' and to find an identity outside the 'linear time of identities', one which is 'exploded, plural, fluid, in a certain way non-identical' (p. 194). Moving beyond this dichotomy Kristeva goes on to propose a third possibility or moment which 'mixes' the previous two: *insertion* into history and the radical *refusal* of the subjective limitations imposed by this history's time' (p. 195). This third position is not, she stresses, a reconciliation of the previous two: the social contract is as 'deadly' as feminism has shown and has therefore to be contested rather than absorbed into some larger unity. But the ability to pose the question of what might lie beyond the dichotomy of her first two positions seems to indicate for Kristeva that a third place, or 'mental space', difficult to define, does already exist or, at least, can be imagined.

Kristeva's understanding of how sexual difference establishes and is established through different positions in relation to the conception of linear time, the 'time of project and history', also allows her to see the subversive potential of unsettling meaning at the very point of their conjunction. Changing subjectivity, for Kristeva, conceiving of a (female) subject moving between divisions, challenges the meaning of both history and identity. The problem with this may be, as Elizabeth Deeds Ermath suggests, 'irresolution' and the difficulty of deciding 'what this implies for linear time and its associated values'; in other words Kristeva's (irre)solution could be no solution and could leave us, in a way similar to other theoretical moves, at a loss, stranded in abstraction[16] Ermath, taking the hints that Kristeva herself provides in her essay, goes on to argue for the unsettling of meaning as a *process*: for a process, while undermining the subject and history as fixed and defined and opening up their multivalence, need not abandon them as meaning*less*, hopelessly dispersed and fragmented. In a sense, Ermath (and Kristeva) seem to be arguing that we may have to think ourselves through history – the time and the place it gives us – in order also to be able to think ourselves beyond it.

Is this what Virginia Woolf has already shown us? Returning briefly to 'The Journal of Mistress Joan Martyn' we can see how, in Woolf's re-writing of history, the two moments, the historian's quest and her historical subject's identity to herself, do not join, cannot be resolved into one story. The subjectivity revealed by Joan Martyn's writing is in excess of her historical place – her negation within history; her journal seems to inhabit another place, a timeless space beyond narrative closure and beyond death. Rosamund Meridew's search, on the other hand, establishes the assumptions and constraints which determined Joan Martyn's

---

[16]'The Solitude of Women and Social Time' in Frieda Johles Forman, ed., *Taking Our Time: Feminist Perspectives on Temporality* (Oxford, Pergamon Press, 1989) p. 45.

invisibility historically and give a particular poignant meaning to her journal. Woolf imagines a complex relationship between subjectivity and history: Joan Martyn is both absent and present, both inside history and outside its subjective limits. Woolf's fiction literally embodies Joan Martyn's absence; what she creates is a ghostly presence – not only absent but real – unsettling historical definitions and the certainty of narrative closure.

The echoes from Woolf carry over into my discussion of Toni Morrison's *Beloved* the novel with which I want to end this essay.[17] Morrison's complex re-imagining of history in *Beloved* is also an exploration of history's absences, of how what is unwritten and unremembered can come back to haunt us, troubling the boundaries of what is known. 'That unrecorded past', Frieda Johles Forman writes, 'is always with us and its absence strikes at odd, unsuspecting moments.'[18] The unrecorded past Forman is referring to is the missing history of women but for Morrison there are other absences too: the only partially acknowledged sufferings of slavery, the (pre)history of Afro-Americans in Africa, and the devastations of the Middle Passage which forms both a physical and a temporal link between the previous two experiences. *Beloved* partly seems to be an attempt to imagine a different relationship between subjectivity and history, to write from the position of a female subject whose connection with the maternal places her outside the socio-symbolic contract in the way Kristeva describes: to write from this timeless place, to attempt to find language (which cannot be found) within an almost impossible void, unsettles all our stable notions of identity, language and history. But Morrison is also aware that Woman, in that psychoanalytic sense, crosses into other meanings of woman, the particular identities of different women determined by our lives *within* history. Even motherhood cannot be separated, as Morrison shows us, from its meaning, or distorted meaning, under slavery. Within *Beloved* Morrison reveals a complicated overlapping and enmeshing of meanings: she moves between history and its determinations to a subjectivity which lies beyond it in an imaginative realm which has yet to find a place.

As she has acknowledged Morrison based *Beloved* on an actual historical incident,

> [a] story I came across about a woman called Margaret Garner who had escaped from Kentucky, I think, into Cincinnati with four children . . . And she was a kind of cause celebre among abolitionists in 1855 or 56 because she tried to kill the children when she was caught. She killed one of them just as in the novel.[19]

---

[17]*Beloved* (London, Chatto & Windus, 1987) All further references to the novel are included in the text.
[18]'Feminizing Time' in *Perspectives on Temporality*, p. 8.
[19]Mervyn Rothstein, 'Morrison Defends Women', *New York Times* (26 August, 1987).

But whilst she researched very thoroughly the historical background of the novel, 'Cincinnati, and abolitionists, and the underground railroad', she also refused to find out any more about Margaret Garner: 'I really wanted to invent her life'. Leaving space to imagine her central character – Sethe in the novel – is also a way of leaving space for subjectivity, for the interiority denied by historical records. 'They "forgot" many things', Morrison has said about slave narratives. 'Most importantly – at least for me – there was no mention of the interior life.'[20]

In order for subjectivity to enter, therefore, there must be space – not only space for Morrison's imagination but for the reader's as well. Morrison has seen a need in all her novels to move away from narrative closure. 'I want to shift the emphasis away from a need for a closed door. I want the door open because I want the reader to think about it.'[21] In *Beloved* there is no authoritative version of history, no single 'truth'. The narrative voice does not offer a transcendent level of knowledge – a position from which the reader can 'understand' – but blends instead with the other voices in the novel. It speaks, like the characters, from within a culture which not only unquestioningly accepts the existence of ghosts but which more generally does not prioritize the rational. It moves freely outside realism and its assumptions about 'truth', refusing the division between subjective and objective, mataphor and fact.

History becomes in the novel the series of stories which the characters tell themselves and each other about their lives, stories which move into and out of each other, merge and overlap. Memory reveals the complex formations of history within the characters; how the subject is constituted in and through history. But the process of remembering also highlights the past as not past, not finished, but as continuously reaching into the present and beyond, into the future. For Sethe, as she tells her daughter Denver, time cannot always be distinguished from the physical reality and permanence of place:

> I was talking about time. It's so hard for me to believe in it. Some things go. Pass on. Some things just stay. I used to think it was my rememory. You know. Some things you forget. Other things you never do. But it's not. Places, places are still there. If a house burns down, it's gone, but the place – the picture of it – stays, and not just in my rememory, but out there, in the world . . . Where I was before I came here, that place is real. It's never going away. Even if the whole farm – every tree and grass blade of it – dies. The picture is still there and what's more, if you go there – you who never was there – if you go there and stand in the place where it was, it will happen again; it will be there for you, waiting for you. So, Denver, you can't never go there. Never. Because even though it's all over – over and done with – it's going to always be there waiting for you. That's how come I had to get my children out. No matter what. (pp. 35–6)

[20]Review, *Newsweek* (28 September, 1987), p. 74.
[21]'Interview with Toni Morrison', American Audio Prose Library.

Leaving the past behind is impossible, in Sethe's view, not only because it lives on in her mind, her 'rememory', to be recalled privately, but also because it has a public existence which makes it real for other people too and able to affect their lives. Sweet Home farm and Sethe's experience of slavery, are presented as ominously indestructible; even though they are 'over', part of time which advances linearly as 'project and history', they are still 'there', existing in another dimension, a timeless place where their power never diminishes. For Sethe their horrifying 'reality' is greater than her own capacity to remember; they go on existing outside her, therefore, as well as within her mind.

Beloved's return, the return of the child Sethe killed in order to save her from slavery, functions in the novel as the return of what cannot be remembered, a repressed memory which in 'real', albeit ghostly, form is haunting Sethe and others at the beginning of the novel. For Morrison Beloved's entry into the novel seems to have been born out of the need to provide another viewpoint on Sethe's conviction that she had to 'get my children out. No matter what'. Killing her child, in the circumstances, according to Morrison, is understandable but 'it's also the thing you have no right to do.'[22] Maternal love is both powerfully enabling *and* excessive in this view: it motivates Sethe to risk a love which as a slave is dangerous to have since it will inevitably expose her to pain. 'And this woman did something during slavery', Morison has commented on the novel. 'She was trying to say something about her children's lives in a slave system that said to blacks, "You are not a parent, you are not a mother, you have nothing to do with your children."' But mother love can also be 'a killer', according to Morrison, assuming rights over the lives of others and 'displacing the self'.[23] No simple judgement of Sethe is possible just as there can be no simple assessment and understanding of maternal love: 'I felt the only person who could judge her (Sethe) would be the daughter she killed' Morrison has said. 'And from there Beloved inserted herself into the text.'[24]

Beloved not only highlights the complexity of Sethe's action she also brings a 'bottomless longing' (p. 58) into the text, an insatiable thirst. She seems to embody the daughter's desire for the mother, a desire which has been unlived and unsatisfied; she also stimulates the desires of the other characters and their own sense of longing and of lack. In the lyrical monologues which form the centre of the novel Denver, Sethe and Beloved all voice the same desire to possess the Beloved: 'She is mine'. But that desire springs first of all from the deprivation they share as daughters, the loss of a relationship to the mother. Earlier in the novel Denver had asked Beloved why she had come back. Her answer is: 'To see her face' (p. 75). This crucial relationship to the mother's face, suggesting a very early stage of merging with the mother, of being contained by her gaze, has been

[22]Mervyn Rothstein, *New York Times*
[23]*Ibid.*
[24]Marsha Jean Darling, 'In the Realm of Responsibility: A Conversation with Toni Morrison', *Women's Review of Books* 5 (March, 1988) pp. 5–6, (p. 5).

painfully destroyed by slavery. Sethe never really saw her mother's face: 'She'd had the bit so many times she smiled. When she wasn't smiling she smiled, and I never saw her own smile' (p. 203). Denver, knowing her mother capable of murdering her children, experiences her mother's gaze as violent rather than benevolent: 'She cut my head off every night . . . Like she didn't want to do it but she had to and it wasn't going to hurt' (p. 206).

When Beloved speaks in this section of the novel she enacts an even more complicated relationship with slavery for she speaks not just as Sethe's daughter returned from the dead but as 'a survivor from a true, factual slave ship.' Morrison has explained that she intended Beloved to function at two levels:

> She speaks the language, a traumatized language, of her own experience, which blends beautifully in her questions and answers, her preoccupations, with the desires of Denver and Sethe. So that when they say 'What was it like being dead?' they may mean – they do mean – 'what was it like being dead?' She tells them what it was like being where she was on that ship as a child. Both things are possible, and there's evidence in the text so that both things could be approached, because the language of both experiences, death and the Middle Passage – is the same. Her yearning would be the same, the love and yearning for that face that was going to smile at her.[25]

The language of both experiences is the same because they both reach from dissolution and loss of identity towards the possibility of a new identification through finding and joining with 'that face that was going to smile at her'. They exist in a pre-conscious or unconscious realm which is outside the symbolic, the time of 'project and history'; making them visible exerts pressure on language, identity and narrative structure. It seems important that these sections in the novel break into, break up the narrative; that they are spoken by tearing a veil, by letting through repressed desire. Stylistically they are set apart; they cannot be related in a sequential, linear fashion to what comes before and after but seem to collapse boundaries between past and present – where do we situate them? – and between internal and external. In the last of these sections as the voice moves between Sethe and Beloved the stability and separateness of 'I' gives way as the primordial need of mother and daughter fuses their identities and the pronouns holding them apart:

> You are my face; I am you. Why did you leave me who am you? (p. 216)

In order to try to make intelligible what history and the social order represses it is necessary to rock their very foundations. At the end of the novel Beloved has disappeared again and it is suggested that her memory has too:

[25]*Ibid.*

Disremembered and unaccounted for, she cannot be lost because no one is looking for her, and even if they were, how can they call her if they don't know her name? Although she has claim, she is not claimed . . .

It was not a story to pass on. (p. 274)

What gets passed on, what becomes 'known' as history, is not all there is to know. There is no closure, Morrison suggests, no point of completeness and understanding to be reached. Memory is open and what is not structured in terms of 'project and history', what is not passed on, may have another existence in the future. Re-imagining history has to be a process without end.

Notes on Contributors

Linda Anderson is a lecturer in English Literature at the University of Newcastle-Upon-Tyne. She is the author of *Bennett, Wells and Conrad* (Macmillan 1988) and a forthcoming book on *Women and Autobiography* from Harvester. She is also an editor of *Writing Women*.

Penny Florence is currently a freelance writer and film maker. She is the author of *Mallarmé, Manet and Redon (Visual and Aural Signs and the Generation of Meaning)* (Cambridge, CUP, 1986). She has contributed essays to *The New International Dictionary of Art and Artists* (London, St James Press, forthcoming) and *Teaching Women* (Manchester, MUP, 1989) and has written various articles and reviews on feminist film practice, painting and word-image studies.

Elaine Jordan was born in Yorkshire and has three children. She studied at Somerville College, Oxford, taught at Durham University and for the Open University from its foundation, and now teaches in the Department of Literature at Essex University, where she directs an MA in Women Writing. Her *Alfred Tennyson*, which is particularly concerned with the representation of gender, was published by Cambridge University Press in 1988.

Alison Light is a Lecturer in Humanities at Brighton Polytechnic; she is currently writing a study of British women's fiction and the conservative imagination – *The Haunted House* – to be published by Routledge in 1990.

Judie Newman was educated at the Universities of Edinburgh and Cambridge, and is the author of *Saul Bellow and History* (Macmillan, 1984), *John Updike* (Macmillan, 1988) and *Nadine Gordimer* (Routledge, 1988). She is a Lecturer in English Literature at the University of Newcastle-Upon-Tyne.

Rosemary O'Sullivan lives and works in Newcastle-Upon-Tyne. Before her two children were school age, she worked in women's education and schools while completing an MA as a mature student at the university there. She has now been teaching English for three years at a Newcastle Comprehensive School.

Pauline Palmer works in the English Department at the University of Warwick where she teaches a course in 'Feminist Approaches to Literature' (previously 'Literature and Sexual Politics'). Her publications include an essay on the fiction of Angela Carter in Sue Roe, ed., *Women Reading Women's Writing* (Harvester, 1987) and *Contemporary Women's Fiction: Narrative Practice and Feminist Theory* (Harvester-Wheatsheaf, 1989). She is at present writing *An Annotated Bibliography* linking women's fiction and feminist theory (Harvester-Wheatsheaf, forthcoming) and a book on *Contemporary Lesbian Writing* (Open University Press, forthcoming). She writes fiction and has a story in Jan Bradshaw and Mary Hemming, eds., *Girls Next Door: Lesbian Feminist Stories* (Women's Press, 1985).

Ruth Whittaker is a graduate of the University of East Anglia. She is the author of *The Faith and Fiction of Muriel Spark* (Macmillan, 1984), *Doris Lessing* (Macmillan, 1988) and a study of *Tristram Shandy*.

Index